TEXAS PRIDE

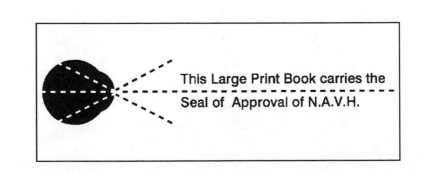

This Large Print Book carries the
Seal of Approval of N.A.V.H.

TEXAS PRIDE

TIM McGUIRE

WHEELER PUBLISHING
An imprint of Thomson Gale, a part of The Thomson Corporation

THOMSON
GALE

Detroit • New York • San Francisco • New Haven, Conn. • Waterville, Maine • London

THOMSON

―――*―――™

GALE

Wheeler Publishing Large Print Westerns.

The text of this Large Print edition is unabridged.

Other aspects of the book may vary from the original edition.

Set in 16 pt. Plantin.

LIBRARY OF CONGRESS CATALOGING-IN-PUBLICATION DATA

McGuire, Tim.
    Texas pride / by Tim Mcguire.
       p. cm. — (Wheeler Publishing large print westerns)
    ISBN 1-59722-341-7 (lg. print : pbk. : alk. paper)
    1. Gamblers — Fiction. 2. Race horses — Fiction. 3. Large type books.
    4. Texas — Fiction. I. Title.
    PS3563.C36836T49 2006
    813'.6—dc22

                                    2006019949

Published in 2006 by arrangement with The Berkley Publishing Group,
a division of Penguin Group (USA) Inc.

Printed in the United States of America on permanent paper
10 9 8 7 6 5 4 3 2 1

To Pat, Marilyn, and Richard

Thank you for all your support and love
for your kid brother during all of this.

ACKNOWLEDGMENTS

Much appreciation to the Daughters of the Republic of Texas for all their information. Many, many thanks to my editor, Samantha Mandor, for her patience and understanding beyond the call of duty. And to all my friends at the DFW Writers' Workshop, whose guidance has allowed me to do this.

1

Rance Cash sat up straight in the saddle and folded his hands on the pommel. He exhaled in relief while gazing down at the grass- and tree-filled valley. "So, that's it?"

"Yes, sir," Jody Barnes replied with pride. The young Texan only glanced at Rance and Les, and quickly returned his view to the settlement below. "San Antone."

Rance couldn't help the swell in his own chest. Not for the sake of Jody, whose affection for his hometown was made plain by his gleam. It was the culmination of the journey that tickled Rance's ribs.

Four months has passed since he was aboard the *Robert E. Lee* on the Mississippi headed to St. Louis. A foolish whim to exploit the prosperity of Kansas cow towns sent him west, encouraged by the threat of a known man killer. A chance meeting with the girl Les masquerading as a cowboy put him on his way to Texas in her pursuit of lost rebel gold. The brothers Curry from Arkansas sought to trump the play and would have succeeded. If not for the heroics of a man who only answered to the name Smith, Levi and Eli Curry would have gotten away with the whole share of the bounty, leaving corpses in their wake including Rance himself.

However, it was the thieving brothers left in the dust, but they took the mysterious Smith, their final partner in the secret, with them. A finger, pointed in death, had this leaderless trio leave their friend Smith in a marked grave under the headstone of Captain Marcus Broussard, veteran of the Fourth Texas Brigade and husband to his beloved Deborah, next to whose side he now laid.

The bounty turned out to be worthless Confederate notes left under the same marker. The entire affair turned out to be folly. Or was it? Even for a gambler, to chase a rumor was a lost bet. Nevertheless, he now found himself seven hundred miles from the nearest Kansas cow town.

The daydream faded with his next breath. "Well, should we go and have a look?"

Jody flashed a smile once and took his hat in hand. "Don't have to ask me twice." With that, he swatted his mount's rump and rode at a gallop down the side of the valley. Les cast only a glance at Rance as if she should follow at the same pace. Rance opened his palm to the front. "Ladies first."

"Don't call me that," she said with a sneer, then kicked the paint mare's flanks to scamper in pursuit of her friend.

Alone at the top of the hill, Rance pondered whether to follow suit. He held no affection for the town and saw no reason to tire the dun or himself at such a gait. However, when he thought of the relief from the relentless Texas heat along with a hot meal and soft bed awaiting him only a mile away, he slapped the horse's behind and raced after his companions.

Once down the slope and across the narrow river, he caught up with Les and Jody as they entered the dusty edge of the once Spanish mission. Jody gave only an impassive glance upon arrival.

"Get lost?"

"Not quite," Rance replied. "I just wanted to enjoy the scenery." Curious at his own remark, he gazed upon the surroundings as the trio ambled their horses three abreast through the narrow street. The architecture was a mix of cragged adobe single-story buildings little bigger than huts placed amid double-floor wood structures resembling those of the East. However, none rivaled the refinement of anything found in New Orleans.

"We came all this way for this?"

Jody didn't respond to the remark. He only nudged his horse a little faster and Les kept pace, leaving Rance to the rear once more. After a moment's consideration, he resolved to keep his opinions to himself and look for more favorable destinations on which to comment within the small town's boundaries.

Dark- and light-skinned locals crossed the street in harmony, each carrying their needs wrapped in canvas sacks or wooden crates to continue their existence for this day and the next. Such behavior of those of mixed cultures wouldn't be seen as civilized in the East. However, Rance was encouraged to see the placid conditions. It was good for business to be in an open town where as many people could cohort together as possible in order to enjoy the games of chance.

While gazing, one particular site at the end of the street caught his eye. Larger than the rest, this white double-floored edifice stood out as a beacon for those seeking better accommodations than a horse stable with a leaky roof. Rance pulled up on the dun's reins. "What place might that be?"

It took a moment before Jody followed the direction of Rance's view. "Oh that. It's a hotel. Menger, I think is the name."

Visions filled Rance's mind. Just as pieces of a puzzle slipped in place he saw the whole image before the parts were even about from which to choose. "Has it been there long?"

Jody shrugged. "Can't say as I know. Been there a good spell building on it. Seems like this might be the first time I seen it without somebody hammering more nails into it."

"Would you know the name of the proprietor?" The question sparked two confused faces turning his way. After few seconds without reply, Jody finally shook his head with a bit of disgust. Rance sneered at their posture, realizing the purpose of his inquiry was so easily seen through. As the three riders wound through the street, Rance again eyed the tall oasis passing by their path. "Where is it we might be going?"

Les turned to him but Jody didn't, although at least he answered the question. "I'll have a stop at the stock pens outside of town. I wanted to have a look at some breeding bulls in the corral. I told my folks I'd have a look on my way back."

The idea was of no interest. "You're not going to stop here? Rest weary bones? Perhaps enjoy some decent food." He paused only to apologize to Les with a bob of his brow. "Maybe see the sights."

"I seen them. Besides, all there is to see is in the center of town." Jody kept the pace of the slow progression. The end of the buildings were nearing, a signal of the resumption of life in the wild.

"What about Les? Neither she nor I have."

With only a glance, Jody turned his head to her, then returned his view straight ahead. "She can stay if she wants."

"I was raised in Abilene, Kansas," she answered. "Cow towns all look the same to me."

"Cow town?" Rance was hoping she was wrong. "Of what I see, I don't recognize all the trappings of a dusty trail stop." The pace didn't waver. "There appears to be *some* culture here. Why not take a few moments to enjoy it?"

Les again turned her attention to Rance, a reaction of momentary intrigue. Just when he thought the idea might be creeping into the back of Jody's head, the young drover frowned and shook his head.

"No. I just want to get back to my own spread. I come this far. Ten more miles can be made before sundown." Les's interest waned with the response. There was no sense appealing to her youthful curiosity. The last three hundred miles from Fort Worth had been guided by the cowboy. Just like a duckling, the girl didn't appear ready to leave the safety of the leader. "You can stay, if you like?"

The question hung in the air like a dare. Rance scanned about the town. This wasn't exactly home. Yet, the promise of leaning against a rail fence watching and admiring the qualities of fine-bred bulls just wasn't his idea of how to spend the rest of the day. Was it time to seek out the finer surroundings of this place? By the tone of Jody's voice, Rance wasn't certain if the invitation to continue to his parents' home was extended beyond just Les. However, the suggestion for Rance to stay in town sounded genuine. There was never a rapport between the two men, although they had remained civil while tolerating each other when they first met at the entrance of the Indian Territory. Upon further thought, he was reminded just how long ago it seemed. He glanced again at his two compadres. They had spent most of the summer together. Maybe it was time to give each a rest. Him from them and them from him. Rance called the bluff.

"I believe I will." The announcement stopped all three horses. Les was first to show surprise, but after a moment even Jody took a breath, waiting more than a second before exhaling with a relieved smile. Rance looked to the cowboy and shrugged. "I think I owe this place at least a chance to get to know me."

Les grinned. "Whether they want to or not."

Rance cocked his head. "Well, sometimes you got to show folks what's good for them, even when they don't think so."

"And you'll be sure to show them the difference between good and bad." Jody smiled after his remark, then after a small pause held out his hand. "I know we haven't always got along, but I can say I learned a thing or two from you, and I'm a better man for it."

Rance accepted the handshake, the men's grip meeting in front of Les's chest. "I guess one of those things would be not to play cards."

"At least not with the likes of you," she sniped.

Rance pushed back his hat. "And you, young lady, I can say I will miss dearly." She didn't appear swayed with the flattery as with most females. However, she wasn't like most females he'd known. "When I first put eyes on you, you were in dingy cowboy duds. Now look at you." He gazed at her modest blue dress with white spots and lace collar. Before she first put it on months ago, she rode double with him wearing only his coat and a slicker after having been harshly exposed as a female by the Currys. Before his very eyes, Rance witnessed the blooming of the teenage girl from the dirty bulb disguised as a boy just to ride to Texas with drovers. However, she still had on the tattered broad-brimmed hat with the chin cord. "I must admit, you do make a far better young woman than you ever did a grubby cowpoke." He peeked at Jody. "No offense."

"None taken," Jody replied.

"I think I made a better cowboy than you a preacher." Her assessment had merit. In order to gain a friendly reception and a hot meal, he used his limited knowledge of the gospel on a Christian family heading to Santa Fe. While on the run from railroad agents, he continued the ruse in order to persuade Les to aid his escape and take him to their camp. However, it wasn't long before the old sage named Smith saw through the lie. The brief recollection brought to mind a few items of unfinished business.

"You know," he said, looking into her eyes and taking off his hat. "As a gentleman, I never did apologize for the way in which I made your acquaintance." The sincere apology spooked Les worse than a rattlesnake in the middle of the night. Her features drooped as in panic. Rance sat perplexed. He wondered if he'd stepped into another verbal gopher hole. Should he not have brought up the incident when, while hiding behind a tree in fear of being discovered by the railroad agents, he had in turn discovered Les's true gender when she answered nature's call?

"What's that mean?" asked a confused Jody.

It was evident by the absence of an appropriate answer ready to come off Les's tongue that he indeed had misspoken. By the sight of her bulging eyes, it appeared she hadn't ever fully divulged the details to the drover nor wanted them known at this time. The only thing to do was to act as the girl's advocate.

"I simply meant to express my regret that I first deceived her as a man of the cloth rather than telling the truth" — he paused, still looking into her panicked face while stuck for a word — "of my true calling."

"Oh," Jody responded, apparently dismissive of the admission. "You mean that you said you was a preacher instead of being a no-account gambler?"

The simple summation was good enough

on which to admit. Rance nodded and put on his hat. "We'll leave it at that." He eyed Les. She blew out her long-held breath. It was a favored sight to witness. During the long trip from Kansas to Texas, even when wearing the dress, she acted more comfortable in the role of a trail hand than that of young lady. Despite her pride at not wanting to admit she was a member of the weaker gender, it did Rance's heart good to see her retain some vanity as a woman. And by the fear in her eyes, there might be reason to believe that the last person she wanted to know about her introduction to Rance was Jody.

A weight pulling on his left hip was also pulling on his conscience. He drew the seven-inch-barreled pistol from his belt and held it out to Jody butt first. "I suppose this is best to be kept with you."

Jody didn't extend his hand, but rather shook his head. "No. He gave it to you. I suppose you're the one he meant it to stay with."

The gesture was a kind one. The pistol belonged to Smith, given to Rance to use in a gunfight that eventually took the old man's life. Rance had kept the pistol for peace of mind during the remainder of the trip, but since he knew the old wrangler the least, didn't feel so honored as to keep it. "Are you sure? He was your friend."

Jody nodded. "I got my own," he said slapping the Remington tucked on the left side of his belt, then did the same to the short-barreled Colt tucked in the right. It was that revolver Rance had stared down the muzzle of when about to meet his maker while gripped by the man killer Colton Schuyler. Had fortune not smiled once again on Rance's behalf by firing all six barrels at once of the unreliable pepperbox now resting in his right pocket, the Colt would have been the gun that took his life and not one he wanted to see again.

Rance accepted the gesture. "Seems a fair trade." He tucked Smith's pistol back into his belt. "So, I guess this is good-bye." He turned the reins of the dun.

"Maybe, you can come out to my folks' place," Jody offered. "It's just ten miles west. That is when you get sick of the food here and want some real home cooking."

The invitation was uncharacteristic and unexpected. Rance allowed the tickle at his lips creep into a full grin when he sensed the sincerity in Les and Jody's eyes. "I'll do that, as long as you remember that the road there leads back here sometimes."

Jody grinned, then tucked his hat tight to his brow and nudged his horse. Les took another moment before doing the same, but not before casting an eye of silent farewell. Rance watched the pair continue down the street toward the far side of town, Jody in his pale blue shirt with stained pale suspenders and Les in her white-dotted blue dress. Rance sensed it would not be the last he would see of his fellow travelers.

He turned his attention to that which had kept him here. A beautiful hotel ripe for a man of his expertise. However, he couldn't decide which he preferred first, a hot meal or a comfortable bed. When he reached into his pockets, all in the world that was left of his once-held eleven-thousand-dollar asset had dwindled to three. The amount was hardly enough to pay for true hotel fare. However, his hunger won out over his aching back. So, sure of his luck, he nudged the dun toward the Menger. Food was a difficult play to get on his good looks, but on more than one occasion it had got him into a soft and cozy bed.

2

Two polished oak wood doors opened into the lobby. Once out of the sunlight, Rance immediately felt the cool breeze provided by the rotating belted wands suspended from the wood ceiling. The relief was delicious. So much so, his spirit was renewed as he strolled to the counter stuck out from the left wall. Behind the thickly varnished partition stood a slim man in a dress coat and string tie with long hair hanging from the sides of his scalp.

"Yes?"

Rance paused at the tone. There was little if any courtesy attached to it. He glanced at his own dusty black trousers, sweat-stained white shirt, and gritty hands. In an instant he recognized the reason for the less than respectful greeting. If matters were reversed he would have gauged the same lack of financial stability.

He opened his mouth, but no words emerged. In one of the few times in his life, the proper approach to a difficult situation eluded him. When catching himself in a lie before he even told it, reflex flashed his bright, cheery smile that had served him so well. As he stood there smiling, waiting for an idea on how to explain he wanted a room with only three dollars in his pocket, the slim man only creased a brow as if examining some strange species theretofore unseen.

"Are you the proprietor of this fine establishment?" The inquiry didn't ease the creased brow.

"No, sir," was the low, cold reply. "How can I help you?"

Rance cast an eye to the foyer further to the right. The opposing embroidered sociables were of hand-carved cherry, the small table of the same wood and equal craftsmanship. An immaculate rug stretched over the major portion of the shiny wood floor. Paintings of the vainly posed noteworthy appeared the work of skilled hands no doubt from the East or even Europe. All about the room opulence permeated except for the lack of one ingredient. People. Patrons. At last, his purpose for coming inside the hotel resurfaced in his mind and his confidence returned.

"I have a business proposition."

The creased brow finally eased only to allow the roll of eyes above. Not the first time witnessing the initial doubt to his ideas, Rance kept the smile in place. "Is there a place where we might discuss the details in private? Over a meal perhaps?"

After a long huff, the clerk leaned against the counter with his palms on the edge. "What do you have in mind?" he sniped.

Realizing he would have to offer more in order to get fed, Rance leaned closer to his mark. "What I have in mind is attracting large numbers of customers into your business, uh, I'm sorry, I didn't get your name." Rance offered his hand.

The slim man didn't offer his. "No, you didn't."

His courage flowing, even though it appeared up a considerable stream, Rance kept his smile and whispered in order to add value to the exclusive proposal. "Might I ask if you are empowered to entertain such prospective enterprises that will enhance the liquidity of the hotel's daily receipts?"

Like on the wrong end of a bar-fight punch, the clerk shook his head, stunned by the twist of words. Rance recognized the reaction. Many a member of the fairer gender had succumbed to the seeming prose of a sophisticate, which usually led to the further twist and tangle of bed linen at a more appropriate time and venue. He didn't seek such an outcome at this time; however, the effect was universal on the weak-minded no matter the gender.

"What is it you are asking me?" the clerk blurted with a confused tone.

Rance subtly shrugged and glanced about the vacant lobby with a bit of a sneer. "I'm only suggesting a mutual agreement that will allow me to parlay my trade to the customers of this hotel, allowing them to engage in friendly wagering on an uncertain outcome."

The slim clerk didn't grasp the subtlety. "What?"

"Table games, my good man. The excitement of risk."

The clerk glanced at the foyer. "You want to set up a card game? In the Menger Hotel?"

"Precisely. You are a man of shrewd observance," Rance complimented. The mark's face didn't reflect the flattery.

"Get out," was the rude reply.

Undeterred, Rance held up a finger in order to get to the universal incentive of all mankind. "It would mean a considerable windfall of cash."

The clerk waved his hand like shooing flies. "There are laws against such things. Get out before I have to call the sheriff."

"There is no law against people exercising their free will to increase their personal fortune. Why would this establishment not be afforded the same right?"

"Do I have to call the law?"

"My good man, I have been a part of the financial success of many a —"The clerk circled the counter and flipped up the bridge. In a few steps he could be out the front door hailing the local law. It was time to play the best card. "I guarantee a thousand-dollar-a-day take with seventy-five percent to the house." The bold prediction froze the clerk in midstep, still holding the bridge. One more card was needed. "With that kind of increased revenue, I would think you would be entitled to a lofty commission."

The bridge resettled in place. The clerk resumed his position at the counter. "Like I said, what do you have in mind?" Although the question was worded the same, the voice was more agreeable. While on a run of winning hands, there was no need to continue bluffing.

"Faro. There is no more profitable a game for the house. I never met a man that didn't want to buck the tiger." He pointed to the open foyer. "We can set up a table right over there. Fine fabric surface, brass railings, nothing to suggest a rowdy nature. It will lure most of the town's notable citizenry. And once they find it to their liking with a few one-sided plays to their benefit, they will never leave. Trust me."

The clerk bobbed his brow in an intrigued manner, then his eyes darted down to Rance's soiled clothes.

"Never fear, my good man. This is just my traveling wardrobe. Once I have all set in place, you'll see me in only the fashion that will reflect this establishment's ambiance." He again offered his hand. "Do we have a deal?"

With still a little apprehension, the clerk scratched his chin. "It does sound interesting. We have been a little weak in our number of guests. But, I would still have to ask the owner."

"Please do," Rance said with open arms and broad smile. "Let's go and present *our* idea to him right now."

"The Mengers are in St. Louis. He's not expected back for three weeks."

The arms came down to the side, but the smile stayed in place. "Three weeks? We can't let this opportunity slip through our fingers."

"I don't know. He's pretty particular about what goes on in his business."

"Well, no doubt, he's left you to act in his stead, isn't that right, uh . . . uh . . ." Rance rolled his wrist.

"Calvin. Calvin Perkins."

The rolling wrist once more took the shape of the friendly offered hand. "Nice to do business with you, Cal. My name's Cash. Rance Cash. Both my name and eternal pursuit." It took a few moments before Calvin finally accepted the often-offered hand. "Excellent." Rance propped an elbow atop the counter. "Now that we have reached an agreement, I must admit that I first was attracted to your hotel for a chance at a good meal."

"Our chef is the best in town."

"So I suspected." The compliment set the hook. "Calvin, since now we are business partners, I was wondering if you could extend to me a small stake in the place. A modest line of credit, of course. So in order to replenish my good health after long months traveling over the frontier to here." The idea didn't get the sought after exuberance.

"You're asking for money?"

"Not money, per se." Rance leaned closer to whisper in confidence. "However, it would enhance my status around this town if

28

I were to mention that I was the guest at the finest inn in all of Texas. And there would be no greater place to start such a gossip than in your own restaurant here in the hotel itself. Of course, the food is delicious, and I would be only so happy to sample some of the cuisine and make it known throughout the confines of this hamlet that a gentleman of my station only dined at the Menger Hotel."

"You wanting to eat for free?"

"Let's call it an advance." He again extended his hand to the bewildered clerk. As if still in a daze from the very first punch in this fight, Calvin slowly gripped Rance's hand. "That is a good man, Calvin. I will mention you highly among the others I come across." Rance released his grip to point to the far end and at what appeared to be table and chairs. "Is it this way?" he asked while nodding. "No reason to guide me." He nodded again. "I'll seat myself."

With the speed of a thief in the night, Rance made a quick pace away from the counter and went into the far side of the lobby. Three small steps down signaled the entrance into the restaurant. Sheer pale drapes allowed just enough sunlight through to illuminate the surroundings. A dozen small tables each with a quartet of chairs dotted the wide floor. As before with the foyer, not a soul occupied the room. No matter. The absence of customers was a welcome sight for surely it meant speedier service. However, another scan showed no waiter either. Not alarmed, he sat at the nearest table, allowing his legs to throb with relief. He inhaled the cool air while removing his black short-brimmed hat and placing it on the adjacent chair to his left. A voice stirred him back to the right.

"Welcome to the Menger. What would you like?"

The feminine voice cast an image in his mind that his eyes soon realized. There, standing next to him, was a tall, fair-complected, statuesque woman. The blond hair was pulled into a bob resting on the back of her shoulders save for a few strands that strayed from the restraint to curl above her blue eyes. Although she repeated the question, there was no need, for he knew what he desired without looking at the bill of fare. When she bent slightly, staring into his eyes with a third request for an order, he noticed the second and third buttons loose from her white stiff-collared blouse, allowing for a stolen peek at her healthy cleavage. He also noticed a slant to her English.

Rance shook his head to snap out of the

daydream. "Forgive me. I was so entranced with your accent. Swedish, is it?" He peeked at her fingers and saw no bands.

"German." She didn't blush at his question. "Now, what do you like?"

"I don't even need a menu to answer that." Quickly, he flushed the lurid fantasy from his head. He paused and grunted his throat clear. "I desire your finest cut of beef," he started, gazing into her face. "Just above a wild flame." He swallowed. "Heating the inside to a soft pink, yet still warm and moist. Do you understand how I like it?" Even though he was lost in her eyes, she was still on steady ground.

"And would you like beer with your steak?"

Never an advocate of the brew, he thought it wise to accept her advice. "As long as you'll join me."

She snapped her order book closed with a sarcastic yet polite smile. "I'm sorry. I am on duty at this time."

"As it turns out, so am I. You see, I work here, too." She stood confused at his mention. "I'll talk to Calvin. I'm sure he won't mind if you take a break."

"Sorry. No." She turned to return to the kitchen, but he stopped her by gently grasping her fingers.

"Isn't it customary for the waitstaff here to introduce themselves to their guests?" He raised his brow to further entice an answer. After several seconds, and several more bobs of his brow, he found himself near begging. Finally, she answered.

"My name is Greta Schneider." She pulled away from his touch.

"A heavenly pleasure to meet you, Greta. My name is Rance."

"Good to meet you." Her tone was formal and cold. Again, she turned for the door to the kitchen. In moments, she'd be gone and chances favored another server would return, perhaps even the chef himself. He chided himself for his forward nature and felt an apology needed.

"Greta?" he called. She took three more steps until finally stopping at the door. When she turned about, words failed him again. Seconds clumsily elapsed as she waited for him to speak his piece. Finally the truth leaked out. "It is an indescribable delight to have met you."

He was certain she would meet the over-wrought flattery with contempt, but she said nothing, faced about to the door, and went through, running her palm along the back of her brown skirt.

3

Certain he had overstepped the boundary of proper decorum, Rance silently chided himself for his brazen conduct. Most women he acquainted himself with often were receptive to his forward manner. However, this tall, blond beauty left the dining room with all the excitement of having stumbled upon a skunk. The choice of words forced him to peek at his soiled clothes. Perhaps the description fit in more than one way.

As he peeked, his eyes strayed to the left enough to see Calvin Perkins, overly greased hair drooping beyond the brow, standing at attention like a child not wanting to interrupt a busy schoolmaster.

"Yes, Calvin?"

"I . . . I . . . I was wondering."

The long pause confused Rance as to whether there was a question coming or there was more to follow. "Wondering? Wondering what?"

"Well, you see. All these plans you mentioned. Just how do you plan to get all this business in here you promised?"

Rance flashed his confident grin. "Calvin," he started in a condescending tone. "Leave that all to me."

"That's what I fear."

The lack of faith startled Rance. "You have nothing to fear."

"Oh, I think I do. There were many great pains that went into making this hotel what it is today. Efforts I don't wish to see washed away by the turn of cards to attract undesirables making this into a dance hall."

With smile still intact, Rance thought of a different approach so to soothe the clerk's qualms. "I have no intention of turning this fine establishment into a dance hall. Besides, there is no space big enough in the lobby to place a stage for one." He chuckled at his attempt to lighten the mood. Calvin wasn't amused. He grunted his throat clear. "But," he started, scrambling in his mind for a way to shift the attention from the uncertainty to anticipation about the enterprise. Flattery was always a favored tactic. "You bring up an excellent point, Calvin," he said with a profound shake of the finger. "And together we will bring only those patrons into our midst who offer the best image reflective of the Menger Hotel. I'm glad you were so astute as to bring that issue to my attention. The Menger has a lot to be proud of to have a man like you watching over her best interests."

The swing of a door swayed Rance's head to the right. Walking into the room was the tall, blond beauty carrying a tray to the table. So enamored by her return, Rance didn't notice the steaming steak she placed in front of him next to the froth-topped mug of beer until after he saw the previously unfastened button of her blouse neatly resecured.

Stumbling for words, he glanced at Calvin, then his manners spilled from his mouth. "Calvin, have you met Greta?"

The duo standing on each side of the table stood as if in a stupor at the question. "Yes," Calvin answered. "I hired her."

The obvious slammed into his face like a punch. "Of course you did," Rance blurted with a grin, thinking of anything else to wipe the embarrassment off his face. He opened a palm. "Join me won't you?"

"I — I can't leave the front." Calvin looked to Greta. "That's it for him today." With that, the clerk sidestepped the table and left the dining room. The shroud of having been dismissed partially paralyzing his hands and brain, Rance slowly looked up to Greta. "And what about you?"

"I have to prepare for the evening customers."

Rance scanned about to see the room still empty except for just the two of them. Finally after looking about in all the corners, he peered up at her.

Her eyes dipped to the chair in front of her. "For only a moment." She pulled out the chair, leaving Rance only time to stand but fail to perform the gentlemanly duty. Without even a notice of gratitude for the attempt, Greta sat, no smile as she appeared every bit the prisoner as his bequest. Rance slowly returned to his seat, taking time to reset his napkin under her stoic gaze.

He cut into the steak. The ease at which the knife sliced into beef surprised him. Most of the meals eaten on this side of the Mississippi weren't this tender. A second later revealed the wall of red meat, juice oozing from between lines. His mouth began to water and his eyes darted to her. She watched as he stabbed the first piece with the fork but showed no anticipation for his opinion. Slowly, he placed the beef on his tongue. Instantly the flavor, like freshly churned butter, permeated his senses. As he chewed, a smoky seasoning ebbed from the savory beef.

"Um," he hummed. He bobbed his brow at her. "My compliments to the chef. Be sure to tell him that I praise his work."

She didn't express any satisfaction at the compliment. "I'll tell *him.*"

He nodded at her assurance to pass along his words, cutting into another slice and hungrily stuffing it into his mouth. As he chewed, her tone slowly crept into his consciousness. Gradually, his jaw slowed until finally it came to a stop. He darted his eyes at her. Her unapproving eyes didn't waver. As a nervous reaction, his lips curled at the end. "There isn't a him, is there?"

She shook her head with the methodical pace of a clock pendulum.

"You?"

Only the motion of her head from side to side to a nod changed.

He grunted his throat clear again, brushed back the hairs from dangling next to his brow, and presented his best apologetic grin. "Might I say that you are a excellent cook." The moment he uttered the word, he knew he was in trouble.

"Cook?" she questioned. "When it was *him,* you called him a chef."

"A thousand pardons, my dear. Forgive my oversight. It's just that never have I ever enjoyed such an exquisitely prepared steak. Of the ones that I have tasted that even could be compared, they were all the result of men. I meant no slight."

"I'm sure you didn't," she said in disgust, rising from the chair.

Reflex had him reach and gently grip her arm. "Please don't." He expected her to jerk her arm from his grasp; instead she stood and turned her head to him. "I don't wish to offend. Especially such a beautiful and talented woman. Not twice. And surely not twice within the same hour." It took several moments before she allowed a hint of acceptance to crease her lips. He released her arm and silently, with just an open palm, asked her to sit. After exhaling through her nose, she sat again. The relief was almost as delightful as the steak.

"This really is a unique taste. What is your secret?"

Greta shrugged. "Grilled over wood."

Rance cut another slice, stuck his fork into the sizable slab. "What kind of wood?" he asked before shoving the fork in his mouth.

Again she shrugged. "Just what they are able to cut and age here. Mesquite."

Once he swallowed, he cocked his head

and reached for the beer. "They should grow them in crops." Once his fingers were around the mug, he paused then looked to her. "Did you brew this, too?"

Now an even bigger grin broke her face. Rance knew he had atoned for his mistakes. When lacking the first one, humor was the second best way into a woman's heart. Since it seemed Calvin may not be forthcoming with complimentary accommodations, and lacking the funds for a room of his own, he may have to earn this blond beauty's good favor in order to earn an invitation into her bed.

He took a sip of the brew. The distinct taste of grain erupted up his nose. Some of the stoutest whiskies he had didn't rival the kick.

"No. It's the Menger brew. Mr. Menger began the brewery before the hotel."

Rance swallowed and gasped for breath. "Tastes like it came from the vat the same day it went in." Once he cleaned his palate, he sunk the knife in the steak, but sank his view into her deep blue eyes first. "So, how does a girl from Germany find the dusty frontier of Texas?"

Hesitant, she took a few moments, watching him slice through the meat, posing as a witness before she answered. "I am from a small town near here."

"What town is that?"

"Fredericksburg." Her short answer left little space for inquiry.

"And so you walked in one day and Calvin hired you?"

She sneered in the direction of the front desk. "He did not hire me. Mrs. Menger did. She did all the cooking before, but became too busy with all the building of the hotel. She is German. I am German. She wanted someone to continue what she had started."

Before he filled his mouth with food, he wanted to give her something to answer. "And how does that bring you from Europe?"

"My brother." As he chewed, he raised his brow to spur her to explain. She took the hint, although reluctantly. "My brother sent for me. He came here with my parents to start a farm." Another pause gave her an uneasy appearance. "My parents were killed by the Comanches. Before there was a peace made."

The announcement seized Rance's jaw.

"My brother, Guenther, found a job as the master of the station for the stagecoach line. I was living with my father's sister and her husband in Munich. So, when Guenther was alone at the station, he sent for me to cook the meals for the passengers."

As he had before with tragic stories of loss, he slowed his gestures, unsure exactly how much sorrow to show. He put down the fork and knife.

"Go ahead," she encouraged. "Eat. You should not feel bad for me. This is your time to eat. Maybe your only one."

Despite her urging, his appetite waned. Rance leaned back in the chair and put his napkin on the table. "And what about your brother?" He feared the answer was the same.

"He is married now." When Rance raised his eyebrows, Greta nodded. "He returned to Germany to get married and bring his bride to America."

Rance was relieved to hear good news. "A long-held love."

Once more, Greta shook her head. "No. Guenther doesn't have any women there."

The confusion made Rance thirsty. He lifted the mug. "Then who is he marrying?" he asked taking a swig.

"The first girl that will say 'yes.' There are many young fräuleins that want to come to this country." The unromantic reasoning stunned Rance. He lowered the mug in surprise. Greta took the napkin off the table. "The rest of the world is not what you have here," she explained while blotting the froth from his upper lip. "Women look for a man who will support them, give them a family and a home. Guenther knows that. So he will pick the best of who he finds."

Her genteel touch to his lips gave him thoughts about giving them a final cleansing against hers. However, when she finished, she abruptly put the napkin back on the table and glanced at the kitchen.

"I need to get back to my duty. Supper starts at seven."

Before she could move, he carefully wrapped his fingers around her wrist. "When does your duty end?"

She paused, taking a long look into his eyes. "When the last plate is washed."

"When is that?"

"After midnight. Maybe even more."

A satisfied grin creased his lips as he withdrew his fingertip grip. "Then, Miss Schneider, I hope to see you when I return."

She first turned for the kitchen but did not take a step. After a moment, she faced him again. "Return from where?"

"Oh," he said modestly, "I have a few items to tend to before we open up."

"Open?" She cocked her head to one side. "Open what? Open where?"

"Well, you see, we're about to open up the best gambling parlor in town. Soon, you'll see a line of people stretching out the door and around the town in here."

"Gambling? You're a gambler?"

Rance confidently nodded. "I've been known to place a bet or two. Anyway, you're about to see a great change in here." The expected excitement for the project didn't surface on her features. Instead, she turned her nose down at him.

"You expect people to pay their money to gamble with you. You? Like that?" She curled her lip as she picked up his plate, shaking her head all the way back to the kitchen.

Rance slumped in his chair. Greta's sharp words cut right through his spirit. The prospect of joining her in a late-night rendezvous seemed further away than those Kansas cow towns. However, the longer he thought them over, the greater resolve built up inside him. He faced around to the front door. There was a lot of work to be done. When he stood, he took his hat and snapped the brim down. The dust popped loose, filled his view, and forced a cough.

There was indeed a great deal to wash over, and that was the first order of business.

4

Nothing spurred on a man to improve like a rebuke from a beautiful woman. Rance marched out of the front of the Menger Hotel on a mission to relieve himself of the grime and dust he had carried most of the way from Fort Worth.

Off the shaded boardwalk and into the temperate evening heat, he strode toward the nearest street. He rounded the corner of the one named Crockett and headed toward what seemed to be the assembly of the town. He first spotted a barbershop among the numerous stores. Remembering the time in Fort Worth, he knew it as a refuge for men to shed the clothes and soil from their bodies. However, before he stepped into the place, he thought it wise to find suitable clothing for the successful man he wished to be considered.

The view from across the street didn't reveal the desired business. Rance walked down the boardwalk sighting a store with traffic of customers both entering and exiting with items ranging from sacks of ground grain to wooden boxes being hauled to waiting wagons. He strolled across the dusty lane and into the business. Once inside, stacks of further crates lined one wall while a row of shelves stretched from corner to corner of the other. Sensing he was out of place, he nosed through the narrow aisles to find a table with piles of dungarees neatly folded for purchase by those used to hard labor with small reward to show for it. He sought another table. He didn't find one.

Wandering to the back wall, he found a row of modest dresses hanging from a wire hooked to the far wall. At first, he let his mind run free, recalling the days when as an adolescent he learned to remove those dresses just as well as the young ladies who were wearing them at the time. However, the more he considered it, the meager cost of any of the garments and the large number of them meant only one thing: there wasn't much money in this town. How could he expect to attract the exclusive clientele needed to propel his venture at the Menger to success?

"Help you with something, mister?"

The question came from the portly clerk with a pencil tucked behind the ear of his balding scalp. The immediate answer in his head was to refuse the help, but since he wasn't sure which way to go next, he decided to accept the offer. "As a matter of fact, friend, I could use some guidance." Rance stepped to stand in front of the counter. "I'm of a need of something a little finer than that I've been able to find in your store." The sutler didn't seem impressed with the remark. Rance leaned closer to the portly man's ear. "You see, I was robbed by bandits while on the way to your little hamlet here among the hills, and all my worldly possessions were taken."

The sutler peeked down at the pistols tucked into Rance's belt. "They robbed you and left you with two guns?"

Rance paused to peek at them himself. "Oh, those. I was able to take these from those masked men and chase them for as far as I could. But, with them on horseback and with me just on foot, they got away with my coat and all my funds."

The portly man cast a suspicious eye at the mention of no money. Fears needed to be calmed.

"I was on my way to meet my fiancée here. And I feel terrible that she should see me in those soiled and torn clothes. I've been able to wire a line of credit to the inn down the street for lodging while I am here and —"

"The Menger Hotel?"

Rance paused only long enough to let the hook sink in. "Yes." He nodded with a shrug. The sutler's face lightened. "And I was hoping to replace the clothes to which I am accustomed."

"Well," the sutler started with a giddy doubt to his voice. "I don't have much call for what I think you're looking for in here."

Certain the next piece of advice was to leave, Rance was surprised when the man began shaking his finger in revelation. "You know. I may have an idea for you. Lester Farlow over at the livery was claiming that some people's things were lost on the stage while coming here. They found a trunk of real fancy duds in one of the trunks and never could locate the rightful owners."

Rance restrained his smile. "What a shame."

"I think if you ask him, he may have something you're looking for."

"And where might I find Lester?" Rance aimlessly pointed. The sutler stepped around from the counter. "Just down the end of Crockett Street. Here, I'll show you."

"That would be grand of you, uh . . ." Rance said.

"Cullum. Paul Cullum is my name."

"Rance Cash, Mr. Cullum," he said, shaking the man's hand as they walked to the door. Rance was careful not to let go until he fully understood where he was to go. When they reached the door, he peered in helpless fashion.

"Here, I'll take you there." Cullum faced around for a moment. "Mary, I'm leaving the store to take this gentleman to see Lester. Be back in shortly."

Glad to hear the offer, Rance opened his palm for Cullum to lead the way.

"Where did you say you were from, Mr. Cash?"

"Please, all my friends call me Rance. And I am originally from New Orleans. But, my business takes me to all points around the globe. St. Louis, Philadelphia, New York, London, and here in San Antonio."

"What business you in?"

Rance hesitated only long enough to think of a better answer than the truth. "I'm in the speculation business."

"Speculation? You mean like land or cattle?"

"Land, cattle, last will and testament."

When Cullum poised his confused face

over his shoulder, Rance huffed a laugh. The tactic worked on Cullum, who also laughed.

After the long walk to the end of town, stepping onto one boardwalk after another, they reached the sickly sweet indication of horse dung. A large barn structure soon came around the corner, with several wagon wheels in disrepair littering the entrance. Cullum stepped through the maze of wheels with ease and opened the door.

"Hey, Lester" was Cullum's call. Soon a thin man wearing overalls and long handles emerged from the dark stench. Rance turned his head, in part due to the overwhelming odor and the idea that anything coming from this barn would be infected with the same. Lester nodded at the introductions while wiping his soiled hands with equally soiled rag. Rance just waved politely. Once circumstances were explained with excited exuberance by Cullum, Lester scratched his thinning scalp and looked to the loft of the livery.

In a few minutes a heavy trunk crashed onto the ground while Lester carefully climbed down the rickety ladder. All three men dragged the trunk from the barn and into the light. Lester had trouble with the thick leather buckles, but when he finally unthreaded the last one and opened the lid, the heavenly aroma of the cedar-lined chest wafted into Rance's nose.

There on top was the wardrobe of a man of some sophistication. Rance went through the white shirts and black trousers, but when he held them up to his frame found them to be as long as the top of his boots.

"Don't worry," said Cullum. "My Mary can let them out a little for you."

Rance gave a grateful smile, then looked to the less-than-sharp Lester. "What would you want for the whole trunk, my good man?"

Lester again scratched his head. "Don't know. By rights it's stage property."

"Oh, come on, Lester," Cullum admonished. "This stuff has been here nearly six weeks. Ain't nobody even asked about it. Now, Mr. Cash here, he's getting married here in our town and hasn't got but what he has on. Now, what use does the stagecoach line got for it?"

Rance was only too glad to have someone make his case for him. He faced Lester like a wounded dog. After only a few silent moments, he broke a friendly smile. "Tell you what, Lester. I would be glad to pay for the storage on behalf of the original owner. Deal?"

Lester shrugged as in agreement then held out his hand for payment. Rance pointed down the street.

"Send the bill in care of the Menger Hotel. I'll see that it is paid." Still fearful to shake the livery operator's hand, Rance patted the man's shoulder. Before any objections could be voiced, Rance grabbed a handle, but the load kept him from budging it. When further attempts met with failure, Lester retrieved a dolly from the barn and the trunk was carted back to the store.

Once the proper thanks were extended to Lester, along with a grateful good-bye for taking his reeking clothes and body away with him, Rance and Cullum managed to get the cargo inside. When the sutler divulged to his wife Rance's impending nuptials, she was only too glad to help with the needed altering.

Rance went to one of the storage rooms in back where he removed his shirt. Normally not shy about removing clothes in front of women, he found himself a bit uncomfortable doing so for a woman over the age of fifty. Mary Cullum didn't seem to mind as she stretched a string over the length of his arms, shoulders, waist, and hips. With the point of her finger, she ordered for him to drop his trousers. Rance complied like a soldier, unfastening the buttons and letting them fall around his boots. When she knelt in front of him, Rance stared at the ceiling and tried to fill his mind with the daunting task that was yet before him and other troubling thoughts while feeling her touch to his loins and a firm push to gauge the exact spot at which seams needed to be sewn.

"We'll need to let some out down here for you."

"Thank you, ma'am," Rance said while still staring upward.

It took more time than Rance first guessed, but in that time, Mary found the measurements she needed to ensure a tailored fit. As soon as she was done, Rance expressed his thanks to the Cullums and headed to the barbershop.

As Les approached the house, her stomach churned worse than when she expected a switching from Miss Maggie. Despite the urge to turn the paint around and scamper back to Kansas, she sat stiff in the saddle following Jody's lead. Ever since she had left home to come to Texas in hopes of finding a lost fortune in gold, supporting dreams of a better life, she had overcome every challenge she encountered. However, those were the unexpected. Now she faced an even tougher fate she'd been warned about for the last hundred miles: meeting a man's family.

"Would you hurry up," Jody barked. "I'd

like to get there before sundown."

Les glanced at the west. By her gauge more than a hour remained in the daylight. She couldn't dawdle that long. Finally her fears couldn't stay buried in her head. "How you going to tell them about me?"

Jody only glanced behind, then shrugged. "I'm going to tell the truth."

"How's that going to sound?"

"What do you mean?" he answered, staring straight ahead.

She hesitated before risking a laugh with her reply. A glance about showed the rolling green hills dotted with trees on the slopes surrounding the spread. A single longhorn in a wood-fenced corral stood guard some hundred feet or better in front of the long single-floor house. This was a home. But not hers.

"You bringing me here. Jody, I'm a girl."

The announcement stopped Jody. He twisted about in the saddle. "Yeah," he said with a nod. "I found that out some time ago."

His casual manner unnerved her. Whatever her fears, they weren't his. "What if they ask me questions?"

Again he twisted about. "Listen here. They ain't going to rip you apart. They might ask you your name, if that ain't too much." Les dipped her head, then again peered at the landscape to avert his eyes. Jody's tone turned mean. "Well then, go on back. Go to San Antone and stay with that gambler you brought. You two will get along just fine."

His words were meant to poke at nerves and they did the job. When she finally turned her view to him, he had already brought his horse to a trot for the last few feet of travel to the house. For her to answer that she held no feelings for Rance Cash, she would have had to shout for the county to hear.

Jody was quickly off his horse. The front door to the house swung open and a woman of some size came out to the porch and wrapped loving arms around Jody as he did so to her. It wasn't a moment later that a man who was the spitting image of an elder Jody stepped out and grabbed Jody's hand as they slapped each other's shoulders.

This was how families greeted. How a real ma and pa and son showed one another how loved all of them were to each other. It wasn't a familiar scene to Les. It was only Miss Maggie's hug she'd ever known, but the woman that raised her since stepping off the orphan train wasn't real kin. Les sat in the saddle for the brief seconds as Jody flashed his bright smile to his parents. This was not where she belonged. If she was to turn without notice, it would have to be in the next instant.

Paralyzed by indecision, Jody finally looked her way and pointed. Les didn't know why she did, but she nudged the paint forward. It didn't take a minute before she was at the front of the porch.

"Ma," Jody said, waving at Les. "This is a friend I met in Abilene. Her name is Les Turnbow." The introduction was more plain than any given a man. Les slid off the paint as she had many a time, but from the corner of her eye noticed the father poke an elbow in Jody's shoulder with a look of disgust. Maybe it was a sign that Jody should have helped her down. Still, with her heart pumping so hard her ears surely must be beet red, Les gradually looked up at the Barnes family.

It took only a moment for the mother to open her arms as a clear invitation to climb the steps. Les did so only to be wrapped inside a loving embrace.

"How do, Les," greeted the mother, tears still streaming down her face. "Thank you for bringing my boy home to me." The comment had Les glance at Jody, who only rolled his eyes. A second passed before the father stepped forward.

"Jack Barnes, Les." He held out his hand.

She took it and squeezed as hard as she been taught by three months on the trail. She wasn't sure if she impressed him, but he shot an eye at Jody. The look of confusion reigned on all faces.

"Well, why are we all standing outside?" said the mother. "Let's all come in. I have supper just about ready and I've got plenty to be ate." With that order, she led the way inside and, once an indecisive moment came and went, Jack Barnes followed his wife. Les looked to Jody. He took a long breath, then motioned to the door with a mixed face of disgust and embarrassment.

"Well, let's get on in or we won't hear the end of it if it gets cold."

Les stepped inside.

By the time Rance arrived, the sign in the window had just flipped, showing the end of the business day. With the urgency of a man drowning, he rapped on the glass, reeling the barber back to the door like a fish caught on a line. When the door was open, the successful explanation of his dire situation convinced the barber to extend his practice for one more haircut and shave. It took extra pleading in order for a bath to be allowed. Most of the clean water had been depleted.

Nonetheless, Rance was grateful to strip

the soiled clothes once more and enjoy the cleansing wash. The young son of the barber fetched fresh water to be poured on the back and earned an extra two bits shining the boots to a glossy luster.

Once all the grime was scrubbed from between the toes and accumulated perspiration of three months was rinsed into the tub, Rance spent his last five cents on the splash of toilet water to his neck and cheeks.

Not wanting to slip on the same dirt he came in with, he used the rear door of the barbershop to discreetly sneak down the alley to rear door of the store, hoping the dim light of early evening would shield pious eyes to a less-than-covered rear end.

A knock at the door took only moments before it was answered by Cullum. Relieved that he would be seen near naked by a man, he soon discovered he'd been shooed into a room with only Mrs. Cullum. With only a bundle cloaking his most private of assets, she casually held up her hurried seam work to his chest with the interest of a carpenter as to the precise measurement, rather than a female in front of a near-naked man. Satisfied the white shirt would fit as planned, she took the bundled clothes from his grasp, tossing them aside with an appropriate lack of regard.

She held the pants to his waist. Rance once more turned his view to the ceiling, forcing the recollection of the discomfort of being shot in the shoulder into his brain while she pressed the pants to his waist and every contour of his body below that point.

Finally, every inch of that ceiling firmly embedded in his mind, she stood and faced him. "Well, I'm not satisfied that the middle seam is right. So, you'll just have to try them on."

"Yes, ma'am," he answered, waiting for her to leave. When she stood firm, he grunted as to remind of the impropriety of a man in the flesh in front a woman not his wife.

She looked him straight in the eye. "Mr. Cash," she said with a firm tone, "I've been married thirty-three years next March. I have bore and raised three sons in that time to adults. Whatever it is that you think it is I haven't seen in my time with men, you're wrong. So get on to it." With that order, Rance proceeded to slip on the pants, then the shirt. She inspected them like a sergeant. "How's the fit down there?"

Rance cocked his head to the side, not wanting to disappoint her despite the tight seam between his legs.

"I only had so much material to work

with. But it will have to do." She went over to a sewing table and tossed him some clean socks and a new tie. "You can think of this as a wedding present." She turned around to leave the room. As she opened the door, she faced around one last time. "By the way, Mr. Cash, your bride is a lucky girl."

"Thank you, ma'am," he replied coyly as she shut the door. With a deep breath, he slipped on the socks and then the boots. Tying the tie, he slipped on the long black frock coat, which fit his shoulders like his own skin. He took another deep breath, tucked Smith's pistol in his belt, and put the pepperbox in his side pocket. He headed into the front room of the store. With a firm handshake he thanked Cullum and told him he would get the trunk in the morning. Then he graciously took Mary's hand as she continued to inspect her work on the middle seam, or so Rance wished to believe.

He strolled through the night air across the street with a uncontrolled spirit to his step, tipping his hat to all the ladies as they strolled by on the boardwalk. When he reached the lobby of the hotel, he noticed the sway of the pepperbox wasn't as comfortable as before. He removed the six-barreled short pistol from the pocket and slipped it into the inside pocket of the coat.

When his fingers touched the presence of a paper object, he pulled out and faced the light. It was a business card.

FLETCHER'S UNDERTAKING AND EMBALMING EL PASO, TEXAS

"Jody Barnes, you've been in this house for over an hour and haven't told us all about your trip to Kansas," said the mother.

Les peeked at Jody sitting beside her, still with his mouth full of the next-to-last fried chicken leg.

Jack Barnes cleared his throat. "Let the boy eat, Jessie. Probably the first woman-cooked meal he's ate in six months."

Jody's mother took the remark as a compliment, then laid eyes on Les. "Oh, Les must have cooked him some good vittles while they were out on the trail."

Chewing on her own mouthful, Les's jaw seized in midbite. Again she peeked at Jody. He arched a brow at her to see if she would answer. The truth was that all the experience Les had at cooking was heating up dried beans. The meal tasted less like food and more like mud. However, as the dare hung in the air, Les felt compelled to answer. She swallowed, but it was Jody that answered first.

"Not as good as your fried chicken, Ma."

The proud proclamation was enough to clear the air. Les inhaled in relief, eager not to answer what recipes were favorites and the like. The peace didn't last long.

"But, your mother brings up a subject I would like to know," Jack Barnes spoke while wiping his hands and face with a cloth napkin. "How was it out there? Run into any Injuns?"

Jody shook his head without hesitation. "Mr. Pearl, the trail boss, he set with all them tribes. Had to give them some beeves on the way north. And some horses on the way back. Weren't no trouble." Jody waited for an instant, casting an eye at Les. She was only too happy to stay silent.

"Hector Simms told us you were bringing back the remuda. I didn't think that was your job going there. How'd that happen?" Jody's shrug wasn't enough to dismiss the question.

"Tell us, Jody," Jessie Barnes begged. "I want to know why all the other folks got their sons home a month ahead of mine."

Les's eyes went wide. She put the napkin to her face in order to hide her fear at the whole truth. Jody looked to his plate for a long moment, then bobbed his brow and snatched another leg of chicken. "Not much

61

to tell. A couple of fellows didn't make it in time. Mr. Pearl, he knew J. S. Cooper wanted them ponies back. He asked me and Smith to help Monty Briscoe with them." He paused a single instant, peeked at Les, then looked back at the chicken. "But, Monty didn't show neither."

"Smith?" Jack Barnes asked. "That the fellow with the small spread east of here?"

Again, both of them paused before answering, until finally Jody nodded. "That's him, only —" He hesitated, words stuck on his tongue. Just like he had the truth he couldn't swallow, Jody told it in a somber tone. "Smith. He didn't make it." The mother put her hand to her mouth, Jack Barnes's brow furrowed, showing his surprise. Jody nodded and continued.

"Bandits that done it. They'd been following us since we first got into Indian Territory and kept after us all the way through and into to Texas." He thought about taking a bite into the chicken leg, but the subject obviously made him put it down. "They took the remuda from us south of Fort Worth." He bobbed his head toward Les. "Me and her. Smith was coming up late after us."

Les held her breath and closed her eyes, not knowing if the next words out of Jody's mouth would tell the tale when the Curry brothers took their clothes.

"Oh, Jody, stop." Les opened an eye at the sound of his ma's voice. "You're upsetting poor Les. I can see it pains her to think of something awful as that."

Les nodded, unsure if the woman really knew how accurate her words were.

"Yes," Jack agreed. "They'll be plenty of time to tell us all about it." He looked to Les. "So, where is your home?"

She eyed Jody for just an instant, not knowing how much he wanted her to say. "Abilene."

"Oh, my," said Mrs. Barnes. "Why did you come to Texas?"

Every muscle in Les's body seized. Should she tell the truth? About the gold she was told about by a man about to drop through the trapdoor of the gallows? About pretending to be a cowhand and coming south to Texas, leaving her adoptive mother behind in Kansas? She couldn't think of which lie to tell. She shrugged. "I wanted to see what every man from here bragged about."

The father chuckled at the comment, allowing a momentary relief, but the mother took a puzzled posture. "Do you run into a number of men often in Abilene?"

Again every muscle seized. The real reason she knew was actually passed on to her by the women she befriended working for the lady called Shenandoah. It was always a risk of a whipping if Miss Maggie found out she even talked to those second-story sisters, but Les took the chance to learn about the ways of females and why she had the feelings she had. Miss Maggie never wanted to discuss such matters.

However, Les had to come up with an answer that would get Jody's mother's piercing eyes off her own. "Some of the men boarded at the house I lived at," she lied. Miss Maggie wouldn't let drovers stay inside the house. "Some of those men talked about what great folks there was in Texas during the night's supper." The lie seemed to be working. Mrs. Barnes's eyes seemed to ease. Les sensed one more lie would provide confidence the story was true. "And of course those that I met during the Sunday sermon."

No one moved. Les feared she had stretched it too far. As all at the table traded glances, Jack Barnes broke the silence.

"Son, I'm sure you're ready for some rest."

Jody broke into his bright smile. "Yes, sir, I know that is true. After sleeping on the ground so long, I can't wait to crawl into a soft bed."

Les couldn't help but agree. The long

months on the trail took over her mouth. "I'm right there with you."

Jessie and Jack Barnes froze stiff, eyes wide, jaws dropped.

"I — I, uh, just meant," Les stammered. "I don't — don't —"

"She just means she tired of sleeping on the ground . . ." Jody said, offering explanation. "With me. I mean like me. She don't want to sleep on the ground with me." With his mother blushing, Jody slapped the table. "I'm just saying we didn't like sleeping on the ground. Apart. Far apart. Y'all know what I mean."

Although the proud mother sat still with some shock, Jack Barnes rose from his chair. "Les, let me offer you a room for the night." His calm tone eased nerves, and Les was only too eager to leave the table. The father led her through the wide den. Les glanced at the varnished columns supporting the thick wooden beams above. Past the den, Les found herself in a long hall. Jack opened the first door on the left.

"This was Jody's older sister's room. She's married off now, but we've kept it up." Les went inside to find the widest bed she had ever thought about sleeping alone in. Clean sheets lay neatly folded at the foot next to a folded wool blanket. As soon as she stepped in, Jack stepped out of the room. "There's a basin and pitcher in the corner if you'd like to wash up," he said as he closed the door.

With a loud sigh of relief, she stared at the ceiling, wondering just how she had gotten this far.

5

An enormous gasp awoke Rance. Instant fear of the unknown brought him to sit up. Eyes scanning left and right for bearings, he found himself in a rear vestibule of the hotel. Ahead was the lobby. To the left was the restaurant. Under him was a small two-seat couch. On him was all his clothes.

As he rubbed the itch from cheeks and eyes, he rambled through his memory in search of the circumstance that put him here. Slowly the unremarkable events filtered back into his head. When he had arrived at the lobby the previous night, he was met with what could be considered little fanfare. The more accurate assessment would be that he was treated like a dog after a run in the mud ready to come back inside. Calvin, ever with his disdainful stare, didn't show much, if any, exuberance over the new apparel. It was evident that the clerk had soured on their arrangement likely just a few minutes since it had been struck.

However, it wasn't Calvin's reaction that gave Rance that queasy gut. He rubbed his messy hair back in place, recalling her glance at him while serving the evening supper's customers. She didn't smile nor sneer. It appeared a notice of indifference, one meant as a gauge of his potential all in one blink his way. By the lack of appreciable approval, the message had to be received as one of huge doubt.

Disappointment sank his spirit. Few times in his life did he enter into a room to be met with such passive results. It was then the journey of swaying and rolling on horseback over the swaying, rolling hills of Texas caught up with him. Retreat out of sight seemed the most comfortable course. Once down the foyer and out of Calvin's view, he thought to rest his weary bones on the small couch.

Now, through the thin drapes of the lobby, the sun announced a new day. Another opportunity to prove himself as a man of means. With renewed resolve, he rose off the couch and picked up his hat. While doing so, the butt of the heavy .44 stabbed his ribs. When he twisted in reflex, the pistol fell from his belt to the floor. It could have been an omen.

Not to be deterred, he inhaled deeply, retrieved the fallen weapon, and replaced it in his belt. However, the sign was a clear one that certain matters needed to be dealt with as soon as possible.

He went to the front door. The desk was abandoned. Calvin must not have started his duties for the day and Rance wasn't sad to not be seen as he left. On the front boardwalk, he stepped from the shade of the short awning and into the morning light while the air was still cool.

The mission to set things straight and secure led him back to the center of town and to the Cullums' store. Sweeping off the front boards was Mary Cullum. Her smile was the last one to greet him almost twelve hours ago. Rance tipped his hat and went back to the routine of the aimless groom-to-be in order to appeal to her womanly instinct to help. Although she wanted to, Mary was unable to supply the needed advice; however, she did take careful notice of the long barrel cinched against his trousers. Rance tried not to be conscious of the woman's intent inspection of the area below his waist.

She summoned her husband, much to Rance's relief. When Paul Cullum emerged from the store, hair frazzled about the top of his thin scalp signaling either a late start to the day or a recent rise from a mattress for another reason. Rance again sought the advice of the elder sutler as to where to find the needs of his long-barreled .44.

As before, Paul was only too eager to help, leading Rance down the boardwalk. They passed corner after corner with the traffic of townsfolk gradually growing in numbers as they walked past. Eventually he recognized some landmarks and realized he was being led back in the direction he came. As they went by the hammering construction of a three-floor edifice, Rance took a long notice of the tall building yet to be and remarked at the emergence of a town right before his eyes. They crossed the dusty street with Rance's eye still yet glued to the large building, then noticed the familiar awning of the Menger Hotel. When they reached the far boardwalk, he twisted his head to the front in order to not miss his step. His eyes caught a peculiar sign above the next building they were about to pass that he had not seen in the previous day and darkness before.

"Alamo Saloon?"

Cullum only peeked at the sign that had stopped Rance.

"Yup. That's the name." He stopped and turned about to join Rance. "Must have

70

been a slow night for them. There's usually two or three drunks passed out in front of the place." Paul was about to start his step again. "Usually the ones bounced from the place after losing at cards and no money to pay their losses or the bottle."

Rance grinned. "That a fact."

Cullum nodded as he gave his lecture. "You don't want to go in there. Only thieves and gun hands stay in the place. Looking to make money without rightfully working for it."

"How much?" Rance asked with a purposeful tone. The inquiry again turned Cullum.

"I don't know for sure. I've heard stories, though. Some say that fellows in there take in as much as a thousand dollars. Some in one hand of cards."

The news made it hard to suppress his smile. "You don't say."

"It's what I heard." Cullum paused with a bit of concern on his face. "Why are you asking? You a card player?"

Rance cocked his head to one side. "I've been known to play a hand or two."

"Well, you ought not go in there. A lot of cutthroats in there." He turned away to walk down the boardwalk toward the Menger, but Rance remained staring at the closed doors.

Another peculiarity entered his head as he once more looked up at the sign. The namesake of the saloon struck a chord. "So where is it?"

Again, Cullum retraced his step to come next to Rance. "Where is what?"

Rance looked at the short man. "The Alamo?"

Cullum cracked into a giddy smile. "We just walked by it."

"We did?"

Cullum, still chuckling, stepped past Rance to round the corner of the street he had just walked while enamored where the new building was being built. Cullum pointed down a dusty alley. At the end stood a small pale crusty face of an old mission. The rounded parapet arched at the top had numerous missing chunks of masonry. The hollow windows gave it a ghostly appearance with overgrown sage scrub emerging from its base. A horse tethered to a post in front took its natural relief as Rance watched.

"That's it?"

"Yup. Still as that day Santa Anna came through."

Standing amazed, Rance dipped his eyes to the dirt. There wasn't a man in the country who had not heard the heroic stories of the defenders of Texas. Expecting a shrine, he again cast his eyes at the tattered structure that looked more a warehouse or barn. He glanced once more at Cullum, who didn't seem to be affected by the depressing condition of the hallmark of Texas legends.

"I was expecting it to look different," Rance muttered.

Cullum just nodded. "Well, that's it." The sutler peeked at the sun. "Look, I've got to get back to the store. I'm sure Mary has opened the doors and is cursing my name for not being there for the customers." He pointed farther down the street. "Around the corner there and another few streets over, you'll find what you're wanting." In a hurry, he shook Rance's hand and scurried back in the direction of the store.

Rance nodded, still a bit dumbfounded over his discovery of the Alamo. He watched Cullum walk out of sight, but once he faced about, found himself lost once more as to which street he was to follow and which corner to turn. For a moment, he gave thought to waiting for the Alamo Saloon to open, but that would mean taking even more time wandering the streets than he planned. The other choice would be to enter the Menger for directions and suffer the browbeating he would surely receive from Calvin. He'd rather have waited for the saloon to open.

While pondering, he noticed across the street from the saloon a lone old-timer under the broad shade of an elm tree seated on a crate with another supporting a flat board. Curious and needing advice, he slowly crossed the dusty lane to come next to the man, who intently stared at a checkerboard with the pieces strategically placed on the squares.

"Excuse me, sir. I was wondering if I might ask —"

"Hush up," came the stern reply from the old white-whiskered man in a long-handled top with suspenders supporting his dungarees and a soiled bowler on his head. "Can't you see we're in a game here?"

The remark steered Rance's view to the other side of the board. Atop a third crate sat a black rooster with a flourishing red comb. Rance shook his head, not wanting to assume the absurd. However, the old-timer made it obvious.

"Ole Chuck, there, he's a-thinking."

Rance first looked at the old-timer, then at the bird, who with an abrupt turn of the head gave an appearance it might be looking at the pieces or on the lookout for a cat. Rance swayed his view from the old-timer to the chicken. From the man to the rooster. From the human being to the animal with a brain the size of a corn kernel. This wasn't what it seemed. Rance grunted his throat clear. "I was searching —"

"Quiet, damn you." The old man leaned closer to the checkerboard, eyes fixed on the bird. "Chuck is a crafty player. Always scheming on his next move, to get the jump."

Now, more stunned than when he first saw the dilapidated Alamo, he stood motionless in part to not receive another admonishment from the old-timer and the other in utter confusion. He watched as man and bird analyzed the placement of the pieces.

Chuck jutted his head. The old-timer mirrored the move. When the bird recessed his long neck, a laugh hooted out. "He's worried now. I've got him."

"I'm sorry I've disturbed your play. I was just wanting to know —"

Chuck crowed and flapped his wings.

"Damn you, you filthy bastard." The old-timer moved the black piece closest to his own red, jumping over three red pieces and removing them from the board to be placed in front of the rooster. The old-timer sat back in a depressed slump. "I was hoping he wasn't watching what trap I set for him." He shook his head. "But, he was too smart," he ended with a nod. The old man turned to

Rance with a puzzled face. "Now what do you want?"

In a stupor over the events just witnessed, Rance stammered. "I — I was looking for a leather-goods merchant."

"Horton Manley has a shop down at the end of the corner." He pointed to the south. "Head down this street, turn at the first corner. Go twenty paces, turn to the left, you'll be at his door."

The simple directions were clear and easy to understand. Satisfied he could follow them, Rance tipped his hat. "Thank you, uh . . ."

"Dudley."

"Dudley, my name is Rance," he said, offering his hand. The old-timer went back to scanning the board without accepting the offer. Rance just wiped his trousers with the palm. "Well, I'll let you get back to your game."

Another shrug came with the reply. "He's got me now. No," he lamented with a shake of his head. "No beating Chuck when he's got you on the run. No better than he."

Rance paused at the remark, deciding to leave the scene before he watched Chuck swipe the ground with Dudley. He walked to the edge of the street and then to the corner. Hesitant to follow the directions of a man

76

who lost at checkers to a chicken, he had no better prospects and so did. He walked what he counted as twenty man-size paces, watching the passersby as they watched him. When at the final count of twenty, he turned left. In front of him was a shop with a sign of leather goods painted on the window. Surprised and amazed that the skeptical advice proved to be worthy, Rance entered the shop amid the chime of bells.

"Can I help you?"

Rance followed the greeting to the front counter. "Yes, sir, I believe you can. Are you Mr. Manley?" The owner nodded. "My name is Cash." He removed the .44 from his belt. "I am needing a proper holster for this."

Manley received the weapon with the awe shown a priceless piece of jewelry. "That's a Walker Colt," he said softly. Rance only bobbed his brow at the reverence. "Don't see many of these around these days." Manley squinted an eye to peer down the barrel then at the chamber. "Appears to be some time since it was last loaded and fired."

Rance thought about the time that had passed since the gun's proper owner sat by a fire and meticulously tended to the task of priming the cylinders. "How did you know that?"

Manley arched a brow at Rance, then

eased it while returning attention to the pistol. "The rust around the bore. Also, the wadding looks old. Turned brown from moisture." He looked up at Rance. "How long has it been since you fired it?"

Stuck for an answer, Rance only shrugged. "It was actually a sort of gift."

"Gift?" Manley again looked at the pistol. "This weapon was made for use by rangers. They were the only ones I ever seen as the ones carrying them around. Now, most men handling a gun use brass cartridge loads. This is still a more powerful gun. Wouldn't think someone would give it away."

"Well," Rance drawled, hoping a satisfactory answer would enter his head. "It was kind of passed down, you might say."

Again, Manley arched a brow at Rance. "Passed down? Like from some sort of kin?"

"An elderly gent who helped me out of a tough spot." Rance was eager to change the subject. "What I was seeking was a holster that might better handle the weight." Manley nodded at the idea and went to a rack of gunbelts that hung from pegs on the wall. When he pulled a hip holster that accommodated the long barrel, Rance shook his head. The vision of sitting with a hogleg strapped to the thigh while contemplating the play of cards didn't feel right. Besides, most of the men he'd seen carrying such guns usually had to place them on the table, making them vulnerable to be seized and used against their owners.

The next one taken off the rack was met with a recollection. At first sight, he was reminded about the time not yet three months old when Colton Schuyler nearly killed him from a pistol drawn from such a gun rest. The black leather loop was meant to wrap around both shoulders for support. The holster was reversed so to rest against the left chest and hold the pistol butt protruding back for easy reach for the right hand.

"This is one I think you may be interested in." Manley walked around Rance and helped him off with the coat. Just as with the coat, Rance slipped on the holster. It fit like a vest. "I can switch out the holster for the forty-four," said Manley while removing the holster and helping Rance back on with the coat. "By the weight feels like something else in there."

Rance smiled, pulling the lapels for the fit on his shoulders. He reached inside his coat and pulled out the pepperbox, anxious for the same respect to be given for his first choice in pistols.

Manley took a long stare at the gun in Rance's palm, then broke out in laughter. "Is that what that was?"

Humbled, Rance nodded. "It is a —"

"Pepperbox," answered Manley. "I know what it is. English gun. And by far, without equal, the most unreliable weapon known to mankind. Has it gone off all six barrels at once yet?"

Again recalling his encounter with Schuyler, Rance remembered looking down the muzzle of a short-barreled revolver. It was the unreliable nature of the pepperbox that nearly got him killed when it misfired, and moments later saved his life when all six barrels indeed did fire at once and ended Colton Schuyler's days. "As a matter of fact, it did just that."

"I recommend you bury that before it buries you."

It wasn't the first time Rance heard the advice. However, it was the pistol he chose when he started out from New Orleans on his own nearly four years ago. No matter its questionable reputation, it was now a part of him. Not something to be parted from. Rance shook his head. "No. I can't do that. No. What I'd like you to do is make another holster on the right hip." He motioned the draw for the weapon.

Manley nodded, then cocked his head in a manner of questioning the intelligence of the choice. "I already got what you're looking for." In a short time, the shop owner brought to the counter a holster proportioned to the size needed. Rance threaded it onto his belt.

"Are you planning on reloading that weapon?"

The shop owner's inquiry forced Rance to stop his quick retreat to the door. "Actually, I don't own powder and supply to do such."

"I can. If you like."

The offer was delightful. "As a matter of fact, I would," Rance accepted with some cheer.

"I can have it done in the next hour. Leave that English peashooter. I'll reload that, too." Rance ignored the remark but did surrender the pepperbox so to include it in the offer. As Manley began to write out the bill, Rance flipped his wrist in a casual manner. "Just send the bill to the Menger Hotel." Manley's eyes widened, but Rance took the pencil from his hand and scribbled a signature before allowing any objection. "Good day to you, sir. I am beholden for your service. And I'll be back shortly." With that said, Rance turned for the door and quickly left the shop.

A huge sigh of relief later, he retraced his steps back to the square in front of the hotel and the Alamo Saloon. Once around the corner he weaved his way through the people on the boardwalk until he reached the front of the establishment. As hoped, the doors were open and a barkeep was sweeping off the planks at the threshold.

"Good morning to you, sir," he said. The barkeep peered indifferently over his shoulder and entered into the saloon. Rance was only too glad to follow, anxious at the chance to practice his trade. Just before he stepped through, he glanced across the street.

There was no sign of Dudley. Or Chuck for that matter. Nor were there any crates stacked on end.

6

Into the dark den of iniquity, Rance walked in the same comfort as if surrounded by his mother's arms. In the brief time the place was open, several patrons already had assembled along the bar at the back of the room. Three of the locals sat at one of the four tables in the center.

Rance pushed back his hat and pulled out a chair. "You gents mind if I join you?" Without an objection, he took the seat and noticed one of them rumple playing cards from one hand into the other. "You fellows looking for a game?"

Stern stares came his way. "Who are you?"

"The name is Cash. Rance Cash," he said, offering his hand in friendly manner. There were no takers.

"You some sort of sharp?"

The reference to those accustomed to cheating passengers on steamboats and trains was understood. Rance flashed his grin. "Me?" He shook his head as innocently as he had in the Cullums' store. "Nah. I'm just waiting on my intended to join me here. We plan to make Texas our home. Just looking to make friends for her to meet." A shrug was needed to further the purpose. "Perhaps engage in a little sport while I'm waiting."

Initially, it wasn't certain if the tale had been bought, but a few moments of scanning faces sold the story. The one with the cards began to shuffle. Reaching into his pocket, Rance was quickly reminded of his meager funds. Although he could be mistaken, he figured these players were used to higher stakes than forty cents.

"I have an idea," he said as the deal was about to be made. "Would you allow me?" With an open palm, he asked for and eventually received the deck. "I thought we might enjoy a neighborly game meant for fun before we engage in serious play." Shuffling the cards, he quickly spotted the five of hearts third in line from the top of the deck. "This is a game taught to me by my wife-to-be." Rance thought the mention of a woman would challenge any man to beat a female parlor game.

In truth, the game was the favorite of a woman. A lovely beauty who had shuffled hands to Union officers during the occupation of New Orleans. Her play had multiple advantages. Never one to risk sparse revenue, she offered her own tokens, minted with a fleur-de-lis on one side and the French image of a bare-breasted Lady Liberty on the other. One coin represented a minute of time with a minimum of fourteen needed in order to be redeemed for her exclusive services. She only accepted Yankee issue as her reward. Those officers with less than fourteen tokens were left to choose from her workers with all of them splitting the bounty taken. Yet, it was the pursuit of her that kept those officers coming back to her table.

Rance reshuffled and squeezed the bridge to flatten the deck, slapping the stack on the table, spreading the deck facedown in a long, arched line. He looked to the dealer. "Ten dollars says you draw the five of hearts." The dealer eyed each of his friends, then reluctantly reached into a pocket. Rance shook his palm. "Friend," he said with a smile, "I assume we are all gentlemen of the South and therefore good for our debts." The dealer took a moment before he nodded, then reached with his middle finger and drew a single card. Quickly, Rance nabbed the card before it was seen by the rest.

With the sole knowledge the card drawn was the three of clubs, Rance nodded at the rest. "Very good." He turned his focus to the one to his right. "Now, you sir. I will bet you twenty dollars that you can draw the three of clubs."

"Wait a damn minute," said the dealer. "Let's see the card."

"All in good time, friend." Rance pointed at the one to the right. "What say? Are you game?"

The dare was enough to spark the man's pride. It only took an instant before the man fingered a card and Rance again casually but quickly snatched it from view. Flipping it toward himself, Rance held the ace of diamonds. He nodded again. "That's what I like to see."

"See what? Let us see."

"Of course," said Rance, about to show the cards of which only one was correct, but he stopped. "Unless, you'd like to double the bet?"

"Double? Hell, son, I'd like to see what I won or lost before I look to bet more money."

With a grin, Rance wiggled a finger at the ceiling. "Yes, that may be so. But among the three of you, I'm sure you can come up with a mere ten dollars more apiece to see the three cards I've picked."

"Three?" they all questioned in unison.

"That's right," Rance said with a nod. "Because I'm going to bet you all the money that I have in my pockets, that I can draw the ace of diamonds out of the pile."

"You ain't proved a thing yet," said the dealer.

"Ah, yes. But you see sir, that's the beauty of cards. You have to pay to see. Do I have a bet?"

It was the dealer, who after a glance to his friends on the left and right, spoke for the group. "All right then. You have a bet."

Rance's smile grew as he scanned over the deck carefully, acting as if he needed to ponder which card he needed to pull. Finally, after rubbing his chin and cheek, he thumbed out the card third from the end. He picked it up, peeked at it, and slid the card between the other two. "Any chance we might be able to call off the bet?"

The dealer leaned over the table and grabbed the cards from Rance's grasp. Snapping them on the table face up were the ace of diamonds, three of clubs, and the five of hearts.

"Gents," Rance said as he reclined in his chair. "Since we've concluded this game, I think it time to let tempers settle and to settle up so we can get on with a relaxing game of poker."

A quick glance about gauged thirty or better patrons had drifted into the saloon in the three hours of play. Resuming his view to the table, the same three originals were still in the game, however, only after leaving for two trips each to a private reserve of cash in order to stay in the game of seven-card stud. Rance kept a modest stack of bills in front of him, stuffing the majority of his winnings into his wallet. It would be rude and risky to count the success, but by his instinctive nature, he had garnered a take of $486, not including the $70 in front of him.

"Call."

The loud announcement brought Rance's mind back to the game. He placed down his three jacks and watched as the once-grumpy dealer surrendered the pot after showing three eights. Rance counted the modest pot of fifty-six dollars, noticing the uneasy nature brewing in the saloon. "Just a streak of bad luck, gents. What say we change the game to five cards. Increase in the likelihood of straights and flushes."

"No," said the dealer as he rose from the table. "That's enough beating for me. It'll be five months before I can earn back what I left here. I never seen a man who can win four out of every five hands, mister."

Rance took it as a compliment, knowing it wasn't meant as praise. "I must confess. I am amazed at the result. All this will go toward a beautiful wedding in your fair town." However sincerely he delivered the proclamation to soothe the loss of the departing players, the heavy scent of restless regret hung over the saloon. Counting the bills in front of him, Rance thought it best to retire for the day. About to scoot back from the table, a voice broke over the noise of the crowd.

"I'll play you."

Rance peered up at the other side of the table. A tall brute in a faded top hat, gold shimmering vest, and long coat stood on the other side. The greedy grin of the man didn't invite for a match. "I beg your pardon?" Rance asked innocently.

The big man pulled out a chair and sat, arms folded on the table. "I said, I'll play you." He tapped his finger. "I'll match what you got in your hand and all that you stuffed in your pockets." Rance grinned at the bold wager, until he heard the rest of it. "But, my take won't be for that."

"No?"

The big man shook his head and opened his jowl like a hungry dog. "No. You see, I've got a lot more I'm after. My name is Red McClain, and you're going to remember that. I've been running the game here probably since your daddy wet your mama, and you are in my chair. So, you see, one of us has to leave. So, you're going to stack them cards," he said with a nod. "And we're going to cut cards to see who goes."

At first, he expected a hearty laugh, but in an instant realized he was in a game for his life when McClain leaned back in his chair to let it be seen he was carrying dual pistols in his belt. In response, Rance matched the play by leaning back and opening his coat. Only after the chuckles from the crowd did he remember the .44 and the pepperbox were at Manley's leather shop being loaded for just such an incident.

Deciding that cowardice was much preferred to valor, Rance let out with a laugh of his own. "As a matter of fact, Mr. McClain, I was just leaving," he said with a smile. "Had I known the chair was yours, I would gladly found another." He scooted back from the table and opened his palm as surrender.

"That's smart of you, son," replied McClain. "I see you got brains." He pointed at folded bills in Rance's hand. "But, there's still the matter of the money that you took while sitting in my chair."

The room fell silent.

Rance looked to the money in his right hand. "But, this is money I played for. It's mine."

McClain shook his head still with his hungry face intact.

With a long, silent snort, Rance realized there was a decision to be made. It was one matter to relinquish the chair, but quite another to allow hard cash to slip through his fingers. He peeked again at the money, then at the pistols in McClain's belt. It may have been time to fold, but this game was not over.

"Mr. McClain, you have me at a disadvantage," he said, opening his coat. The plea didn't serve to sway the big thug. "So, I will have to relent to your terms." He dropped the money in his hand to spill onto the table.

"What about the rest? That you got in your pocket," McClain said, corralling the loose money.

To concede any money was painful enough, even though it could be reasoned that the tactic was less costly than accepting a bullet. However, there was a line to be crossed. As long as it was stood behind, it would always be drawn further to the rear. As he stared into Red McClain's eyes he decided it was here he had to make his stand.

"No."

The murmur of the crowd showed the surprise at the decision.

"No?" asked a stunned McClain. "What are you saying, son?"

"I'm saying —" He took a long breath, waiting for an answer to come into his mind. "I'm saying no, I am not going to give you the money." The murmur became louder. "You see, Red — may I call you Red?" He inhaled and thought about the peculiar name. While pondering that insignificant fact, another single-word name crept into his mind. Suddenly he had all the answers he needed, if he played them right. "You see, Red, a good friend of mine wouldn't think much of me if I was to give you money that I promised to pay him."

At first starting with a giddy laugh, then a chuckle, McClain glanced about the room, unaccustomed to hearing a refusal. "Friend? Boy, I'm the only friend you got to have in this town. Now, I don't care who this friend is, but I —"

"Marcus Broussard," Rance interrupted. The murmured voices fell silent. "Captain Marcus Broussard." He glimpsed the confusion of the locals as to the name. A loud introduction was needed. "Of the Fourth

Texas Brigade. Hero of the gallant sons of Texas during the fighting at Gettysburg on behalf of the Southern cause." The murmured voices now grew. Rance sensed they were in his favor as McClain scanned the reverence given by the locals.

"What's he to you?"

When asked a question about a lie, it was best to back it up with another. "I saved his life."

McClain arched a brow. "Saved his life? How did a scrawny fellow like you save a war hero's life?"

While holding a strong hand, it was best to bet big. "I pulled him out of a river when we were in Indian Territory together a few months ago. If I hadn't, he would have drowned." It was an easy lie to recall. The roles of the two men were the exact opposite when Smith had saved Rance's life. Despite the actual truth, the fable was holding all in the saloon's attention. It was time to call. "I was just going to have dinner with him. I need to tell him why I was delayed."

For the first time since they had met, McClain's face now held the pose of apprehension. He scanned left and right, perhaps in effort to establish any merit to the story from the faces of the patrons. "Is he coming back with you?"

Rance shook his head. "I would expect a Texas Ranger, as he is, to leave me to settle my trouble myself. However, I may need the loan of his Walker Colt." His blood pounding through his veins, his nostrils flared, Rance Cash turned for the door.

"Are you going to leave this money here?" asked a nervous-voiced McClain.

Rance paused only long enough to peer over his shoulder. "No, Red. You keep it here. It will give me something to come back and play for." With that said, Rance faced straight and went in the sunlight.

7

Once out on the boardwalk, Rance turned right and out of view of those inside. Only then did he inhale. When he let out the breath, he quickly took another just to be sure he wouldn't faint dead. As conscious thoughts of what to do next slammcd into his head, the first of reason was to retrieve that which he'd bragged so much about.

He crossed the street at a hurried pace, dodging the horse traffic and spooking one mount to the curses of its rider. Once around the bend, he threaded his way through wrought-iron pillar supports, tipping his hat to the ladies in his best attempt to show his casual nature while he stepped quickly. Finally, as before, he arrived at Manley's shop, although this time in less than twenty paces.

He grabbed the knob, but it wouldn't move. He tried again with the same result.

The door stood locked. He peeked into the glass. Even without the benefit of a sign, he figured the shop owner had locked up for the midday meal. Rance would have to wait on the .44 Walker Colt.

He took another deep breath, realizing it wouldn't be long before the stunning boasts given to Red McClain would wear away. The big man had been shamed by a dude from the East and that likely would eat away at any fear of Rance. Only the presence of a pistol would back up the play. However, that ploy was at least one hour away.

Plans of leaving San Antonio crept into his head. He had made some money. Certainly considerably more than he had when he arrived. He could make his escape and still hold some honor at his success. The more he thought about it, the less sure he was about the idea. He knew nothing of the surroundings. How far he would get without a guide couldn't be certain. It was a poor risk. At least that's how he came to decide to stay. It was a good excuse.

While retracing his path, he silently admitted the real reason for remaining in San Antonio. Despite leaving the Alamo Saloon with his life, he had left a noticeable sum on the table. The facade of an experienced gunman was a performance worthy of a shower of applause, but like many actors, he lost himself in the performance. In doing so, there was hard-earned money that belonged to him that wasn't presently in his pocket. He couldn't leave it behind. It was a matter of principle. A matter of pride.

While in thought, he absentmindedly rounded the corner of Crockett Street, back to the place where he was least comfortable. Upon sighting the Alamo Saloon his stomach churned with each step. However, as he neared the Menger, he rationalized the queasy feeling could be from hunger. Carefully, he stayed from view from the saloon's door and slipped under the narrow portico of the hotel.

When he stepped inside, Calvin stood at the front desk. When their eyes met, Rance's shoulders slumped. Calvin came around the desk. Convinced he was about to be run from the premises or, worse, given a bill for his night's stay on the couch, he stood confused as Calvin broke into a welcoming smile and offered his hand.

"Rance! I missed you this morning. It's good to see you."

For an instant, Rance looked to the vacant front desk just to be sure he hadn't mistaken this gregarious person for the strict clerk. He took the man's hand, still in shock. Calvin continued, "Are you hungry? I didn't notice you at breakfast this morning. Greta has dinner ready. Let me join you." They faced about to the restaurant with Rance still in a daze over the change in Calvin's attitude.

When they reached the table, those patrons already seated stared in near fear over his arrival. Rance and Calvin sat at the same table where Rance first ate almost twenty-four hours before. Just about to tuck his napkin into his collar, Calvin's head turned back toward the lobby. With a smile, he excused himself to perform his duty at the front counter. Still dazed, Rance faced around as Greta came to the table with a pot of coffee.

"What's got into him?"

The tall, blond beauty kept her eyes on the porcelain cup as she poured the java. "He is trying to be nice to you." The initial explanation was obvious enough even for Rance. However, further details took him by surprise. "Now that you are the *big* man in the town."

"Big man?"

Once the cup was filled, she lifted the saucer beneath and placed it in front of him. "Gossip has spread that you challenged Herr Red McClain at the Alamo Saloon. The people's talk is you called against his honor bravely without a gun. Everyone thinks you are a hero of the war and rode with Texas Rangers. I've heard you've killed sixty men, all bare-handed, and that you plan to be the next governor of Texas."

Upon hearing the news, it was little wonder at Calvin's new attitude. His charade in the saloon had swelled in distortion, as was the habit of most townsfolk anywhere. Nevertheless, it wasn't all bad. "Governor, huh?"

Greta looked down her nose at him. It was enough to slam him back into reality. He nodded at the prudence of her reminder.

"Well, it was something like that." He quickly slurped the coffee to help cure his cotton mouth. The steaming brew singed his lip, but the strong taste slowed his mind enough to ponder. Greta remained at the table and refilled the cup.

"So. You are pleased? It is good for you now?"

Rance considered the question, cocking his head from side to side. "Things are better. Not good I would call them. But, they may be getting that way."

His words hung in the air, and although he didn't take much more from the cup, Greta stayed. It was enough to have him pause while thinking of his next move and peer up at her. She stood straight, eyes avoiding his. "It is dinnertime. But, you look like you need a good breakfast. I will bring you eggs and some ham." She still didn't look him in the eye, but rather faced about and went to another table to refill the other patrons' coffee cups and retrieve empty plates.

Rance sat in a stupor. First, he saw the ramshackle Alamo to his dismay, met a man engaging in games with a rooster, hustled a few locals in poker, nearly goaded another man to shoot him in the back, and learned the experience had made him the legend about the town. Yet, what he most remarked about the day so far was the momentary glimpse at this woman standing above as if looking for an excuse to stay. It had been an eventful day.

Breakfast was just the remedy for his nerves. Even though most folks had finished dinner, the opportunity to start with a morning meal and the solitude to enjoy it provided Rance with a clear enough head. Greta kept herself busy and out of sight for the most part. He need not bother her nor spoil the hum in his soul over what he felt was, at least, her mild interest in him.

However, day was more than halfway done. It was time for him to continue what he started. Quietly, he rose from the table and was careful to exit while she wasn't about. Had she seen him, he would have expected too much from their parting and read far too much in her slightest twitch. He'd rather leave without being noticed where he could imagine what he liked to think her reaction would be, reasonable or not.

He used the side door of the hotel to begin his path to Manley's. As he walked, he noticed a different spirit to his step. He went to the shop and found the knob unlocked. The familiar chimes signaled his entry. The shop owner recognized him and had the two freshly loaded pistols tucked into their respective holsters.

With his encounter with Greta still in his mind, he struggled to concentrate on Manley's instructions on the use of the .44. He was already well experienced on the finicky pepperbox. Manley helped him off with the coat and on with the new leather. Once the coat was back on, Rance tipped his hat to the merchant who had bestowed greater confidence in this young gambler. Rance turned for the door and headed to the Alamo Saloon to reclaim his chair.

During the walk, he readied himself for the confrontation, but when he crossed the street and passed the white frontage of the Menger glistening in the western sun, his heart began to pound. Finally he stepped up to the boardwalk and went through the open doors of the Alamo Saloon.

The place held a bevy of locals, all with their eyes turned his way when he entered. The hush guided him through those standing around the one table he had left earlier in the day. Once by the last of the spectators, he saw Red McClain seated in the chair of dispute. The two gamblers by trade eyed each other for a moment, then Rance moved to the far side of the table from McClain.

"I see you have sand there, Cash," said McClain as Rance pulled out the one empty chair. As he sat, he was careful to pull open his coat and reveal the weapons he'd brought to back up his play. "That there's Captain Broussard's piece?"

Rance scooted the chair closer to the table, keeping his eyes on the deck in the center of the table, then he nodded. "It is."

"Think there's going to be reason to use it?"

Rance slowly lifted his head and forced a grin across his lips. "I don't know, Red. That depends on you."

The two men stared into each other's eyes. Rance had no idea where he garnered the courage to keep his eyes locked on McClain. If there was to be gunplay, he surely would be last on the draw and decidedly sorry if not dead from it. Nonetheless, he was playing the part hc'd bccn cast. As long as he was alive, he was on a winning streak.

The tension was measured by the silence of the surrounding patrons who no doubt had come to see a showdown. Red McClain didn't change from his steely face, at least at first. The long mutual stare slowly eroded away on McClain's face. Like a bubble, he huffed a single chuckle, then another. Three more followed until the big thug erupted into a huge guffaw. Rance let his smile show his acceptance of the truce.

"Let's play," shouted McClain, slapping the table. Rance reached for the deck, but McClain snatched the cards as an exhibit that he hadn't completely relinquished the table. Rance leaned back in the chair while watching the shuffle.

The hands were dealt facedown to the five players. As Rance made a motion to assemble the cards, he was met with a sharp order from McClain.

"Leave them lay." As he continued tossing cards in front of each player, a sly grin crept over his lips. "We're going to play a little game known here as Mexican Sweat." He finished the deal and slammed the deck in the center of the table. "A hundred dollars buys into the game. You show your hand one card at a time."

The rule had Rance take another deep breath, but he did his best not to show his concern. He'd played this game before, although the name changed according to the locale. The challenge was to play the hand when even he didn't know the value of the five cards. Only after each round of betting could one flip over a single card and form a strategy on the potential of the remaining unseen cards.

Rance threw in his hundred-dollar ante and after the player to his right showed the ace of clubs to the awe of the assembled crowd, he turned over the center card of his five. King of diamonds.

The two to his left followed with each player showing a jack. With all eyes watching intently, Red McClain rolled over his center card. Five of hearts. The small card brought renewed confidence to Rance. The player to his right tossed in twenty more and flipped over the jack of spades. With three of the one-eyed gentlemen already showing, Rance hoped he had one of the last two remaining to escort his king. He called the bet and turned over the deuce of diamonds. Normally his enthusiasm would sink with a card so far away from the other, but two in the same suit kept him in the game.

The two players to the left didn't provide much drama. Each of them produced small cards but not in the same suit. With that disappointment both folded their hands.

McClain spent little time matching the amount and showing the seven of clubs.

The play was now to Rance. He eyed Red and the other player. It was about to get to a point where the stakes were painful. Always looking for an edge, he decided to employ a tactic that every player despised.

"Well, well. What to do." He took his time to allow the aggravation to set in. After several seconds of silence and inaction, he pricked McClain's nerve.

"Get on with it, Cash. You in or you out?"

He smiled inside, careful not to show his delight at the success. "I don't know, Red. This game is new to me," he lied. He fumbled with the bills in front of him. Finally, allowing as much time to pass as possible, he raised the pot with another twenty. "I'll go another round." He flipped over the three of clubs. His heart did sink this time. Wrong suit.

McClain went through the same tactic, arching a brow at Rance, then the other player. Back and forth went his eyes from the cards to Rance, to the other player, back to the cards, and so on that Rance had to bite his tongue to not fall victim to his own ploy. Finally, he threw in a pair of twenty-dollar coins and nudged over the eight of spades. His gap-toothed jowls slipped open in delight. "You fellows sweating yet?" He looked to the player to the right. "How 'bout you, Hank?"

Rance took notice of the player's name but paid even more attention to the building straight Red was composing. Normally when he was nervous, he let his mouth do some distracting. However, it didn't appear needed with the big gambler's needling of Hank.

"I'm fine, Red," said the calm Hank, as he dipped into his pocket and drew three silver fifty-dollar pieces and stacked them onto the table. "I'll raise." Without much consideration for the stakes, which appeared by all likelihood the entire amount he was carrying, Hank turned over his fourth card. King of clubs.

8

The turn of the card was met with giddy laughs and individual cheers of support from the surrounding crowd. Rance sat concerned, yet intrigued. There was a sense that Red McClain and Hank had a history and he was glad to see it. It would take the burden of carrying all the play from his shoulders.

Red didn't appear intrigued, but rather perturbed. He appeared wanting to bully his way into a win. Now, he was forced to make a decision whether to stay in his own game. While Hank had the royal family on his side, Red had only the threat of a flimsy straight. Again, he went through his routine of shifting his gaze from cards to opponent.

"Them half-breed kids will need feeding. Remember that, Hank."

The remark turned Hank's view to the big man, who didn't seem sorry for the insult.

Without words, Hank slowly looked back at the cards, then at Rance. With all the buzzing in the crowd, it was apparent that, instead of a history, these two had more of a long feud. Yet, the play was to Rance and the stakes were getting out of hand for his meager holdings. Figuring it might be more to his advantage to stay out of the middle while these other two settle their differences, he held up his palm.

"Fold."

The announcement brought McClain's face at him like a shot. "Fold? Hell, Cash, I thought you were more game than that. Are you going to let him scare you?"

"Too little for me to play with, Red. Besides, I think you two can get along without me," Rance said with a smirk. He enjoyed the strain etched over McClain's face. It wasn't quite as easy reading Hank's features. No doubt quite a few years younger than McClain, there was a great sense that his time here in Texas had not been an easy one. The modest wide-brimmed hat and plain, dust-stained white shirt were testament to the hardworking labor class. Despite the presence at a poker table, something told Rance this was an honest man of means. It may have been due to the wide shoulders, or the straight posture just as if he were sitting in a pew. Since Rance himself was out of the game, he would use the disarming tactic of questions when it would benefit the most.

McClain continued to dawdle. With each thumbing of the paper money, he contemplated the risk of staying in the game. Finally, he peeled off the matching amount and tossed it into the pot. With a slow, deliberate move he pushed the five of hearts to the center of the table. "Dealer takes one." He took the top card from the deck and turned it face up. Four of spades.

The cringe on McClain's face warmed Rance's heart. The play of discarding a higher card for a lower one didn't improve the big man's hand. Hank didn't show any delight. Rather, he dug into his pocket once more and produced a single five-dollar gold piece. Although a substandard amount in poker, it was enough to keep him in the game and allow for the turning of another card. Ten of spades.

Just like a welcoming parade, the crowd applauded, although be it briefly. McClain's scowl sprayed the spectators with a gruff, silent order to be still. It was, however, clear who was the people's choice.

The odds were against the big gambler. As he surveyed the cards on the table, it was obviously a poor risk to stay in this game. The modest Hank was a queen away from an ace-high straight while McClain worsened his hand with a four. Despite the loss of pride at losing, the big thug showed he hadn't lost his mind. He waved his hand at the pot to the delight of the those surrounding the table. While Hank drew the pot of money toward him and McClain looked to his remaining hand of the six of hearts and deuce of clubs, the big gambler couldn't let it go without a few parting words.

"That ought to buy a few more beans for them Mexican runts you're raising."

The insult was loud enough and made even more so with the hush of the crowd. Poor losers were common in games of chance and their nasty comments were a nuisance to be shrugged away. However, if they were to shake an opponent's wits while playing it was considered fair game. When they were used after the game was over, it was a message of spite. Hank appeared to take it so.

He lifted his view from the pile of money and stared directly at McClain. "You leave my kids out of this."

Big Red chuckled and gave a mock look of surprise. "Oh, is that what you call them." He paused only long enough to allow Hank to stack the bills and coins. "I call them mud-grubbing greasers."

The two players on the left scampered away from the table. Hank didn't make a move much to the disappointment of Mc-Clain and Rance. The idea of chasing the winner from the game was confusing, unless McClain wanted all that money to leave the room. The other strategy was to make the man so mad he would fall into a slump. However, Rance's dismay was over Hank's lack of action when McClain had no intention of stopping. As the buzz of the room fed the tension, Rance felt it necessary to resume the game. If for no other reason than to recapture the money he himself lost.

"Red, I thought you a more gracious host?" The question posed brought all eyes his way. Rance seized the opportunity to assemble the cards for his turn at the deal. "Normally, it's customary to welcome the winner to a new hand. I didn't think you would want Hank here to leave with all your hard-earned money. Do you?" He shuffled the cards while the confused McClain looked to both he and Hank. The tension seemed to ease as Rance flashed his smile about the room. "What say we continue in a more gentlemanly fashion."

With a sense he had restored some decorum to the game, he shuffled and reshuffled the cards, tossing them from one hand to the other. The crowd peeled back off the table. Red McClain allowed his sparse-toothed smile to show, and Hank appeared willing to have another hand. All seemed well. Before the mood changed, Rance dealt the cards. With only three of them, it seemed appropriate to get to know each other. "Hank, what might be your family's name?"

"Baines," was the simple answer as he lined the facedown cards in a row.

Rance peeked at McClain, who seemed more in a trance looking at the card. He knew the peace wouldn't last long, so to get the game started, he threw in his hundred-dollar ante. The other two did the same. With all in order, Rance turned his first card. Queen of clubs. Encouraged, Rance didn't want to scare off a game, and so only took a modest bill. "I'll raise twenty."

Hank didn't seem worried, but the play was next to McClain. As before, he took an inordinate amount of time to respond. Finally, he called the bet and turned his first card. Six of hearts.

Hank didn't waste any time. He put in twenty and flipped his card. Ace of diamonds.

The haste of the play didn't allow for Rance to bring his most favorite tactic. He'd have to make up for lost time. "So, Hank, if you don't mind me calling you that, what is your line?"

"I work twenty-five acres about fifteen miles from here." The answer wasn't important, but it was a start.

Rance eyed his dwindling stash, but he wanted to keep the game moving and interesting. "A farmer. A noble profession. I never had the patience to work soil. You're a man to be admired. I'll raise another twenty." Queen of hearts.

With the discovery of the twin sisters, Rance was hoping he held the whole family. He spied a glance at McClain, who didn't show much interest in Rance's hand, but showed more attention to Hank. "I heard you had a poor harvest. Lost your crop with that hailstorm a few weeks back. I'll call and raise fifty." McClain tossed in the money and turned his second card. Four of hearts.

With suited cards so close, McClain held a threat, but Rance still had a standing pair and felt no pressure yet. Hank looked to his cards, let out a long sigh, then grabbed the stack of coins he previously risked. "I'll see the bet and raise three hundred." He quickly flipped over his card. Ten of clubs.

The spectators buzzed at the bold bet and the same suit. Rance needed time to think.

"This reminds me of a time when I was in Memphis."

"I don't want to hear no talk about Memphis," McClain interrupted. He leaned closer, elbows on the table and peered at Hank who didn't match eyes with the big man. "Are you sure you know what you're doing, boy?" Rance felt the reason for doing so was to intimidate the younger player. However, the longer the words hung in the air, the more he sensed it was a personal matter. "Seems to me you still have a heap of bills due around town. Do your creditors know you're in here risking their money?"

"It ain't their money," Hank sniped, but McClain wasn't finished.

"Oh, I think it is. Once they learn you're in here losing *their* money, they're going to be mad. Probably call the law on you. Have them kids run off that barren place you have."

"Gentlemen, please," said Rance. "I'm trying to play a nice game of poker." He wanted to ease the tension, but the attempt failed. McClain remained a hulking presence over the table. It was best to resume the attention to the cards before they and all the money was spilled all over the floor. "I'll call the bet," he said, his blood pumping a little faster with the huge amount being pushed to the middle of the pot. However, if he was going to risk, it might be time to test the others' mettle. "And go another hundred." He turned the card. Nine of clubs.

The bet didn't seem to deter McClain. He lifted an elbow and counted out the matching funds. "I'll call." He turned the card in the center of his row. Five of clubs. Upon sight of the burgeoning straight, the crowd hummed their concern for Hank, while Red let go with a hooting celebration.

"Things got a heap worse for you, boy."

Rance wasn't sure if the warning was for him or Hank. Soon it became clear that his harassment of the farmer was unrelenting. "Could be the second-worst mistake you made." The assessment only begged the question of the worst mistake made. Rance was curious, but knew that should he ask, he might spark the fight his way. Preferring to remain neutral, he watched as Hank stared long at the small assets he held. McClain didn't keep silent. "We all know what the first was."

Just as the words left the big thug's mouth, Hank pushed what he had into the pot. "I'll see it. And raise seventy-five."

"The worst was plugging that little Mexican whore, then marrying the trash when she turned up plump with his bastard."

Hank rose from the chair, standing over McClain, fists clenched, but he had no gun. "I've had enough, Red. You want to settle this here and now?"

"Take it outside," was the shout from the bar. That was exactly what Rance didn't want. He wanted to finish the game, then the two could have at each other all they desired.

"Gents," he said, trying to seize their attention. "Let's get back to the game. Mr. Baines has yet to show his card." Hank's scowl was met with the unconcerned if not amused face of Red McClain, goading the modest farmer to take the fight to the next step. There appeared little chance of success against the big man. However, Rance had seen men of smaller stature whip larger foes when it came to defending their honor. Only after several silent seconds passed did stares wear down. Hank took his chair and carelessly turned his card. Ten of hearts.

The hand of a pair of tens was met with supporting comments from the spectators. However, Hank placed his entire holdings into the pot. Normally it wasn't sporting to simply out bet the opposition, but there was a lot of money on the table. It would be foolish not to use all the advantages. Just in case Hank dipped into his pocket for a secret stash of cash, Rance opened his coat and pulled out what he needed. "I'll call the bet and raise another hundred." Rance turned his card. Nine of spades.

The crowd hummed.

McClain abandoned his normal caution. He took little time to put in the matching amount, but only after rocking to one side to pull out a worn wallet from a back pocket and ripping out the bills that would suffice. "I'm going to stay in this," he said with some spite. He slapped down the money into the pot and flipped over the card. Four of spades.

With the pair of fours, McClain slapped his hands together. Rance still held the advantage with two pairs, but the matter of Hank's place in the game seemed doomed. It didn't take long for him to look at Rance with a solemn face.

"Mr. Cash, I have a favor to ask."

The proposition at first alarmed Rance; however, it might have been another opportunity to better his holdings. "Please go on." A peek at McClain showed his giddy mood had vanished.

"Mr. Cash, I don't have the money to stay in this game, but I do have something of value."

9

"Don't listen to him, Cash," McClain blurted.

Hank ignored the rude interruption. "I own a horse. A racehorse."

Despite the rise of voices around him, Rance wasn't enthused. He looked to his money and cards on the table. He really didn't want to know more, but common courtesy required him to listen while Hank continued.

"I didn't come here to sell," he said, removing a rolled parchment from inside his shirt. He took a long look at it just as one would a loved one. "I haven't had him but a short while, but he means a great deal."

"Ain't nothing but an old nag, Cash."

McClain's warning only served to interest Rance. Yet, the notion of owning a racehorse wasn't on his list of notable assets. Having grown around those with investments in the

sport of kings, he soon found the investments constantly ate money while leaving
behind large piles of unrecoverable losses.
He shook his head. "I'm sorry, Mr. Baines.
I'm not a man with the patience to own a
horse. Other than for relocation, of course."
As soon as he uttered the refusal, he saw the
sparkle in Big Red's eye. Second thoughts
were a bad idea to one who made a living
with his gut feeling. When he saw Hank's
continued stare at the parchment, he
couldn't help himself ask a simple question.
"Just what are you proposing?" McClain's
sparkle faded.

"What?"

Rance raised his palm. "I'm just letting the
man finish what he had to say, Red."

"But you already turned him down. You
can't go back on that. Let's get on with this
game."

"We're still in the middle," Rance said,
then facing Hank. "What is it you're asking?"

The reprieve not only brought Hank's eyes
off the paper to look at Rance, but showed
Red McClain's sparkle. "I can't say how
much it means to me to stay in this game."
He pointed to the pot. "If you were to stake
me for the rest of this game, I'd be willing to
let you hold the ownership of the horse."

119

There were still conditions that needed to be discussed. "What's in it for me?"

Hank nodded. A good sign of a man wanting to make a fair deal, or a grand facade for a swindle. "If I come out on top in this game, then I'll pay back all that you risked for me with a ten percent profit." Rance kept silent, knowing it wasn't necessary to address the counter side. Hank, to his credit, took little time to provide the entire offer. "If I don't," he said, holding the paper for Rance to take, "then I deed the horse over to you."

"Hell, boy," McClain hurriedly spoke, pointing to the money on the table. "Why not go ahead and place it into the pot. Cash already said he didn't want that animal."

Hard to figure, it was obvious Red McClain wanted a chance to own the horse. Despite an aversion against owning anything that had to be fed, it was worth the entertainment to spoil the big thug's plans. Hank made the point clear.

"Because I don't want you to get your filthy hands on him."

The spiteful words furrowed McClain's brow. "After all I done for you?"

"You mean done to me," Hank barked.

Before matters erupted again with talk of a fight, Rance raised his voice. "Whoa, you two." After tempers simmered briefly, it was time to make the deal or break it. "Mr. Baines, I'm not a man that likes looking too far ahead of where I'm at. Before me is a pile of money that I confess I wouldn't mind taking with me." He inhaled, unsure why this idea remained in his head. "But, I am also a man that doesn't mind risk." He leaned closer to Hank and took the paper. "I accept your offer, Mr. Baines. If for no other reason than to get on with this game."

"No!"

"Yes, Red," said Rance, tucking the parchment inside his coat. "Now, I do believe, it was Hank's turn to show his hand." A peek showed the modest farmer holding an ace and two tens. Slowly, he flipped over his fourth card. Eight of diamonds.

McClain's giddy laugh only irritated all the saloon. "Ain't going to see that horse no more, boy."

As Hank locked eyes on the worthless eight, Rance thought it time to conclude the matter. Without raising the stakes, he turned his fifth card. Queen of spades. The full-house hand left little to rejoice. Normally, his heart would be warmed by the strong showing. As the crowd murmured their disappointment, Rance averted his eyes from the somber Hank and caught sight of McClain's steely look. He still had a card remaining.

With only a pair of fours, McClain didn't hold much hope of stealing the pot. After several rubs of the chin, he finally reached for his card, but then stopped. "What if I was to trade you what's in here for the horse, Cash?"

Rance peeked at Hank, who only hung his head. "I don't think so, Red." Scowling at the refusal, he flipped over his card while keeping his mean eyes on Rance. Four of clubs.

Three of a kind didn't top Rance's full-house hand. As others in the room offered their wisdom over Hank's proposal, Rance kept his eyes on the modest farmer. Without much ceremony, or even the graciousness of congratulating the winner, much less showing appreciation for Rance's willingness to finance his continued play, Hank Baines rose from his chair. McClain stopped his own sulking only long enough to take an interested notice in the silent man's methodical march toward the door and out into the autumn's early darkness.

Rance sat as the winner, but the gloom over the saloon provided no reason to indulge. While he raked in the pot, it was McClain who satisfied the curiosity of all in the room. He flipped over Hank's remaining card. Eight of spades.

With Hank's hand lined in a row, it was an ace that spoiled the hand from another full house. Rance took the notice that, perhaps instead of his hand, it was his ace that brought him the win.

"Let's have another," McClain suggested. "Just you and me, Cash. We'll play for the horse."

Usually more poker meant more opportunity to line his pockets with more money. However, two-handed games weren't as interesting and in the past hadn't been as profitable. Besides recovering his forfeited money from their first encounter, he had won more than he originally held and by his account, gained a certain status as a worthy rival of Red McClain. All in all, it had been a good day and he thought to take a rest for the night. He shook his head. "No, Red," he said, somehow infected with the melancholy left by Hank. "I believe it may be time to let the cards cool down." He peered outside. Visions of a meal cooked by the tall German blond entered his mind. Perhaps she would make him something special. Surely, if he was to parade into the lobby with money dripping from his pockets, she would have to take notice. It was what every woman noticed.

He kept his eyes fixed on the stars illuminating through the open doorway. Visions of the foreign beauty swam about. *He would be at a lone table in the corner of the hotel. She, dressed in a long, gold-colored satin gown, would hold the meal on a tray, slowly taking steps toward him, to serve him as a king. Bending to a knee and head bowed, she would offer the tray for his approval, hanging on his every motion as to whether she had pleased him. Once he nodded, she would place the tray on the table, then rise to stand, awaiting his every whim. He would cut into the steak, sample the soft, succulent red meat, and peek into her sky-blue eyes, which truly longed for him to take her. As he enjoyed the warm butter-like taste, her narrow fingers slowly would rise to her front, slipping buttons free of their bounds to part the gown like a curtain, revealing her bosom, restrained by the meager confines of her white ruffled bodice. She would slip the top from her shoulders, then, one by one, unfasten each clasp of the cotton undergarment until all but the last at the bottom remained firm. It was for him to take. For him to release the final binding that would open the barrier that all men sought. She stepped closer to the table, her white flesh shining like a beacon in the candlelight. Closer and closer, she came toward him. More steps and more steps. So many steps, but she didn't near. The clomp of boots rang with each step. The candlelight dimmed and from out of the darkness,* Hank Baines strode toward him.

Like a snorting bull, the once-modest farmer grimaced with revenge. Rance shook his head to shield his eyes from the delusion. When surrounding light and loud shouts crashed into his ears, he saw the pistol firmly in Hank's grasp. Without words he marched to the table.

Rance's reflexes sank his right hand into his pocket. Only money met his fingers. In an instant, he pulled his hand from the pocket and put it inside his coat. His fingers met the butt of the .44 when Hank raised the pistol, but the aim wasn't at Rance.

"Now, you're going to get what's coming to you," Hank yelled.

From the corner of his eye, he saw the stunned face of McClain. The loud blast rang through the place. A wood pillar splintered from the errant shot. Chairs tumbled by the side as the patrons scurried and leapt from the path of the aim. Hank recocked the hammer. McClain crossed his arms and drew both of the pistols tucked by his ribs.

With the hammer back, Hank pulled the trigger once more, but before he steadied the barrel. The table cracked from the piercing lead. McClain put both weapons in line with Hank and fired. Streams of red flame exploded from the barrels. Rance flinched from the loud shots. Hank still stood, no doubt from Red's equally poor marksmanship.

Not knowing where the next bullets or where the next shots would come from, Rance instinctively leaned back. His chair cracked from under the weight and he fell on his right side. The .44 slipped from his grip.

With some steps of retreat, Hank used both thumbs to recock the hammer of his pistol. "This is for my wife," he yelled over the clamor. "And for my kids." Before he brought the pistol to an aim, his clenched finger on the trigger dropped on the hammer. The shot rippled wide and high.

McClain already pulled back the hammers of both his pistols. With two arms outstretched, he let fly with both barrels. The first shot Rance noticed hit the frame of the doorway. An instant later, he saw the red splatter in Hank's dust-stained white shirt.

At a staggering stance, he gritted his teeth and aimed the pistol again. Red McClain already had two shots ready. The big thug fired twice more. One shot found Hank's left shoulder, the other hit his knee. Hank did not fall.

Now bent from the pain, Hank Baines sucked in breath, stood straight, and pointed the pistol at arm's length. He steadied the aim right at Red McClain's head. His right finger wrapped around the trigger. The shaking muzzle waved back and forth. A moment later, Hank cringed, but fought through the agony, reopening his eyes and huffing in air. McClain still sat, smoke wisping from each barrel, but he made no motion to prepare for another shot. The wobbling legs spun Hank around in Rance's direction.

On his back, his eyes wide, he watched as the wounded man looked into his eyes. Blood streamed down from his belly. The pistol in his hand gradually rose to a position where he came in line with Rance.

In panic, Rance rolled on his shoulder and retrieved the .44, rolling back so to put it to aim. Hank panted quickly just as if he'd run for a mile. Blood trickled from his lips. Rance didn't know the intent of the motion, but no good would come from a gun pointed in his direction. He cocked back the hammer and lifted the big revolver at Hank.

As Rance matched the aim of Hank's weapon, one of them was likely not to miss. About to pull the trigger, a loud shot rang out. A cloud of white smoke shrouded all light in the place.

As the haze cleared, Hank's figure was frozen, back arched in a pose of every nerve having been pricked. He let out a gasp and with that, his body went limp. His eyes met with Rance.

"Take good care of the Lone Star."

Like a tree having been felled, he slammed face-first into the wooden floor. It was more than a moment and maybe two before Rance finally took a breath. He looked to the open stare of the dead farmer who only minutes earlier had begged for a chance to better his holdings. Fate had turned him from alive to dead faster than the turn of the cards.

"You all saw it." McClain's voice boomed through the place. "Weren't nothing I could do. The boy came into here to kill me. It was a clear case of self-defense."

Rance rose to sit on the floor and peek over the shattered table. There McClain still sat and looked about the room at the scattered patrons who hadn't fled for their support. Despite a yearning to believe otherwise, Rance had to admit to witnessing the truth of his claim.

For a long moment, Rance stared at the body with blood sprawling underneath. He then peered at the .44 in his right hand. As much as he hated to confess, Red McClain may have saved his life.

10

Mid-morning light was harsh for eyes that had been trapped in the confines of the Alamo Saloon through the night. The events had sapped the strength to find more suitable lodging. While a doctor was summoned to confirm the obvious truth, and the local law collected his reluctant but accurate testimony as to how matters unfolded, Rance stood as one less frisky than normal for the fortune gained at cards, unable to clear his mind of the guilt for his contribution to poor Hank Baines's demise.

The few hours spent in a hard wooden chair didn't help his mood. Long after the corpse was removed and taken to the undertaker and big Red McClain's departure to brag about his bravery to all ears listening, Rance still stood, breathing the cool air, wondering if this was an omen to leave San Antonio, or to stay and pay respects for the young modest farmer at the wake, perhaps even offer the one good black suit designed for the dearly departed.

As he contemplated, the clop of hooves at a quick gait, jangle of metal, and hum of wheels rolling pulled his attention to the left. A single carriage came toward him with great haste. In the distance he saw an elaborate bronze-colored carriage pulled by a dual team of white horses.

He didn't see a reason for the fast pace. He saw no fire, heard no gunshots, and the weather was pleasant. While searching for the possible cause, he looked past the formally dressed driver and caught sight of a passenger seated on the near side.

Dark hair waved in the wind. The fair skin drew him to the angelic features. Thin brows, a slender, proud nose defiantly turned up, well-defined lips, and brown eyes casting out temptation louder than a siren's song.

The open coach neared the boardwalk. Rance took a slight step forward as she turned her head his way. He looked deep into her. So near he reached to take her hand. Surely she would take his, for she was the delivery from the divine, come to the mortal ground to sweep him into the heavens into her eternal bonds of pleasure.

She locked eyes with him, turning her head as the coach continued to move. She turned and so did he, taking another step. She twisted her head about, the once-approaching carriage now leaving. With another step, he found there was no more boardwalk. Gravity showed its ugly presence. He hit the street face first.

He spat out the mouthful of dust and pushed himself up so to sit. A single hooting laugh crashed into his ears. Across the street atop a wooden crate sat the crusty old Dudley and his checker-playing rooster.

Rance sat for a moment, angry at the ridicule, embarrassed for finding himself on his behind in the middle of the street, and finally cracking a smile in realization he was deserving of the treatment. Slowly, he rose and brushed the dirt from his clothes. "Go ahead, laugh all you want. At least I'm not playing games with farm animals."

Dudley spoke through his chuckles. "I've heard of bowing to royalty, but that looked mighty extreme to me."

Once free of all the dust he was ever going to slap and pat away, Rance walked across the street. "What do you mean royalty? Do you know who that was?"

Dudley's brow rose. "Of course. You mean you don't? My, you have been in town a short time. That was Señorita Catarina Cuellar de Meyor."

"And just who is that?" asked Rance, still flicking dirt granules from his lapels and peering in the direction of the out-of-sight carriage.

"Well, besides being a handful of thorns, it is said she is the sole child of Don Pedro Cuellar de Meyor. Now, don't tell me you don't know who that is?"

Rance shook his head. "Not the first idea."

Dudley leaned back farther on the crate and slapped his knee. "Well now, you do have a thing or two to learn." As the old stubble-faced man prepared to tell the story, Rance thought to get out of the sun. He shooed Chuck from the other crate despite a few squawking complaints and claimed the seat under the shade of the tree. "Don Pedro owns over five thousand acres of prime land north of here with the San Antonio river running right through it."

Rance shrugged. "From what little I know of Texas, there's many men that own great amounts of land."

Dudley bobbed his head in agreement. "Yes. But none so mean and calculating as Don Pedro. It's said that he charged a high price for the water he allows to travel off his land and down to other spreads. If someone

132

doesn't pay him proper tribute, then he'll just dam the flow a mite to bring people around to his way of thinking."

The idea of holding water as hostage wasn't a new one, but solutions to the matter had been solved elsewhere. "Doesn't the law intercede? Surely the politicians of Texas must pass laws preventing such extortion."

With a look to the branches above, Dudley squinted at the filtered sunlight. "You don't get to be a man like Don Pedro without having a few friends in the right places."

The influence of money also wasn't a new idea. "Oh, I see," said Rance. "My mistake."

"That ain't the only one you made, sonny." Rance prepared for another admonishment. "You see, you referred to this fine place as to where we're now living and breathing as Texas."

Rance scanned about for a moment. "Isn't that where we are?"

Dudley leaned closer and arched his left brow. "Not to Don Pedro. As far as he's concerned, this is still a colony of Spain."

"Spain?" Rance questioned. "Mexico I thought was the previous owner."

With a dismissive shake of the head, Dudley continued. "No. Don Pedro is of a Creole line dating back to land granted his family from the court of Philip II. He hated the

133

Mexicans when they won independence. His papa was one who fought against Mexican rule before the Texians ever showed up from the American states. When Don Pedro took over, he kept up the fight, but when the Texians won their independence, he thought the land would return to the rightful owner, the Spanish crown."

The story didn't seem to make much sense. Rance looked to the ruts in the street from that bronze carriage, following them as they led out of town. Then he glanced at the townsfolk as they meandered their way about the day. "You mean this old boy still thinks of this as Spain?"

Dudley nodded. "And he himself the acting governor in their stead until they return. Of course most people around here just see him as an old buzzard still hanging on to the past. But, he still holds a few cards to make them pay notice."

"And what cards might those be?"

"Well," said Dudley with a cock of the head. "Mostly land and water. He holds most of the deeds in town. One thing he doesn't mind is being paid by those he despises. The Germans in the Casino Club tried taking over his holdings but he's fought them off so far. No. There's only one weakness Don Pedro has. His love of horses."

Rance was expecting another result. "Horses?"

"Yup," Dudley replied. "Folks about town say there is one thing Don Pedro wants."

A longer-than-normal pause allowed for curiosity to boil inside Rance. He recognized the ploy, which he himself had used so often in the past and hated to fall victim to. However, just like his breath, he couldn't hold it very long. "And what is that?"

A wry grin grew over the old-timer's face. "It is a nice day, isn't it?"

"Dudley, tell me, or your checkers partner is dinner."

Apparently the threat was taken more seriously than it was meant as the old man gave a distinct expression of shock. After a few moments, he faced away. "Number of years back, Don Pedro held the deed to a place of a few hundred acres worked by a man named Hawkins. Tom Hawkins Hawkins was a good man, but he liked to drink. And drink he did."

"Got himself into debt is my guess."

Dudley turned his head and winked. "Yes, sir, he did. More than fifteen thousand dollars. Most of it was against Don Pedro Cuellar and there was a few more notes held by some creditors. But, old Tom Hawkins didn't have the money to pay him. But he had something else."

"Let me guess. A horse."

"Don't get ahead of me, sonny," Dudley snapped. "You're going to want to hear this."

"I'm sorry. I was just hoping to hear the rest of this story while I'm still able to breathe this fine air you were bragging about."

"Get ahead of me again and you'll be breathing it by yourself."

Fully rebuked, Rance learned his lesson and nodded. "Go on." It took several moments before Dudley resumed his tale.

"Yes. A horse. But, not just any horse. This was a thoroughbred stallion. Reputed to be seventeen hands high, descended from the Arabian breed, brought over here by the British. Don Pedro wanted the animal the first time he set eyes on it. But Hawkins wouldn't sell. So, it didn't take much figuring to see that old Pedro would use another way to get the horse."

Rance had an idea as to the method, but he'd been warned.

"He used the power he held over the banks to urge them to foreclose. And when they did, Tom Hawkins had only one thing he could sell." Dudley dangled the answer in front of Rance. Still unsure whether he was allowed to speak, he finally took a chance.

"The horse?"

"That's right. The horse. But it was not just any horse."

"Yes, yes, we've been through that —" Rance's impatience was again met with Dudley's snarl. Thus again, Rance surrendered. "All right," he replied with palms held out. "Go on."

"Well, he was a champion, damn it. A real champion. Known to be undefeated in twenty races, some of them run in Tennessee and Kentucky. Cuellar, when he took possession of the horse, named it *El Magnifico Uno Por Siempre.* The Always Magnificent One. But, everyone around here knew the real name. The Pride of Texas."

Rance muttered the name, not quite sure why it sounded as if he should have known it. The longer Dudley spoke, the heavier the weight on his inside pocket. "It's bad luck to rename a ship. Or a horse."

"Hawkins died soon after. Some say from heartbreak. Others say he just drank himself to death from the despair of his losses. His wife and daughter left him long before. Years earlier the daughter, she married a man named Baines."

Rance's pulse quickened.

"They had a son. They named him Henry."

"Oh no," Rance murmured. "Don't tell me."

"Yup. It is the truth." Dudley shook his head. Both of them sat silent for more than a minute. Rance looked across the street, remembering the card game with Hank Baines. Dudley's voice broke the silence. "But there is more to the story."

Still in a somber mood, Rance replied, "And what is that?"

"Don Pedro, he brought over the finest Spanish mares, with Cuellar looking for the best of the bunch. He finally got what he wanted. A colt with the same spirit as The Pride of Texas. He named it *El Hijo Magnifico*. The Magnificent Son." Dudley paused. "But, there was another."

The weight in Rance's pocket now felt like a lead ball. "Don't tell me."

"Cuellar accused the Baineses of lying, then of stealing, but before Old Tom Hawkins died, he wanted his descendants to have a horse from the bloodline of the original. It ain't known for sure, but Hank's papa claimed that The Pride of Texas got loose and sired a foal from one of his mares. The foal was a young colt. A colt they named —"

"Lone Star," Rance blurted.

Dudley nodded. "That be the name."

Rance opened his coat, but the old-timer's voice stopped him. "The same horse that Hank lost to you last night."

Surprised, Rance cocked his head and crinkled his nose. "How did you know that?"

With his head down and eyes looking up, it took Dudley a moment before he answered. "It ain't exactly a secret. There were a few witnesses in the room."

Rance nodded as to that truth. Other matters became obvious. "That is why McClain wanted the horse."

"A fact that is. Don Pedro, it is said, has put out a reward on the Baines horse, claiming it is his property to begin with. Word is that it may be worth over ten thousand dollars."

"Ten thousand dollars!"

Despite the old-timer's voice mumbling, Rance sat entranced over the staggering sum.

"Hey, you listening to me?"

Rance shook his head to clear his mind. "What were you saying?"

"Don't let yourself get took. There's plenty that know what I just told you, looking for the same as what you got now. They'll all be looking for a way to get it from you. If you let them, you'll look like a fool."

The warning sunk into Rance's head, but

didn't lessen the bubbling in his veins. He rose off the crate and glanced at the hotel. The news should make him a welcome visitor to one tall, blond beauty. As he took a step, another curiosity stopped him. He cast a wary eye at Dudley. "How is it that you know all this?"

The old-timer huffed a laugh. "Weren't me that knew it all." He pointed at the rooster. "Chuck there. He's the one that told me most of it."

Rance turned to the chicken. After a moment he shook his head. "Yeah. Well, tell him I appreciate his advice. I wouldn't want to go about town looking like a fool."

"Tell him yourself. It ain't like he ain't got ears and can't understand English."

It took a half minute before Rance finally resumed his step. "Of course not."

11

Rance marched across the street with re-newed spirit to his step. Up the steps and under the portico, he entered the Menger with one thing in mind. Before he could find her, Calvin approached from the left. Rance was in no mood to accept more praise. He was in a hurry.

"Mr. Cash, I need to discuss an urgent matter with you."

"Hello, Calvin. Have you seen Greta?" While searching in the restaurant, the clerk's nasal tone broke his concentration.

"I've received some bills with your name attached to them. They want the hotel to pay them. Are you using us as your personal bank?"

Rance kept walking. "Oh, I may have a few markers around town. I told you I would mention this establishment every chance I could." He looked to the kitchen.

"Yes, but this isn't what I had in mind. I need you to pay these immediately and don't —"

Rance twisted about and pulled out a twenty-dollar greenback. The action was so sudden, Calvin stared at it with the same awe as a gun muzzle. "Here. I don't have time to settle the matter now. Use this as an intent to pay. I'll have the rest to you soon. Can you do that for me, Calvin?"

The clerk snapped the bill from Rance's fingers. "I suppose we can go about this further." Once inspecting the bill thoroughly to be sure it was genuine, Calvin looked up at Rance. "Are there any more? I would have to include a service fee."

"Yes, yes. Do include a substantial commission for yourself," he said, backing into the unlatched kitchen door. "But, I'm going to be occupied for the next few moments. Excuse me, will you? Thank you, Calvin." He spun into the door and shut it behind him.

There over the kitchen labored Greta, scouring the stove. She looked over her shoulder, blond strands dangling in front of her face. "What are you doing in here?" she asked in a huff, pulling the hair from her eyes. "You shouldn't be in here."

"Don't worry," he said, removing the document from his coat. "With this, I can gain a major stake in this town and take you away from this."

She looked at the paper and didn't appear enthused. "Is that the ownership paper you won from Hank Baines before you had him killed?"

Rance's shoulders slumped. "How did you know about that? And, I didn't have him killed. He tried to kill Red McClain and myself included."

She wasn't deterred from her duties, reaching for a pot and scrub brush. "It is not exactly what I heard. But, it is blood money just the same." She didn't look at him.

His heart in his throat, Rance tried to get in front of her to gain her attention. "That is not it at all. I tried to talk him out of risking the horse. I never really wanted to own the horse. But, a bet is a bet. And here it is." He took a deep breath, expecting her eruption of delight with the announcement. "I should be able to sell the animal for near ten thousand dollars!"

She scrubbed the pot with vigor, speaking through gritted teeth. "I'm very happy for you." Her tone was all but sincere.

Rance was at a loss. Since he first met this striking woman, he sensed she sought a man of capital. Now that he had it in his hand, he now sensed she'd prefer he grab a rag and dry the pot. With Greta leaning forward he had to prop himself to her side and crouch in order to look her in the face. "Don't you understand? This can take you away from all of this."

She paused her duty for a single moment. "No. It can take you away. Not me away." She resumed cleaning the pot.

"Then I don't understand."

"No, you don't," she sniped.

"So," he asked with open arms. "Tell me."

Several moments passed with Rance not budging from his stance. With a decisive snort, Greta put down the brush. "There are children."

Rance nodded. "Yes, I heard that."

"Did you also hear that they are poor, and that they have no mother? And no father, now."

The news took away Rance's wind. "No. I didn't know."

Greta nodded with spite rippling her lips. "It is true. And that is not all." The fire in her eyes was easy to see. Rance couldn't help enjoy it, until she continued the story. "Hank Baines married Theresa Maria Lorenzo. She was not a rich girl. Not a white girl." She paused. "And, she was not a pure girl."

With that, Rance stood straight and

turned away, scratching the back of his neck. "Oh." Despite Greta's chopped English, he understood her meaning.

"It is true." She paused, taking a rag to dry her hands. During that time it appeared she contemplated whether to resume. Only after a time did she do so. "Every man in town who went to the streets could pay money and have her for a turn. With all that, she still didn't have much money. She didn't have a home. She didn't have her pride."

The story was a familiar one. Many women Rance had come across had lost their innocence years before he met their acquaintance. Yet, he seldom considered their circumstances. Only during dressed occasions did the subject of purity arise on the minds of the men who had previously enjoyed the lack of dignity with the maidens of the mattress.

Greta went on. "Hank Baines was another one of those. But, he loved her. And he married her. His family did not approve of their son taking a wife who was not the same color skin. And who was also a girl that every man had already had. So, Hank moved from his family's house when Theresa Maria had a big belly. Many women talked that it was another man's baby, but Hank kept his promise. When the first girl was born, they soon

145

had another. It wasn't long when one more baby came. A boy this time." She inhaled deeply. "But, Theresa Maria did not survive."

The tragic story sapped some of Rance's enthusiasm. Women dying in childbirth was never easy to dismiss, but it wasn't an unknown fate. Especially in a frontier town. However, all this made Rance feel as bad as watching Hank's body hauled off to the undertaker. With the windfall in paper wrapped in his hand, he didn't want his renewed spirit dampened.

"Yes. That is terrible to learn. But one has to look at the fickle wind of fortune. What is one man's despair is another's prosperity." When he shot his smile, she didn't respond. The grin shrank. "Well, what would you have me do? I didn't cause any of this."

She crossed her arms and it took just a few moments for her reply. "You should give the horse back."

His eyes fell as wide open as his jaw. "What?" He shook his head at the notion. "Give it back! I can't give back the horse. It was won fairly in a game of cards." He struggled to think of a reason. "If I were to give it back I would be defiling all the rules and honor of the gambling profession."

She rolled her eyes and grabbed the next

pot in line to the bucket. Rance stood as if alone in the room. She didn't bother to take up the fight for her side, to allow him to further make his point. She was having none of it. For him to bring himself back into her view would be to forfeit one of the strongest hands he'd ever held. It was too much to ask, even for the most beautiful woman he'd ever seen.

He inhaled deeply, steadfast in his resolve to keep the hand. As she continued her labor, he dipped his head, tipping his hat as he turned for the door. Quickly out to the lobby and through it while Calvin was occupied with other guests, he went outside of the front door. Standing under the portico, he took another breath. With a peek at the document, he thought again what it meant to his future. A glimpse over his shoulder provided a moment what it might have cost him.

"Pardon me," came a voice from the right. "Might you be Mr. Rance Cash?" The inquiry came from a short-statured man in a pale brown long coat with black trim. The tall hat was cut from the same material with a black band. A ruffled white shirt was handsomely finished with a string tie. A hand was offered with charming smile surrounded by the neatly trimmed goatee.

"That might depend on who's asking?"

"Of course. Allow me to introduce myself, sir." He doffed his hat. "Rodney Ambrose Sartain at your service."

Rance recognized the act. He shook the man's hand. "And what service might you be offering?"

"I'm what you might say an intermediary between two parties. Two parties that might have mutual goals in their interest. A broker might be a term with which you're familiar."

The definition was clear the first time. Rance resumed his walk. "You're a go-between."

"Yes," Sartain answered while trying to keep up with Rance's longer gait. "And you're quite right. And at the moment I'm trying to intercede on one of my client's behalf."

With an abrupt stop, Rance twisted about. "Let me tell you something, Rodney. I am accustomed to the part."

"Part?"

"Yes, the part. The false courtesy, the formal manner, the swirl of words of a proposed gentleman. So, let's not waste each other's time. I do all my own negotiations. With the other interested parties. And, although I am an admirer of your tailor, I see no reason to retain your services. Good day to you, sir." Rance twisted about and started across the square.

Despite not sensing Sartain on his heels, the voice found his ears. "Mr. Cash, I don't think you understand. I don't wish to be your agent. I am working for another client."

In midstep, Rance twisted about again. "Who?"

Sartain looked to the side, then came a subtle grin. "I am not at liberty to reveal their name. That party wishes to remain anonymous. However, they have instructed me to offer a substantial sum."

"Substantial sum? For what?"

With the opening in the conversation, Sartain didn't waste any time to close the distance between the two. "Why, for the stallion, of course."

"Let me get this straight," Rance said, standing perplexed at the speed at which his ownership of the horse had become common knowledge. "Don Pedro Cuellar has sent you to make me a deal for the animal?" Sartain glanced to the side, but before he could reply, Rance continued. "I can't believe how fast news travels. Hank Baines's body isn't even cold yet, and already I have people that know more about the transaction than I do."

"If you let me —"

"Well, Rodney, I have to tell you. I haven't even set eyes on the asset myself. And one of my old rules is not to play a hand that I haven't yet seen." The memory of the game of Mexican Sweat came into mind. "Well, at least part of it." Although Rodney opened his mouth, Rance didn't want to hear it. "So, I am going to find this horse and give it a look. Until then, I have set no price for the horse."

Sartain's eyes lit up. "Well, I would be honored if I could escort you there."

Initially, Rance was ready to refuse the offer, not really comfortable with the company. However, with just a few seconds before he spoke, he realized he had no idea where the horse was. "You know how to get there?"

"Of course. It is at the Baines farm. I know right where it is."

The prospect of a guide was too good to pass on. Rance arched a thumb. "I've got to retrieve my horse at the livery. I'll have it saddled and we'll be on our way."

"I have mine already saddled. I'll meet you there."

Without anything to object to, Rance turned about and went to the edge of town to the livery. The price of returning to the reeking stable was a large one paid for by his nose. He called for Lester from outside of the structure and it took a short time for the overall-clad stable master to appear from inside.

With a palm over his nose, Rance ordered his dun saddled, then insisted it be done from outside the livery. With his best face managed despite the smell, Rance watched from a distance. Once the dun was ready, Rance paid for the service and mounted.

He steered back through the center of town where Sartain sat on his horse. With an open palm, Rance gestured for the dapper man to lead the way.

12

The long prairie grass had lost some of its rich green color. Rance tried to make it an omen. He turned his concentration to the dwindling daylight. At the pace of their ride, they would be trying to find the farm in the dark. Sartain rode just in front in relative silence. Only occasionally would a comment be made about the beautiful scenery of rolling hills and the brisk air in the small valleys; however, Rance was content not to engage in the meaningless banter. He needed to keep his concentration.

With a virtual gold mine in his pocket, he was wary of exactly where he was being led. The number of people already aware of his holdings was alarming. Bandits could be behind any tree.

Up a small ridge, Rance kept the left hand on the reins and the right on the .44, waiting for any twig snap to draw and fire, although he was unsure if he could stay on the horse from the blast.

Atop the ridge, Sartain pointed toward a shack in the center. "I believe that is it."

Below lay more prairie grass. A ramshackle corral stood to the side of the dilapidated building. A simple lean-to awning stood in one corner with wide, flat boards nailed to the posts. The more Rance observed, the less he recognized a farm. After several moments in silent shock, Rance nudged the dun down the slope. When the two riders approached the shack, Rance saw a little girl standing in the doorway. Her raven-black hair contrasted with her relatively white complexion. The fact alone didn't intrigue him as much as the fact that she appeared to be alone, near the age of seven, maybe six, showed no fear, and wasn't smiling.

"And what is your name, little lady?"

She didn't answer. Perhaps men on horseback were an intimidating presence. Rance dismounted and slowly approached the girl.

"Are you alone here?"

Again, the only response was her hollow, almost indifferent stare. Rance scanned about to the right, but saw no one. When he turned to the left, he saw Sartain ride to the corral. Rance didn't like abandoning the girl, but he did have an interest to maintain. He led the dun the small distance to the pen and tied the reins to a post. He stepped through the rails. A loud neigh broke through the mild breeze.

"Do you think that's it?" he asked.

"I do believe so," Sartain answered. "I don't see any other animals to confuse it with." The remark, despite being sarcastic, was very accurate. Gradually, Rance approached the awning. When he cleared a side post he was able to peer inside. There, tethered to one of the support posts, stood a bony nag.

"Oh no," sighed Rance. His dreams of owning a sleek thoroughbred, galloping across a wide pasture with the speed of a spring breeze vanished. This horse wasn't worth *ten* dollars.

"Oh my," Sartain said. "Perhaps we were wrong. That could be one of the work stock."

Rance shook his head. "Do you think that thing can pull a plow?" Slowly he approached the horse. The skittish animal shied away as far as the tether allowed despite an attempt to calm it with a hand over the rump. Rance's fingers felt the bone under the hide. As he came to the side, ribs bulged out, the back sagged and the spine rose all the way to the neck. He looked about. Dung piles surrounded the animal but they weren't as large as were seen with a healthy horse nor did they appear the same color. They didn't even smell as bad. "I think he's been tied up here some time." Rance again patted the rump as he walked around to the other side. Sartain's chuckle drew attention. "What's funny?"

It took a moment for the small man to finish the laugh before he could speak. "I was expecting a great racehorse." He finished by pointing his palm at the animal. The gesture boiled Rance's blood, but he had to agree.

He wasn't sure which was in worse condition. The little girl and her unseen siblings appeared in near as bad shape. When he looked again at the prized animal, he wondered if it would even make for a decent meal for the three of them. His curiosity piqued, he returned to the shack. When he got to the door, the girl was gone. He walked into the one-room home. A single table stood in the center. Two beds lined the far walls, but there was no sign of the children. Dusk was settling and a lantern wasn't to be seen. "Hello?"

"Where are they?" Sartain asked.

"I can't find them." The longer he stayed in the dim room, the more his eyes adjusted to the light.

"There's a rider coming." Sartain's announcement came at the same time when Rance spotted a peculiar square cut out in the floor. He knelt next to it and squeezed his fingers between the edges. He pulled up what was a door, but he could only see black.

"Mr. Cash," Sartain called. "There's someone here that is asking for you."

A distant memory urged him to put his hand in his coat pocket. He found what he remembered and drew the match. He struck it against the wood floor. The flaring luminance revealed the three children, the young boy in the arms of the oldest sister. In an instant it became all too evident why they had sought this hiding place.

"Mr. Cash. You have a visitor."

"I'll be right out." Although giving long consideration to extracting the children from the hole in the dirt, he thought better of the idea. They must have felt safe in the place. He took a breath and put his finger to his lips. About to close the door, he changed his mind, left it open to ensure air for the children and rose to leave for the door. Once outside, he saw a rider in a short-brimmed hat and a tight-fitting coat trimmed at the lower chest.

"You are Señor Cash?" The accent was

Spanish and formal.

Playing games might endanger the children. "I am."

"I have been sent by Don Pedro Cuellar to invite you to his hacienda. It is only five miles from this point. We can arrive there safely if you follow me."

"That sounds like it might be a great affair," Sartain said. The rider turned his head toward the dapper broker.

"The invitation is for Señor Cash *solo.*"

The stern slight soured Sartain's face.

With the light dimming, Rance didn't care to be wandering too far in the dark. Since it was more than five miles to San Antonio, and the longer they lingered about the greater the risk that the children might be discovered, he made a decision. "I'll go. But, we have to leave now." Rance went to the dun.

"What about me? I mean, I thought I, uh, we had an arrangement," Sartain protested.

"We do," said Rance, stepping into the stirrup. "You arrange to go back to town, and I'll arrange to follow this gentleman."

Darkness made it difficult to follow the single rider. Rance attempted to quell his rapid heartbeat as they approached two distant points of light. Uncertain if he was riding into a trap, he assured himself that he could always rely on the one asset he always carried with him. Guile.

The closer they came to the lights, Rance recognized them as two torch lanterns on each side of a gaping masoned arch. The escort calmly rode past the open pair of wrought-iron gates. Rance didn't pause the dun as they continued up a cultivated pathway through the landscape and toward a massive mansion.

Despite the dim light, the distinctive architecture of spindly columns, arched windows and doorways, along with the squared roof, showed the European influence he'd known in New Orleans rather than the mudbrick trend of the natives.

The escort dismounted at the front, waiting for Rance to do the same. It took a moment before leaving the safety of the saddle. It was the last chance he would have to gallop away. Instead, he trusted his senses and slipped off the dun.

Quickly his mount was led away. A sudden shiver ran through his nerves. He stood alone at the front of the unknown. Would he be welcomed or persecuted? As more thoughts flooded his mind, he inhaled deeply, deciding to roll the dice.

Up the short set of steps of red tiles he

walked beneath the enormous portico amid the light of the hanging lanterns. Another deep breath was needed before he clenched his fist to rap on the door. About to pound, the varnished door opened and a black-suited man stood just behind it.

"Hello," Rance greeted with a bit of fear.

The stoic-faced person silently opened his hand for Rance to enter. Cautiously he did, barely able to observe the interior before the door closed behind him. The echo eerily sounded like a vault being slammed. He rid his mind of the thought and followed the silent man whom he presumed a servant, perhaps the butler, from the front entranceway. As they entered another room, the butler pointed at the .44 in the holster. It wasn't unusual for the house rules to exclude firearms. Although, he'd rather have the pistol handy, he couldn't refuse and surrendered the pistols.

The initial attraction to his eye was the cavernous room. The ceiling was higher than most buildings with multiple floors. The walls had pillars sculpted into the masonry extending all the way to the top. In between lay pale wallpaper striped with gold-colored tapestry. The interior was lit by oil lamps hung from chains of the same gold pigment. Rance, curious about the elaborate adornment, examined the wallpaper closer to determine if the threads were actually spun from the precious metal. The illumination didn't allow for the proper inspection, but the texture was coarse. There wasn't a way to dismiss that it was not the genuine article.

Just when he was ready to put the issue to rest, he turned and found formal sitting chairs surrounding a low table. Beneath lay a rug embroidered with designs depicting what appeared to be crests of royalty. Resigned to the reality of waiting, he removed his hat and tossed it on the table.

His eyes were drawn to the far wall. Portraits hung of noblemen, which weren't immediately recognizable, although they were no doubt important to the host. He shrugged and allowed his view to wander. To the left was a large hearth of a size that could accommodate a bed. He wondered that despite the fact that there was no current flame, the heat must be enough to make the entire room as warm as a wool blanket.

Just above the hearth hung another portrait. Equal in size to the actual person, the painting was of a young woman. He recognized the eyes, the proud nose, the dark hair, and the enchanting firm lip. The pose made it unavoidable to stare.

The shoulder gown appeared made of

gold lace, which explained the reason for the surrounding decor. The neck was long and elegant. He couldn't help but follow the creamy skin to where the gown covered the chest. He took a step closer and noticed the stroke of a brush above the low neckline of the garment. He took a moment and dipped his eyes. If forced to guess, it appeared an original replication of the natural bust that had been clouded by vanity. However, he sensed the order for the alteration likely didn't come from the subject. Perhaps from one too jealous to allow a view to the many that was reserved for just one pair of eyes. Rance shook his head and thought how lucky the artist was.

He looked about the room. Still left alone, he proceeded to peruse about, admiring the ornate sculptures that were placed about the corners and base of the walls. Some of the busts appeared to be those of historical royalty, judging by the presence of a fluffed lace collar.

Dudley's story came to mind. His tale of the man's fixation for the days gone by was evident. Almost an obsession, this home was more in the mode of a castle inhabited by the dignitaries of history, and Rance's guess was these were all from Spain's past in the region.

During his thoughts, he had wandered toward the center of the room. For the first time he noticed the threshold from where he entered. Above the entrance hung another portrait. However this one had four legs.

He approached for a better look. The farther he went the less light allowed for a clear view. Nonetheless, this image too was as large as the subject.

The chestnut color held a sheen as the drawn sunlight cascaded off the shoulders. The forelegs stood straight and sturdy with white markings just above the hooves. The hind legs, too, appeared strong, providing for a proud stance. The tail was groomed and perfectly shaped like a spearhead.

However, it was the neck and head that projected the essence of the animal. The flared nostrils showed the same proud arrogance of the other portraits. The eyes were focused ahead and the ears perked at attention. The most alluring feature was the marking on the forehead. A white star with four points, the bottom one extending beyond the rest.

A notion emerged in back of Rance's mind of exactly the subject in the painting.

A voice crashed his concentration. "I see you are impressed, Señor Cash."

13

Rance twisted about. Before him stood a distinguished gentleman in a white ruffled shirt under a shimmering gold vest. Rance gauged the age of more than fifty years old in part due to the gray-speckled black hair, but the face was spirited with vigor and a warm smile.

"Welcome to my home," he said extending both hands. Rance accepted the handshake, which he found clasped between both his host's. "It is a pleasure to have you here."

"Well," Rance replied with some surprise and pleasant relief. "I can't think of a better place to be. Certainly the best offer I had tonight." Both chuckled at the levity.

Don Pedro's eyes angled up. "So, tell me, what do you think of *El Magnifico*? Truly magnificent, yes?" Rance faced around and again looked to the painting. It wasn't difficult to agree.

"Oh absolutely. I can see why now he was said to be the pride of Texas." The compliment didn't have the intended effect. Don Pedro's smile slowly slid away.

"I do not prefer that title." He paused and dipped his head a moment. Quickly he lifted his eyes to the painting. "No. To me he represented what is truly remarkable about a lineage, a history, an ancestry," he said, turning his view at Rance. "A bloodline." The mention wasn't by mistake and Rance recognized the ploy to divert the subject. However, his host was as smooth as any riverboat gambler. To rush the hand when only one card had been shown wouldn't allow for an increase of stakes. Rance was willing to wait. Don Pedro motioned to the chairs. "Please, let us sit down."

Rance settled in one of the upright chairs. His host picked up a small wooden box.

"So, Señor Cash, what is your business?"

The answer required confidence. "I'm a sportsman. And, please call me Rance."

Don Pedro paused. Rance wasn't certain if it was the answer or the lack of formality. Again, he smiled politely and opened the lid to the box. "Cigar?"

A glance showed an undisturbed row. Although they weren't the thin cheroots he preferred, he graciously accepted the offer and took the one on the far left. "Kind of you, sir," he said, about to bite off the end until offered the use of a cutter. Attempting to reclaim some of his dignity, he took the cutter and snipped the smoke's end.

Don Pedro struck a match, cupping it between his palms. He leaned to allow Rance to char the end. "You are not from San Antonio. From where do you come?"

"New Orleans, originally."

"I see. And what brought you to Texas?"

Rance took time to let the end burn. The practice made for an even burn of the smoke and gave him time to consider his answer. Sensing there was a reason for the question beside the courtesy of conversation, Rance tried to keep from showing all his cards. "I heard of excellent opportunities here."

After charring the end of his own cigar, Don Pedro lit the smoke. Each puff sucked flame into the tobacco. Each exhale sent leaping flame and a cloud of smoke rising up to the tall ceiling. Once the end was at a red glow, he cocked his head in consideration of Rance's explanation.

"I see." He gestured with the cigar like a king with a scepter. "And you thought there were many opportunities in the Alamo Saloon?"

The remark was cold and calculated. If the

wealthy land holder gauged him as a simple card player then the price likely would stay low. There was a matter of protocol to be observed. No man of prominence could be rumored to pay a sizable sum to one without a respectable reputation.

"Oh, I just stopped in the place for a brief libation after the long travel. I saw there was a friendly game, and to pass the time I played a few hands." He attempted a modest smile. "I even won a few, and not seeing a reason to end the fun, I continued." The expression on Don Pedro's face wasn't one of the whimsy expected. It was time to change tactics. Time for a somber face. "Then, of course there was the terrible tragedy of Hank Baines." He shook his head in as solemn a motion he could muster. "If I'd known it was to come to that, I'd never engaged in the game."

Don Pedro didn't appear moved by Rance's sense of loss. "Yes, it is a tragedy, indeed, as you say." He paused, like he had a piece of gristle caught in his throat. "Rance." It didn't disturb his next play. "However, those like Hank Baines cannot be expected to supervise such an undertaking as what was willed to him."

While in the middle of sucking flame through the wrapped leaves, Rance choked on the comment and not the smoke. "Willed to him?"

"Of course. His grandfather bestowed to him a rather important item. One I have interest in acquiring."

Rance took another puff. "Do tell," he said, pretending not to know the host's intent. They both smiled at each other. Rance was sure each knew the other's play. He would have been more comfortable with the feel of cards. Nonetheless, this was the same game: bluff and raise. "What might it be that you have interest in?"

Don Pedro's smile didn't waver. He simply nodded and with a cock of his head, he winked. "Please accept my apology," he said placing the smoke in an ashtray. "I didn't ask to take your coat. I am sure you would be more comfortable without it." He slightly faced to the side and spoke in a casual tone. "Alfredo." From around the entryway, the butler came into the room. "Why has Señor Cash's coat not been taken care of?"

The butler took the verbal slap with great dignity. When he turned, Rance tried to project an apologetic pose.

"Please, don't take any offense on my account."

Don Pedro was very reassuring. "Oh no, please. It is not your responsibility to ask."

With that, Rance stood, feeling obligated now to shed the coat in order to spare the servant more grief. The butler folded it over his arm, picked up the hat from the table, apologized in Spanish, and promptly left the room.

While always maintaining a smile as if there had been no harsh words expressed, Don Pedro Cuellar stood. "Shall we enjoy our meal?"

"Meal?" Rance asked, confused.

"Yes, of course," was the answer while leading the way. "You have the look of a man who enjoys the finer pleasures." He went to the right and through another open doorway. Inside was a brightly illuminated room with a long table in the center. Plates had been set with the host taking his customary position at the head. Rance sat to the left, but there was one other place setting across the table.

"I see we are expecting company?"

"Oh," Don Pedro said with a smile. "Yes, my daughter Catarina will be joining us."

Rance wasn't surprised, but he acted the part. "Oh, how delightful. I believe I had the privilege of seeing her in San Antonio earlier. You should be very proud. She's every bit the image in that painting."

"Painting?" Cuellar asked as Alfredo

168

brought in a platter of beef.

"Yes," answered Rance, eyeing the steaming meat. "The one in the other room. Above the fireplace."

Don Pedro hesitated, taking a few moments before pointing at a particular steak, which his servant delicately placed on the plate. He looked to Rance, but not with the customary smile. "That is Catarina's mother. My late wife."

With the platter dangled near his nose, Rance gulped, but his mouth wasn't watering from the aroma. Unsure what to say, he took the reprieve of being allowed to select his cut of meat. Once done, he thought of the apology, but Don Pedro spoke first to Alfredo.

"Dónde está la niña?"

"No lo sé, Don Pedro."

A look of disgust encroached over the host. It was no time to worsen it with worthless regrets. It didn't take long before the host's smile resumed. "My apologies for my daughter."

Rance smiled in relief. "None necessary, sir." While feeling confident, he thought to embellish. "I'm very familiar with the unpredictable nature of the gender." He capped the remark with a smile, but that quickly shrank with the concerned face of Don

Pedro. In less than a minute he'd managed to perturb his host twice. Footsteps from the doorway saved further embarrassment.

Through the doorway in a bright bare-shoulder red gown, hair neatly pulled tightly in a bun, cheeks shaded with rouge, and eyes artfully accented with black mascara, Catarina Cuellar entered the dining room. Rance immediately stood. She kissed her father's cheek, although it didn't seem to dismiss her tardiness. She looked to Rance and those eyes lit up.

"This is Señor Rance Cash, my dear."

Extending a hand, he took it with the gentle touch due a lady. "Enchanted, Señorita. And please, call me Rance."

She giggled. *"Muchas gracias."* She paused as her father had before. "Rance." He stared into her eyes and she didn't seem to mind, until Don Pedro politely cleared his throat. "Please, sit down." Rance bowed at the comment, but waited until Alfredo pulled her chair out and seated her. Within moments, the butler placed a small steak on her plate. Soon, the host picked up his knife and fork as a signal to eat. Rance eagerly did the same.

"Catarina, our guest tells me he saw you in San Antonio. Why were you there?" The question was asked like a lawyer probing for an answer to be used against the witness.

Rance stopped in midslice.

The girl peered up at Rance for only an instant, then changed to an impish smile. "San Antonio, papa? What a grand idea. I would love to have gone." She shook her head. "But, it was not me that was there." She flashed her grin and devilish eyes at Rance. "Señor Cash must be mistaken." With that, her father turned his attention to Rance while still holding the sharp knife in his hand. With words being exchanged, it was plain that the young woman was in need of his assistance.

He looked to Don Pedro with his most regretful face. "I beg your pardon," he said with a nod toward to Catarina. "I'm obviously in error." Once more, when in need of wiggling off a hook, he flashed his grin and looked to Catarina. "The sun is so bright here. Perhaps I mistook this beautiful lady for another one of those in town."

Without any sign of acceptance of the story, Don Pedro picked out a slice of the steak, put it in his mouth, and chewed quickly. Rance took the moment to also fill his mouth before any further embarrassments leaked out. As Alfredo doled out creamy mashed potatoes on everyone's plate, Rance chewed harder and waited to learn whether his explanation was believed.

The host looked to him and swallowed. "You see," he started while plunging the knife into the delicate meat. "I never allow my daughter to go into San Antonio unescorted. There are far too many dangers that would await a woman of her age. It would trouble me to learn that she had traveled there without my permission."

"Why, of course —"

"Please let me finish." He paused with that choking motion. "Rance." He stabbed his fork into the portion he sliced. "The only issue I would have more disappointment with than learning that she had disobeyed me" — he cast his eyes firmly at Rance — "is to learn that I was not being told the truth."

With the same scowl of any angry judge, Don Pedro Cuellar pressed Rance for a reply. In an instant, he glanced her way. Catarina, her impish grin mildly in place, beamed those enticing eyes into his, begging for his corroboration. Another glimpse at her father ensured a painful fate should it be found that he supported a lie. And why should he? He was there to close on a deal for a horse, not become involved in a family squabble. Little doubt stood that this was not the first occurrence of what appeared to be a spoiled child's game with her overbearing father, and she was using Rance as a pawn in the game. If he were to play along, his complicity might injure his chances of capturing a tidy sum for a single day's work. The risk was a poor one.

He averted his eyes from hers, knowing they would sway him in the wrong direction. With clear judgment, he was ready to rid himself of this burden, to air the truth and be done with this affair so he could get down to the transaction at hand.

"I understand completely, sir," he said, allowing himself one final peek at her big, engaging hazel eyes. Rance cleared his throat and looked directly at Don Pedro. "Your daughter was not the one I saw in San Antonio."

14

What had he just done?!

Don Pedro took only a moment before his courteous grin cracked his face. Rance saw it as an acknowledgment of another player recognizing a blatant bluff. Without further hesitation, father and daughter Cuellar went about enjoying their meal. However, Rance's appetite was lost with the lie. He stared at the tender beef.

Was it his incurable nature to take a risk despite how poor the odds, or just a weakness for female eyes batting at him? Whichever, he now sat as the mark between two seasoned players of cat and mouse. He wasn't sure which side he preferred. However, there was another reason. All the while his eyes were locked onto the steak, it still didn't capture his interest. Did it lack the same savory taste as the first one he enjoyed while in Texas, or was it the enjoyment of the company of who cooked it? A question interrupted his thoughts.

"Is there something wrong with the beef?"

Rance politely grinned. "No. Of course not. It is exceptional." He took a bite and did his best to display a confident facade. The host turned his attention to his daughter.

"So, how did you spend the day?"

She looked to Rance for only a moment. He tried to sample the potatoes while anxious how she would spin another tale. Catarina showed no distraction by the surprise of the question. With a greater ease than any man she casually answered.

"I stayed in my room and embroidered, papa. You remember, the tapestry of the Madonna." Her reminder only served to install a proud father's smile. She was an expert on what to say to please him. Had there been cards instead of plates in front of she and Rance, he would fold his hand and seek another game.

Don Pedro took a final bite and put down his knife and fork. It was signal that he was finished and Rance didn't mind following suit. Catarina on the other hand ate like the horse in the painting. While watching her voracious attack, slicing the steak into smaller and smaller pieces, then stabbing with the fork through one after another in a stack, her father's conversation crept into his ear.

"You mentioned that you came to Texas for the opportunities here. Are there not the same opportunities in New Orleans?"

"New Orleans?" Catarina's eyes lit up.

"Why, yes," Rance answered with a nod.

"What a glorious city. I have heard so much about it." She swooningly gazed at the ceiling. "I want to visit there so very much." Her desire didn't reflect well on her father's face.

"It is not a place for a young woman." His reminder soured her happy face. Before allowing any effect, her father turned away to Rance. "Why would you not stay there, may I ask?"

With a smile, Rance reclined in the chair. "Actually, I was traveling to Kansas. I learned of greater opportunities there. What with the railroads, the cattle market emerging, the recent transcontinental line, I felt that there was so much happening there, I didn't want to leave it all to the locals." He chuckled, catching Catarina's wink and lean forward from the corner of his eye. Before he allowed further distraction, he locked eyes with the host. "You know the times are changing. This is 1869. The riverboat is no longer the exclusive form of travel or trade." He paused, trying to ignore Catarina's exposed cleavage. "And I believe strongly that any man of vision might need to associate himself with those" — he snuck another peek — "burgeoning" — another peek — "well formed" — one more — "firm" — a last look couldn't hurt — "busty."

"Excuse me. What did you say?"

In an instant he snapped out of his fantasy. "Bustling. I said bustling. As in busy, the, uh, the commerce of the region." He chuckled to ease his host's concern. He was fearful he would have to explain further, but Alfredo entered carrying a silver pail. Don Pedro noticed, but his mood hadn't changed.

"No. I don't think I wish dessert. Perhaps our guest?"

Rance held out both palms. "Oh, please, no. The meal was too much for me. So well prepared."

Don Pedro, still with a puzzled face, quickly changed his expression to the one he welcomed Rance with. "Very well." He looked to Catarina. "Excuse us, my dear. I must discuss business with our guest."

It took a long moment before she responded by putting her napkin on the table. "Of course, Papa. I wouldn't want to interfere with business talk from men. I am only a woman. I'm sure I wouldn't understand a word." Her tone held a hint of sarcasm; however, her father seemed pleasantly pleased at her understanding. As she rose from the chair, Rance stood. She kissed her father's cheek as she left, then whispered in his ear while giving Rance another wink. The action sent Rance's heart pounding when Don Pedro cracked a satisfied smile. When she left the room, the host motioned for Rance to reclaim his seat.

"Children," Don Pedro said, shaking his head. "It is only the young that can afford to be so foolish."

As Rance sat, he smiled in agreement, still a bit terrified at what the daughter told the father. "Yes," he said with a cleansing breath. "Foolish, indeed."

"Yes, now," Don Pedro said with a new enthusiasm. "Shall we retire to the den and resume our discussion?"

Relieved to change the subject and to get along with getting rich, Rance happily nodded and both men stood and left the dining room. Once back to the den, Rance wandered over to the chair he vacated while Don Pedro strode about the room as a king would his palace. Retrieving the cigar he'd abandoned, he was stopped with Don Pedro's offer of a fresh one. Impressed by the host's sense of quality, he accepted the gift of a new cigar, and with the box still open, he took two more for later. After the owner took one himself, the lid snapped shut. It was a signal to get down to business.

"Nothing so well as a cigar after a good meal."

Rance took a match from the holder and struck it. "Couldn't agree more." He cut one end, charred the other, then lit it. As Don Pedro did the same, plumes of smoke rivaling any gun battle rose to the ceiling. "So, sir," Rance started, feeling the hour was getting late and anxious to know the stakes of the game. "I have learned you have offered ten thousand dollars for the Baines horse."

The direct approach seemed a surprise. "At one time. Yes, that is true."

The hedging alarmed Rance. "That is no longer the case?"

Don Pedro took a long drag off the smoke. "There was a time when I believed the animal was worth the price. But no longer. No. It is not the same animal now." The position was disappointing, but the game wasn't over. Rance took another puff before his cigar went cold.

"You are referring to the condition of the horse?" A nod sufficed for the answer. "I see. Yes, well, I am aware of that." It was time for assurance. "But, I am confident that with some proper care, the horse's health will return and be as good as it ever was."

"That is a matter of opinion. And I may say that if I was a seller such as yourself then I would share it. I am not the seller and my opinion is the horse will never regain its condition. Not to run."

The cigar had lost its taste. "Then why would you invite me here? Why did you say you have interest in attaining the horse?"

A smug grin grew over the host's face. "Let us say that I have a sentimental attachment." He slowly faced around to the painting of his beloved horse.

It was encouraging to know there was still a buyer, but at what price? "And just how attached are you?"

The offer came stern and firm. "I will pay one thousand dollars for complete ownership of this son of *El Magnifico*."

Rance's eyes widened. His shoulders slumped, his fingers trembled, and his spirit was shook. In the hour he'd spent in the house he'd lost nine thousand dollars. As he inhaled deeply to calm his rapidly raising pulse, he did his best to show a calm demeanor. There were still some cards to play and some dealing to yet do.

"I must say that I am disappointed at the offer." There was little remorse shown for displeasing a guest. In fact, there was a hint of a triumph with the rise of the brow. It was enough to stir the innermost disdain. While keeping his own lip level, Rance thought it might be time to call. "I will keep the horse."

Don Pedro sat motionless for more than a moment. It was a pose reflective of a man not used to not getting what he desired. He bobbed his head with pursed lips. "I must say that, although I admire your determination, it is a mistake you are making."

"One I will have to live with," Rance said with a swagger to his tone. It wasn't the money anymore. It was the contest. He still owned something another man wanted. "Well," he said while rising, "as you said, the hour is getting late." When he was at his feet, his host also got up. "I want to thank you for a delightful time in your house. Please pass on my compliments to your daughter for me." Rance sensed the more he rushed, the less Don Pedro was anxious to have him leave. He offered his hand. Don Pedro gripped it tight.

"Please, allow me to invite you to stay for the night."

At first the invitation was welcome news. Despite the anticipation of a night in a soft bed, the first in near five months, he didn't want to appear too agreeable. "Very kind of you, sir. But, I have business still yet to tend to in San Antonio. And . . ." He paused to spike Don Pedro's gut. ". . . I need now to seek another buyer for the horse. I believe Red McClain still has interest. Do you know him?"

For an instant, the smile vanished with the speed of an imaginary slap. "I have heard of the name."

Without letting the sting cool, Rance attempted to take the first step toward the door. However, Don Pedro had not released his grip. The smile returned. "You would do me a great favor by staying in my home."

"Favor?"

"Yes. It is a long way to San Antonio. It will take you the rest of the night in the dark, especially since you are not familiar with the area." He put his left palm over his heart. "I would feel badly if anything should happen to you during the travel." He paused and the smile momentarily froze Rance's tongue. The lapse was enough of an opening for an ace. "Please. It would be only for the night, and you will feel so much better in the morning."

The hesitation in answering was enough of an acceptance as any words.

"Then it is so." He led Rance by the hand and toward a rear foyer from the den. With a wide arm motion, he welcomed Rance to the rear area of the house. "Alfredo will see you to your room. Perhaps with a good night's rest, we can talk more about the plans you have for the horse." Before Rance could answer, Don Pedro seized Rance's arm and paraded him down a long hall only alight by candles mounted on wrought-iron stands mounted on the wall. "The room we have prepared for you is at the top of the stairs to the right."

"Prepared?" Rance questioned as he saw the dimly lit staircase. It held all the warmth of the final steps up the gallows. About to reconsider the offer, Rance turned to the right. The grasp to his arm was missing and so was his host, no doubt retreating back into the den. Rather than follow his host to safety and discreetly depart, he inhaled and proceeded up the stairs.

As with the den, paintings adorned the walls, all portraits of dignitaries of the past. Once halfway up, he couldn't help the feeling of the eyes on the canvas watching him. At the top, he went to the right and saw a door ajar. Cautiously, he went to it and nudged it open. Inside amid the light from a single candle lay a spacious bed with a pair of pillows fluffed against an oak headboard.

The scene was inviting since it reminded him he'd not enjoyed a decent night's sleep since June. Now in late October, his legs ached at the anticipation. There was no time to be wasted.

He sat on the edge of the bed and slowly eased off his boots. The rush of blood to those deprived joints had the same effect as a good massage in a Chinese bathhouse. About to shed his pants, he noticed the open door and decided not to share the show to those roaming the halls. He went to close it when the butler emerged from the dark. Eyes wide, surprise seized Rance's hand on the knob. Proper manners kept him from slamming it shut.

"Do you find all you need?"

Rance glanced at the bed. "That's all I need." Thinking the comment would conclude the conversation, Rance stood disappointed when the butler entered. While still at the door, Rance watched as the butler turned down the pristine sheets, went to the armoire and removed a large wool blanket, placing it at the foot of the bed. Alfredo pointed to the wash stand. "The pitcher is full and there are dry towels in the drawer."

Rance smiled. "Kind of you. Please express my gratitude to the master." It took a moment for the stiff-legged servant to understand that no more service was needed nor wanted. With a bit of a bow, he went directly to the door.

"*Buenas noches.*" With that, he exited the room and Rance wasn't shy to close the door behind him.

Finally, he turned for the bed. A minor thought to wash was overruled by his need for rest. He unfastened his trousers, letting them drop to the floor. As fast as he had ever been with a woman, he unbuttoned the shirt and threw it from his shoulders. Almost in a stumble, he fell into the bed, the force of the fall providing enough wind to extinguish the flame.

His body melted into the sheets. His muscles eased their tension, soothing their ache. His head felt like a boulder as it sunk into the pillow. Despite the thoughts provoked by his conversation with Don Pedro, they paled away in his mind.

Barely able to perceive his opaque surroundings, a creak of a hinge piercing the silence sent his heart racing. A weight on the left tipped the mattress. Something came into the bed at his back.

15

Rance rolled about, hands in front of him to fend off the knife he was certain to be plunged into his throat. His fingers met with flesh and cloth. He grabbed and yanked the intruder, throwing a body over him and rising to his knees. Hovering over the attacker, he clenched a right fist where his left fingers told him was a jaw.

"No! Don't!" The voice was panicked, sincere, and feminine.

Rance's heart pounded his chest, his adrenaline flowed with fury. It was all that he had to pull the punch. "Who is this?"

"Catarina," was the nervously panted reply.

"Señorita, what are you doing in my room?"

"Saving your life." She struggled to get from under him. He wasn't anxious to have an unseen stranger about, even if it was a beautiful woman. However, he allowed her to squirm free and heard rustling of wood near where he thought was the nightstand. A moment later, a struck match erupted, sending light throughout the room. She lit the candle and blew out the match. "Do not worry. I am here to protect you."

"Protect me?" he replied loudly, trying to concentrate on exactly why she was there and ignore her long dark hair lapped over a thin purple robe.

She put her finger to her lips. "The walls have ears," she whispered and pointed. So to be heard, she leaned closer to him and he settled onto his side. "You are in danger here." Rance, his eyes fixed on the silhouette of her bosom cast through the robe from the candle, thought differently.

"To tell you the truth, I've been in worse places in my life."

"No. You don't understand. My father is not pleased with you. He doesn't enjoy when other men don't do as he wants. So that is why he has insisted you stay here."

The words brought him out of the trance. "He means to kill me?"

She frowned. "Of course not. He is not a killer." He was relieved, but for only a moment. "My father sees killing as a sin. He will just have Alfredo come to this room and

187

drug you while you are asleep hours from now. Then he will take you to the barn, where Stefan will tie you to a chair, most likely beat you, and if you still refuse to sell the horse, then he may have you whipped." She shook her head. "He would not kill you. If so, you cannot sell him the horse," she finished simply.

Rance was frozen still. "Well," he uttered. "At least he's a civilized man." Before he found himself subdued by her beauty once more he rose off the bed. With his body still attracted to her feminine wiles, propriety forced him to grab the blanket to drape his front. "So, how do I get out of here? They obviously must be watching this room." The thought brought another question. "How did you get in here?"

The question brought that impish smile. "There is a passage to my bedroom." She rose from the bed and opened the closet. With a wave, she brought him to view a small tunnel cut into the wall.

"That's how you got in here."

"Yes. It is important that we leave this room and go to mine. And quickly."

Thinking it sound advice, he went to retrieve his pants, but he couldn't juggle the blanket while slipping on the trousers. He eyed her and she immediately understood, turning her back all the while giggling. Quickly, he dropped the blanket and slid into the pants, glancing at her as she snuck peeks over her shoulder. He did the same with the shirt and sat on the bed to pull on the boots. Finally dressed, he rose and motioned for her to lead the way.

She knelt to crawl on all fours. His view was another distraction, but he averted his eyes so to keep his concentration. Once she went into the tunnel, he did the same in the same manner; however, the tunnel was meant for a small girl who hadn't grown much except in noticeable areas. He, on the other hand, was no small girl and found himself wedged into the small opening more than once. Determination along with the fear of a whip forced him through.

She helped him up and out of her closet. The room of the señorita was as elaborate as the rest of the home. A large bed with four posts supported a white lace canopy. Lamps on nightstands on both sides of the bed lit up the room. A desk made of wrought iron and glass sat on the same wall as the closet, which itself was as big as most rooms he'd ever stayed the night.

"Now, where do we go?"

As he asked, she moved behind a partition. "For now you are safe. This is a forbidden place for everyone in the house. Not even Alfredo is permitted in here. Later, we are going to leave the house."

"We?"

"You do not know the house as well as I do. How are you going to leave if you do not know? And get to your horse?"

The reasons were valid and welcome, but he still didn't understand one reason. "Why are you doing this? I would think you would want to help your father."

She approached him, projecting her captivating eyes into his, spinning a spell not only on his mind but other parts of his anatomy once again. At his front, she gazed up and slipped her palm through his unbuttoned shirt to rub against his matted chest. "I owe you for a great deed."

"Great deed, huh?" Normally when women made their intentions obvious, he was only too willing to oblige. He gulped with visions of exactly what her father would put him through if he found him in her forbidden place.

"Yes. You protected me in front of my father. If he had known that I was in San Antonio, then he would not allow me out from the house for another year." She hugged him, placing her cheek against his chest. "I want to repay you."

"Repay me? Oh, that. Well, I think you have done more than enough. Saving my life and all. If you could just point the way, I'm sure I can make it myself."

She looked up at him with a doubting face. "No. You cannot. And your weapons, you will need." Her palms brushed the front of his trousers. He pushed against her shoulders gently.

"Señorita, I find you a woman of extraordinary beauty. But, I think I'm in greater danger by being in here. I don't think your father would approve. And I've already angered him once tonight. I'd soon not go for the daily double."

Although it took a moment, it appeared by her nod that he had made his point. "I agree. You may be right about this room." She took him by the hand. "Come. I will take you to the place where you can get your horse and your weapons." She stopped him at the door. "Then I will ask you to do a favor for me."

Puzzled by the odd request, he was eager to agree and get on with his escape. "Of course." With the acceptance, she turned the knob and peeked through into the hall. Once secure, she nodded and reached for his hand. He took it and went with her into the hall. The candles still burned as they had when he had gone through before. From door to door they crept closer to the stairs.

The creak of steps froze both of them. Rance turned to retreat to the safety of her room, but Catarina squeezed his hand and led him into an inlet cut into the wall and behind the metal sculpture of a conquistador.

Rance's stomach churned as the creaks became louder and through the twists of metal he saw the dim image of Alfredo stepping onto the second floor and walk the hall. The butler turned in their direction and halted his pace in front of the sculpture. Rance closed his eyes in wait of the sound of a gun being cocked, but once one, two, three seconds had passed, he peeked between his squinted lids to see Alfredo appearing puzzled. Perhaps it was the dim light. Maybe it was the artwork that was the focus of the attraction. Whichever, soon the servant quietly resumed his step down the hall. Rance resumed breathing.

Catarina squeezed tighter on his hand and led him from the wall inlet and toward the staircase. "Do you know what you're doing?" he whispered.

"I know every inch of the house. I've been sneaking about it since I was a small child." They went down the stairs. Rance was unsure of his footing in the dark but that didn't slow the anxious señorita, who went down the steps with the surety of a mountain goat.

Like the end of a tunnel, the light from downstairs grew bigger with each descending step no matter how clumsy. At the bottom landing, Catarina bobbed her head from around the corner and with the speed of a cat scampered into the long foyer, dragging Rance from behind. Once in the cavernous den, Rance couldn't help catching a glimpse of the portrait above the hearth. The resemblance to the woman tugging him across the room was remarkable. At that angle, the longer he stared at the painting, the more he recognized that impish smile.

While his head was turned, he crashed into the back of Catarina. "What happened? Why did you stop?"

"Someone is coming." She looked to the front entrance. "It is Stefan. Hurry," she said, pointing. "This way." Again the young woman pulled him, only this time to an area of the house he'd not seen. They passed the arched entry to the dining room and to another adjacent door. Catarina pushed it open with her right hand and Rance quickly followed. Almost as fast as she opened it she twisted about and closed it.

A moment passed before Rance recognized the pots and pans hanging from a center island in the large room. "The kitchen?"

"Yes," was her answer, she said, still peeking through the door opening.

"How are we going to get out of here?"

She turned around with a scowl. "Do not talk."

Rance stood stymied by her warning. Normally he didn't pay much attention to orders from females. However, since his life might hang on her words, he decided it a good idea to comply. While he stood, he noticed a basket of fruit on the island. Since he hadn't enjoyed dinner, he picked up an apricot with his left hand and thought to take a bite. A second thought stopped him. His concentration might be needed any moment. Since it might be a while before he next ate, he stuffed four into his right pocket. They fell into the long pocket creating a noticeable bulge.

Catarina faced about and immediately her eyes dipped. She arched a brow and cocked her head. "Señor Rance, I am flattered. But, this is not the time."

"What?" he answered, unsure of her meaning.

She shook her head. "No time." She went to him, grabbed his hand and continued to the back of the kitchen. "Stefan is in the den. He will talk to my papa, who will tell him to

194

convince you to sell the horse." This time he was sure of her meaning and followed her willingly into another dark passage. Fear again pushed him into her back and his hands somehow found soft supple flesh. "I said this is no time," came out of the darkness.

Just as he pulled his arms to the side, the creak of a door allowed the outside moonlight into the dark. They went out into the cool, crisp air. From one corner of the house to another, they crept. Once past the corral, they crouched and waddled their way to the back of the large structure, which appeared a barn in the light of the half-moon.

Catarina slipped the board from the cradle and opened the tall door. Rance angled into the doorway and she pulled the door closed behind them. A few moments later, a match flared light into the barn and lit a wick of a hand lantern. Despite the dimness, Rance saw the reflection off the steel of the Walker Colt. He went to it and quickly noticed the pepperbox and his coat hanging from a hook next to a stall. A glance spotted the dun still saddled. "All my things are here?" he said with a puzzled tone.

"Yes," she answered. "I saw Alfredo bring them here. In case you didn't survive."

Gradually he faced about at her. "Survive?"

She nodded and shrugged. "The beatings. If you did not live, then they would have to have all your things to bury with the body. They could not have them discovered here."

Rance shook his head and exhaled. "Of course not." In a moment he regained attention to his escape. He took the gunbelt and began strapping it on.

"Señor Rance," she said in a much softer tone.

"Yes, Señorita," he answered with his head down, buckling the belt.

"Now is the time." Confused by her meaning, he looked to her. Catarina leaned against one of the support beams. She peeled the robe from her shoulders. "I want you to take me. To make love to me. I want to know what it is like to have a man."

His eyes widened at her flimsy chemise and thin bloomers. "Here? Ah, ah, Señorita. Are you sure what — what you're saying? You know, in English it may not be the same as what you mean."

"Yes. I am sure." Her face changed to one of anger. "My papa, he has arranged my marriage to Miguel Alamanzar de Medellin, a nobleman from *España* who is nearly thirty years old." She shook her head. "I do not want to be bred like some horse." She leaned her head back against the wood. The light flickered in her eyes. "I want to experience love. That is why I was in San Antonio. *Pero,* my father is very powerful and when young men learn of my name, they treat me like a disease." She looked to Rance. "I want a man who will stand up to my papa. I want you, Señor Rance. This is the favor I ask." She tucked her shoulders inside the loops of the chemise, sending the garment past her thin frame and crumpling on the dirt. Her long raven strands dangled over her front. Despite the urge to fulfill her wish and his growing desires, he stood still. "You do not want me?"

He gasped for breath to speak. "Señorita, nothing would make me happier than to enjoy an evening in your company." He gulped air again, trying to build a reason in his own head why he shouldn't. He wasn't coming up with any ideas. He went to her. "Catarina, as I said, you are a beautiful woman. And yes, we could mutually bond as a man and woman," he said with voice quivering, peeking at her tender white skin, feeling her bare chest against his, then snapping out of his primal urges and shaking his head. "But I would be stealing what belongs to another man."

"I said I do not want to give myself to the man my papa chose."

"Not that man. The one you choose to love. The one you will spend your life with."

Her shoulders slumped. "I will spend my life with Miguel Alamanzar. I will be his wife."

Rance put his fingers under her chin and peered into her teary eyes. "Maybe you will be his by law, but he will not have your heart. I must say, I believe, he will have his hands full. You will find a way to get exactly what you want, Señorita Catarina." He thought to end his speech with a simple peck on her lips. When he kissed her, she instantly wrapped her arms around him, caressing his mouth on hers, sinking her right hand to squeeze his apricots.

Rance gently pushed her shoulders and picked up her robe. He pushed it into her hands despite her protest. "I may be strong enough to stand up to your father. But, I don't know if I'm strong enough to stand up to you. You are not mine to have." He fought the urge for another kiss, but didn't want to tease her. Quickly he retreated to where his coat hung. He slipped it on, then led the dun to the rear of the barn. He mounted and steered the horse to the un-latched door. He gave her one last look and gave her a wink. "We will meet again."

The night air chilled him. He turned the lapels against his neck. He steered the dun toward the gaping arch that marked the property. Once he was quietly through it, he kicked at the flanks to make his escape. During the ride in the middle of the night, he reflected on what he'd done and the fortune he may have cost himself. A thousand dollars wasn't the windfall he hoped for, but it was still cold cash, and not bad money for the simple transfer of a title. Yet, the more he thought, the more he resolved there was a greater purpose he'd been chosen for, and he wasn't sure why. Over the ridges and swales he pondered exactly the tactics needed for what appeared to be the only plan available. By the time he came upon the rickety fence, he'd made up his mind.

He dismounted and cautiously crept to the house. He pushed open the worn door and went inside. Moonlight allowed him to find what he looked for on the floor. He sunk his fingers between the creases and lifted the trapdoor. When he flared the match, the three squinty faces he expected looked up at him in fear. He took the apricots from his pocket and tossed them to the children. "Now, what do we do?"

16

Rance squatted some fifty feet from the house. He peeked at the midafternoon sun, begging for some sleep, but was content watching Greta bathe the children in the large round metal tub. After only three hours rest on the floor, he knew he couldn't leave these kids to fend for themselves much longer, nor could he balance all three on the back of the dun. Although it wasn't sound, he managed to keep them calm enough to leave and seek the help he needed.

Greta was the perfect choice for the duty. He snickered when recalling her disgust upon setting eyes on him once more just hours ago. However, he enjoyed her genuine smile, the first such he could remember since he first saw her, when he told her he was keeping the horse and then invited her in the rented buggy to come to the farm. She didn't seek a reason to refuse. He even let himself believe she might have shown more than she wanted when she hugged his neck. He thought to steal a kiss at the time, but her proper manner kicked in quicker than his devilish instinct.

About the time his mind wandered to the subject of the last time he was so close to a woman's lips, he spotted a rider approaching from the direction of the Cuellar hacienda. He waved at Greta so not to alarm the children then signaled her to take them into the house. She did so in haste. Within a minute he recognized the single rider as the one that had come the night before.

"Good afternoon," Rance greeted, squinting from the overhead sun. "I don't think we were actually formally introduced. Are you the one called Stefan?"

The answer was terse and brief. "My name is not an important matter."

"Well, something has dragged you all the way out here."

"Don Pedro Cuellar is very angry. You left his hospitality without proper respect and he demands that you return."

Rance bobbed his head to the side. "Well, I had urgent business to attend to." Both men looked at the disaster that was the farm. Rance thought he needed to change the subject. "Please pass on my sincere regrets for my absence. I will make every effort to meet with the don again as soon as is practical." Thinking the matter was settled, he found it wasn't when Stefan didn't turn the horse.

"That is not acceptable. It is not wise to keep Don Pedro waiting, señor. You should mount your horse at once and follow me."

Rance stopped his step, irritated by the rider's tone and his own lack of sleep, and put his hands on his hips, careful to draw back the coat and reveal the Walker Colt. "My friend, let me give you some advice. When you turn around and ride back to your boss, I suggest you keep going and don't bother wasting time peeking back. I hope you understand my meaning." Rance concentrated on Stefan's eyes, which dipped back and forth from Rance's eyes to the pistol strapped to his waist.

"You are making a mistake, señor."

"Not as big a one as you're making by staying here longer than you're welcome."

It took a moment before the rider decided to pull the reins about, but not without a curled lip scowl before he kicked the flanks and galloped back in the direction of the hacienda.

Once it appeared evident Stefan wasn't stopping, Rance let out a long-held tense breath. Greta emerged from the house, leaving the children inside. While also watching the rider's rapid retreat, she came to stand next to Rance.

"What did he want?"

Rance resumed looking at the now-distant Stefan. "Oh, he invited me back to his boss's house. I didn't really think I would enjoy myself there as much I would at this place." He waited a moment, expected a slight grin on the blond's face, but when he snuck a peek at her, her stern lips were still in place.

"The children cannot stay here. It is too dangerous here."

Rance took a quick scan of the open prairie. "And leave all of this?" His attempt to lighten the mood met with the same result. He took a long breath and huffed it out. "Yes, you are right. But where? I don't think Calvin would approve of them at the hotel."

She shook her head. "No. He would not. He doesn't approve of you." Her frank judgment turned his head to her. She finally looked at him. She shrugged. "He doesn't think much of you. Look how you are dressed. It is something people wear when they are buried."

Rance took another long deep breath, trying to bare the needle that had just been jabbed into his gut. Perhaps she was airing her own opinion in disguise. Despite the cut to his own pride, a gust of chilled wind reminded him of their current plight. Words weren't able to roll off his tongue. He ambled aimlessly over to the bony investment still tethered to the post.

The horse jittered slightly at his approach, but he calmed it with a pat to the flanks and ran his palm across the knotty back, then the shoulders. Was this what all the fuss was over? It was difficult to imagine why so many folks wanted this animal. Even harder to believe was the thought that it could actually run a race. Maybe it was the reason poor Hank had risked so much. To attempt to rehabilitate it into the proper condition.

When he got to the head, he saw the unmistakable star. Reminded by the image in the portrait at the hacienda, he shook his head at the differing fates of the colt to its sire. A notion struck him as he stared into the eyes. What if he could run again? But who? Who could turn this sack of bones into a champion? Who really knew horses as he himself knew the games of chance?

She swayed on the back of the paint as she had before, which gave that awful queasy churn in her gut. "I ain't sure I should be going."

Jody twisted his head about. "Would you

quit your bellyaching and think about not washing clothes and doing other chores? I know I am. This is the first I've been able to not think about mending fences, digging postholes, and nailing new boards to the barn. Just think of it as a holiday."

"Holiday? How do you think of messing with bulls and horses as a holiday?"

" 'Cause it's you got a choice in doing it, that's why. You ain't going to understand none of it thinking of it that way. Just watch and you'll understand. The Folsom ranch is just over the ridge there."

Les continued following his lead as always, unsure whether the reality would meet the promise. Once atop a hill, she gazed down at the many folks gathered at the spread. They wound down the slope and onto the dirt trail cut through the tall grass. All the while she made a point to keep as close to Jody as she could for fear of meeting the type of men she wished to avoid. Those which would ask the many questions as to why she was there.

She had to nudge the paint to keep up with Jody as he brought his horse to a trot nearing the edge of the rail fences. People waved at him as he rode by, calling his name with wide smiles. Les now wanted to keep her distance from the thought that she would only confuse the folks and start them talking. Finally, Jody reached a corral where three men stood next to a large roasting pit. Even though she wasn't next to him, she could still hear them talk when they gripped each other's hands.

"Jody Barnes, good to see you, boy."

"Thank you, Mr. Folsom. I'm glad to be here. Looks like you picked a mighty fine day for October."

Les pulled the paint to a stop and dismounted.

"It's good to see you, too, Mr. Basham."

"Jody, my lord, you are a man now. You was just knee-high to a grasshopper the last I think I saw you. How old you be now?"

"I turn twenty just after the first of the year."

With nowhere else to go, Les gradually came to stand behind him.

"Where's your ma and pa?"

"They coming later. Ma had some things she wanted done before she thought she could leave. And my pa, he's a doing them as fast as he can so he can leave." All four men laughed, until the one with the black Stetson noticed her.

"And who might you be?"

"This is Les Turnbow. A friend of mine." All three of them gave a moment's stare. She peeked down at the dungarees and man's shirt loaned to her to see if they were soiled. However, the men weren't staring at her front due to any stains.

Folsom extended his hand. "Les, it's good to know you." She took his hand, which was like sticking it into a slammed door. "This here is Harlan Basham, and that is John Thurman." The other two tipped their hats, which after an instant required Folsom to follow suit. Jody had left his own on and shook his head slightly.

"Les is from Kansas. She's just staying with us a spell." Jody's explanation stole the wind from her lungs, but she knew no other way to explain her presence. She peeked up at him just when he prodded his nose in the air. "Smells good."

Folsom glanced about. "Yeah, slaughtered a yearling for the occasion. Should be good, too. Nice and tender."

Les looked to the meat on the spit. Her stomach churned worse from the thought that what was now there once had legs, a tail, and a head when the morning broke. Even with the savory taste of beef wafting in her nose, she averted her eyes from the pit.

"So, Jody, what have you been doing all these years?" asked Folsom, drawing a wad of chaw from his shirt pocket. Jody accepted the offering and bit off a sizable piece. As before, whenever he spoke with tobacco in his mouth, it sounded like a sheet flapping in the wind.

"Well, I've been back from the trail drive about a week."

"That the one put together by Frank Pearl?" asked Basham.

"Yes, sir. Went all the way up to Abilene." He bobbed his head to the side. "Long ways."

"Bet it was," Folsom agreed. "But, I bet it was worth it. Made you some money. Seen things you hadn't seen." Folsom held his hands out from his own hips and waved them. "Some pretty things not so bad to look at it. Know what I mean?" Laughter from all four soon ceased when they peeked at Les. "Sorry 'bout that," Folsom said.

Les shrugged. "Don't be. Some of those girls are my friends. They like stupid Texas cowboys. They get them drunk and take their money while they're sleeping." Like a bucket of water on a fire, she doused their silliness and soon had them searching for a new subject.

Basham grunted. "So, Jody, you going to rodeo?"

"Yes, sir," he answered with a nod. "Thought I'd give it a try."

"Get his head knocked in," Les muttered

for only Jody to hear.

He spat next to her boots. "You know, there's women over on the other side of the corral. Why don't you see if you can strike up a conversation with them. Ten minutes with you and they'll all be wanting to move to Travis County."

"I ain't going over there. I been with them type. All they want to talk about is their men and quilting."

"Maybe you ought to go. Might find you a man, they might."

"Don't want one. If'n I did, he wouldn't be thinking of jumping on the back of a mad horse." She stared into his eyes, but he soon turned and spat again. When he did, they both saw the fire pit and none of the three men.

"See what you did? Now I got to apologize. These are my friends, Les. These are my folks' friends. You can't come in here and make fun of things they do. It's what they do, it's what they like." He turned once again and spat. "And it's what I like." He twisted about and left her standing next to the rail.

She watched him march off in search of the men, no doubt to express his regrets for their quarrel, and maybe for bringing her in the first place. She glanced at the calf on the spit. She knew how it felt.

When she had headed to Texas, it was for a fortune in gold promised by a man on the gallows. Now where was he when she wanted to tell him it was all a lie? Yet, during the trail she didn't allow herself to sulk in self-pity, and it wasn't going to get her any closer to Kansas than she was now.

17

She wasn't certain, but an unseen force pushed Les closer to the folks she was trying to avoid. Despite the yearning to ride back to the Barnes place or even start on the return trip to Kansas at that very time, she found herself creeping in the direction of the large corral where all had gathered for some kind of show.

As she neared, a sort of aisle appeared with the women seeking the shade of the trees on the left and a row of ranch hands, all with at least one boot on the low rail, to the right. With the wall of shoulders blocking her view, she looked for a gap in order to see what was happening. As she bobbed her head about from the left to the right, she caught sight of Jody's familiar sky-blue shirt with pale suspenders. She wasn't sure why it was now that she recognized it as the same one he had worn when she first met him. It took a moment, but she swallowed what pride she had and went to stand in the same gap next to his shoulder. Jody only glanced at her while he hung both elbows over the top rail.

She had to say something, but while she pondered what, a wooden gate opened in the pen. Out rode a cowboy on the back of a horse, which jumped and skipped across the corral. Twisting and snapping its rear in every direction, the horse soon discarded the rider to the ground, sending a thud to all ears.

Les winced. "Is he dead?"

"Nah," Jody answered casually. The rider got on a knee, wrapping an arm around his chest, then rose to limp to the rails as the horse continued jumping and bucking. "May have cracked a rib, though."

Les's eyes widened at the guess. The man appeared in pain, but masked it with a teeth-gritted smile. "This is supposed to be fun?"

"It is fun. Ain't nothing says fun ain't going to hurt a little."

"A little? He looks to be shot."

Jody laughed. "Well, sometimes it might feel like that. It will wear away sometime next month." When she shot him a look for another dismissive remark, another rider climbed the railed gate and climbed atop another horse. Within seconds the gate opened. As though prodded with a branding iron, this one bucked even worse, hooves flying behind high into the air like lightning. The rider rode with chin tucked into his chest. His hat flew off like blown from a tornado, chaps flapping as wings, as the horse bobbed up and down without all fours on the ground at any time. As she watched, it took a moment before she realized, despite the wild motion of the horse, it was actually jumping toward the fence. The fence she was leaning against. The violent thrash of hooves and shoulders entranced her, freezing her every muscle as it neared.

A grip to the shoulder tore her away from the rail. The horse crashed into the fence, spilling the rider over the rails and onto the very spot where she once stood. When able to breathe, she looked at Jody's hand on her shoulder. "Thanks," she panted. He didn't acknowledge her gratitude. As a few of the spectators helped the rider to his feet, Les shook her head. "What makes them do that?"

A chuckle came from Jody. "That cinch around their privates. Gets them to hop like toads."

She watched as the second rider walked away, favoring his left leg, to the applause and appreciation of those surrounding him. If it was fun, Les couldn't see it. She recalled her own terror at being jerked up and down at the end of a mule's tail. Her back still felt the ache. Why these men would want to put themselves through the pain didn't make sense. It wasn't an idea from a normal mind. Perhaps she could talk Jody out of taking the risk. She spun about. Jody was gone.

Peeking through the maze of arms and paunch bellies, she spotted the sky-blue shirt heading for the swinging gate. She ran after him, but the head start he had was too great for her to make up. About the time she arrived at the gate, Jody was already straddled across another mad mustang.

"What are you doing?"

He looked at her, preferring to concentrate on wrapping the leather and hemp twine over his palm. She looked at the path of the twine, which wrapped around the saddle and under the horse. All during the preparation she saw no worry on his face but rather the ever-present smile that she was first to notice whenever setting eyes on him. Jody took his boots out of the stirrups, huffed a quick breath, then nodded. Les wanted to shriek out to be careful, but suppressed the urge so as not to distract him. The gate swung open.

The horse bolted to the right, jumping,

twisting, bobbing, and bucking. Jody, his chin tucked into his chest, held his free hand high over his head. His body thrust forward and back like a leaping flame that held no form. The horse bucked its way near the fence. Les winced, expecting the same fate for Jody as the one before, but he leaned right and for some reason the horse followed the direction.

With giant skips, the animal charged across the pen, but Jody was still aboard, his boots flung higher than his waist, back slapping against the rump, smile still in place. A loud whistle came from the lips of a man at the gate.

"Time!"

It was over. Jody was still on the horse. Les was confused why nobody stopped the horse. "Get off, stupid!"

Jody's head shot at her. In that instant the horse veered to the right. Jody shot over the top, tumbling headfirst toward the dirt, chin tucked to his chest, and finally back slapping on the dirt like a flat sack of flour. Dust plumed into the air. When it settled, Jody lay motionless. Les's heart sunk.

A moment later, both his arms came up and hands slapped together. He sat up with that smile still in place. Les inhaled, the first air her lungs remembered in more than a lifetime. She unclenched her fingers from the wood of the gate and hopped down to meet him where he climbed over the fence. An urge boiled inside her to grab him about the chest, but when she arrived next to him, Jody stood surrounded by admirers — the most noticeable was Jack Barnes.

The thick-mustached father shook his son's hand with gleeful pride. However, that didn't match the affection shown by Jessie Barnes, who gave a thankful maternal hug. There wasn't any more room for Les.

A moment later the congratulations subsided and soon Jody stood alone. Les hadn't moved as he came her way. "Are you hurt?"

Jody shook his head with the same dismissiveness as with the others. "What'd you yell?"

About to repeat her loud message, she held her tongue only a second, then rethought. "I was cheering you."

"Oh," he answered with surprise. "Well, see, I told you it was fun."

"So, are you done?"

"Heck no," he said with a single shake of the head. "I'm going to rest a spell and give it another try. There's fifty dollars goes to the one that rides the most. I already got one, but I'll need more."

Les tried to keep up with his long stride as

she bumped shoulders with the crowd. "But, you fell off."

"Yeah, but I got my eight seconds. Stayed on long enough to get my ride to count. I'm the first one." His face turned proud, like he'd won the whole ranch as a prize. Still struggling to keep up with him Les faded as Jody continued his walk back to the gate, only mildly watching the next rider suffer a quick and unwanted dismount. The last concern on his mind was talking to Les. She was caught in the wash of people walking about the fence. She finally gave up and watched him walk back to the gate.

Her chest was seized hard, but she wasn't certain as to the reason. Why was she fretting so much?

She inhaled deeply to settle her nerves, content to find a good place to watch. Like a crow, she climbed onto the fence and watched as one contestant after another failed to stay on their bucking horses.

More than ten minutes must have passed before Jody was again settled onto another horse. Les tucked her own chin between her crossed wrists with elbows drooping over the top rail. As before Jody came roaring out of the gate on the bronco. The ride was a repeat of the first; however, what drew her notice was the hoots and hollers from the crowd. It may have not been true, but she swore every-body cheered a little louder for him.

This time, he swung his leg off the animal and landed with both boots firmly on the ground. Les shut her eyes, thinking she was the reason he was thrown the first time. She waited for the rest of the cowboys to ride. Some made it all the way to the end. Most did not. The afternoon passed as one fol-lowed another.

About thinking it was at an end, the men went to their horses. Les followed, relieved the contest was over and they could return to the Barnes's home. However, just when she got to the paint, Jody rode not on the trail home, but back into the pen.

Her spirit sunk at the thought she would have to stay. This wasn't what she imagined when thinking of Texas. She didn't hold with the smell of sweaty flesh and freshly dropped dung surrounding her. All she wanted was a home, and now she was trapped with this cowboy and his family who didn't seem to know what to do with her.

All during her soul search, she moseyed back to the corral. In little time, the men had lined up a small calf behind one of the gates while a mounted wrangler waited with a lar-iat. About the moment she resumed her place on the fence, the gate opened and the calf darted across the pen. The rider spurred his mount and looped the lasso in the air, twirling it above his head then throwing it just in front of the calf for it to run into. In an instant the loop closed like a snare and then the calf was ripped from the ground to crash on its side. The wrangler was off the horse like a shot and pulled all four legs to a point and rapidly wrapped twine around them. Once done, he stood and stopped. All applauded. Les could only think of the animal that lay on its side in the glaring sun, likely pondering what had happened. She shook her head, but a voice came from her left and interrupted her thoughts.

"You going to give it a try, cowboy?"

Les slowly faced him, the brim of her hat slowly revealing the face of someone she hadn't met yet. He had a cheerful face, which gradually faded upon getting a longer look. It was a shock for both of them, worst of all to the kindly older gentleman. When he tipped his hat and retreated from the embarrassment, Les considered again her place. Even without trying she appeared the boy to most. What if Jody still considered her so?

With that man on her mind, she saw Jody now poised to take his turn roping the calf. When the gate opened and the calf broke, Jody was quick to throw his lasso and fly off the saddle. In a blink, he had the calf on the ground and the tether around its legs. Again, everyone cheered.

She couldn't help think that he was their favorite. Was it his smile? She knew it had stamped a place in her mind, and might have in her heart. She shook her head. Jody was a stupid man who didn't think further than the day after the next. He wasn't the type to get all giddy about. There had to be someone else. Maybe that unknown man was here at the Folsom place. She started to look around.

The first man she came across without wrinkles or silver hair was the one she saw bucked off over the rails. She settled next to him. Not used to thinking up things to say, she tried to comment on the other riders. "That one was pretty good."

The young cowboy didn't even look her way. "Nah, too slow. Jody Barnes is the fastest."

"Oh." She thought to infuse interest. "He ain't that good. I bet you could beat him."

The cowboy pointed a puzzled face at her. "You must be loco," he scoffed. "Jody Barnes is the best cowhand in these parts. Ain't no fellow as good as him."

About sick of hearing that name, Les tried to think of the best approach to gain this man's name. After two discarded ideas, she settled on just asking him. However, just as she was about to open her mouth, a young woman in a yellow party dress sashayed by his side and put her arm around his waist.

"I'm hungry. You promised to feed me," the woman whined.

Les receded away without a word, confident she didn't have the charm to steal away this girl's beau. After another moment's thought, she didn't have the looks of that woman, nor maybe a woman at all.

Her heart sunk even further. Resolved to failure, she rested with one boot on the low rail like all the other cowpokes.

18

With all the events over, the sun decided to set, or so Les thought. All about were smiles and happy laughter. She couldn't fault the folks for enjoying themselves. She just desired to be part of it. As people milled about, some nursing wounds suffered during their fun, she showed a polite smile to most as she searched for the one that brought her. Finally, she spotted Jody surrounded by his parents and Folsom as they were in the midst of the memories of the day. She didn't have the gumption to barge in.

When the story ended, the small party began moving toward the house. Les stood her ground as Jody approached. "I'm happy for you."

"Good to hear," he answered as he kept walking, forcing her to do the same.

This time she wasn't content to let him walk away. "Where you going?"

"Get something to eat. I'm starved for some good food."

Food didn't sound like a bad idea. She followed him through the maze of people, feeling like she was following Moses as he parted the Red Sea. While in his wake, she noticed the faces confused about her place with him. With a queasy bubble in her stomach, she considered it just hunger and so went to the long table where the chow line formed.

Handed a plate, she edged spot by spot next to Jody. "What are you supposed to do?"

"Pick and choose. I just want one thing."

Les scanned the table. Peeled potatoes, shucked corn, diced squash, and beets had some appeal. A boiling pot of beans was quickly passed. Once at the end she saw the main attraction. Folsom, with long fork and carving knife in hand, sliced into the still steaming carcass. "How big do you like, Jody?"

"As much as you're giving, Mr. Folsom." With that, Folsom plunged the knife deep into the meat and sliced off a four-inch-wide slab. He plopped the cut onto Jody's plate, who then stepped aside. Les stepped to the end, her mouth watering for a sizable portion.

"I know just what you need, little lady," Folsom said with a smile and carved off a puny slice of less than an inch. When he slipped it on her plate, Les looked to the cut, feet frozen in place and unable to speak a word. "Come on back if you're still hungry," Folsom added, then greeted the cowboy behind her as a sign to move on. Les gave thought of picking up the small piece with her fingers and chewing it right in front of him with plate still outstretched.

Not wanting to make a worse impression, she forced a grateful smile and went to find Jody. He found a place near one of the standing lanterns. When she got closer, the darkness peeled away enough for her to see two young girls who had found places by his side on a long bench. Usually content to find another place and sulk over the crushing sight, Les sucked in breath, resolved to find her own place. Right next to him.

She marched to his front and stood. Jody, his smile aimed at both of the young women, finally noticed Les standing only inches away. "Something wrong?"

"No." A pause and silent curse was enough to goad herself to nudge one of the young women away and take her perch next to Jody.

"What are you doing?" he asked, surprised.

"Eating," she answered in the same casual tone as he spoke before. The girl who was moved took the intended offense and flew off into the night. With half the objective solved, she leaned forward in order to see the girl on the right. "How do. My name is Les. What's yours?"

"Lizbeth," was the confused and uneasy answer.

Les picked up the meat, bit off a piece, and while still chewing, licked her fingers, then offered a handshake. "Nice to meet you, Lizbeth."

The tactic had its intended effect as the girl repelled from the gesture. "What an ugly thing to do."

"Les, what are you doing?"

"Making friends. That's what you told me to do. I was just trying to meet everybody you know." She looked again at the girl. "Just how long have you known Jody, Lizbeth?"

"We've been friends since we were little children, if it's any business of yours," was the terse reply. "We went to Sunday school together."

"That's funny. Jody told me he was no churchgoer." She looked to him. "I don't remember you telling me that." Before he could reply, she looked again at the girl. "He was telling me that while we were sleeping under the stars. Just him and me."

"What?"

"Les, stop it," said Jody.

It was no time to stop. "That was after him telling me about all the girls he was bedding in Abilene."

"Les!" Jody's shout was enough to make her stop, as well as all else around the ranch. Soon, they resumed their business. Lizbeth, shocked more from the loud voice than Les's story, or maybe not, decided to stand. Jody did as well for the girl.

"It was nice talking to you, Jody. Congratulations on winning today." She went back toward the others. Jody beamed his smile at her, then shrank it away when he faced Les.

"What did you do that for? Are you plumb losing your mind?"

Les shrugged. "Could be."

"If you were a man, I'd give you a good punch for what you did."

"Go ahead. You've been thinking of me as one." She tossed the plate on the ground. "I don't know what I am." She hung her head. Tears welled in her eyes, but she breathed deeply trying to hold them back. It was a moment before she felt another weight on the bench.

"I thought when I brought you here, you'd have a good time. See a little what Texas folks are like. If I'd known you'd be a pest, I wouldn't have brought you."

She shot her head up. "If I'd knew I was going to be a pest I'd not come." She shook her head and dipped her eyes once more. "If I knew I was going to be left by myself, I'd soon be by myself, Jody."

"What do mean, by yourself? There was plenty of folks here for you to talk to."

"You mean the ones that think of me as a boy? I found him."

Jody sliced into the slab of beef, stuck it into his mouth, then shrugged. "Can't blame 'em a bit. What you wear."

"You gave me these clothes."

" 'Cause you wanted."

" 'Cause I wasn't riding with my leg wrapped around the saddlehorn under no skirt," she angrily replied, wagging her head side to side. "I have a hard enough time with a leg on each side." Her sharp tone hung in the air. She didn't know what to say next, and the truth of what she said hit her like a punch, sparking at first a snicker, then a chuckle. She glanced at Jody. He broke a smile, then laughed louder than her. Finally she let a loud guffaw. She looked into Jody's eyes and they both laughed together. It was the best moment she had all day.

■ ■ ■ ■

Les rolled over. The call to breakfast filtered into her ears, but she was still feeling the effects of the long ride home in the dark. By her sleepy recollection, she just crawled into bed ten minutes ago. However, dawn had long since broken by the bright sunlight shining through the window.

She rose to sit on the edge of the bed. She quickly threw on her dress while wiping the sleep from her eyes and went to the table. Jody appeared in the same state as she. Rolling his shoulder, he soon rubbed the ache.

"Yesterday still fresh in your muscles?" asked Jack Barnes, who wiped the sweat off his brow as he entered the house.

Jody nodded. "Yeah," he complained. "Didn't hurt then. But now my arm feels like it was tore from the shoulder and Ma sewed it back on." Les couldn't hide the smirk growing across her face, nor stop Jody from noticing. "You think it's funny," he said as he sat down.

Les shrugged. "Maybe Lizbeth will come by and help you rub it."

Jody's mother's eyes lit up as she delivered the skillet of eggs to the table. "Did you talk to Lizbeth, Jody?" The question wasn't one that Jody wanted asked. He curled a lip at Les.

"I did." He puffed out his chest. "Had me a fine talk with her." He cocked his head to the side. "But a pest chased her away." Now, Les curled a lip at him.

"Pest?" asked Jessie. "What kind of pest?"

Jody slid the big spoon into the eggs and slapped the helping onto his plate. "Oh, you know, Ma. One of them varmints that buzzes about. No matter how much you swat at it, you can't get it to leave."

Les stopped eating. Even with his words made in jest, she felt there was some truth to his meaning. Maybe he thought of her as a pest that wouldn't leave. As she pondered the remark, Jack Barnes commented on the matter. "Shouldn't let no pest get in the way of what you want. If Lizbeth run off, I would have run off after her." The words like salt in a wound, Les dropped her fork from the sting. Jessie Barnes looked her way.

"Les, you feeling poorly?"

She wiped her face and shook her head. She didn't want to say much. Her gut wouldn't let her. "No, ma'am. I think I'll get to the chores. Maybe the air outside will be better than what's in here." Les tossed her napkin on the table. When she picked up her plate, Jessie shook her head as a sign she

229

didn't have to wash her own plate. Jody sat and chewed without looking her way. She didn't want to stay. She wanted to leave, and so headed for the door. Once she burst out the door she went to the tub and board. On the porch sat the basket of clothes and on top was that sky-blue shirt. She picked it up, ready to tear it to shreds. Instead, she doused it into the dirty water. Tears dripping into the tub, she rammed the shirt against the board. Up and down, up, down, over and over, punishing the threads that first caught her eye.

"Are you trying to put a hole in it?" The voice didn't come from behind, but in front. Les looked up. In a long-cut dusty black suit sat Rance Cash on his dun.

"What are you doing here?"

Rance shrugged and gazed about. "I was invited to visit. I thought I would take a Sunday ride and come and see two of my best friends."

"You're lying," she said with confidence. Jody came out from the door, first looking at her, but she pointed at Rance.

"What are you doing here?"

Rance rolled his head in frustration. "Don't you remember? You said come and visit and so, I'm here."

Jody looked to Les. "You're lying," they

both said in unison.

"Jody," Jessie Barnes said, emerging from the house with her husband. "What's going on out here?"

"Just another one of them pests I was telling you about, Ma." Les arched a brow at him, but when she thought about it, she couldn't find much fault with the judgment. "What are you needing, Cash?"

Rance dismounted off the horse and casually went to tether the reins at the corral. Once he approached the fence, the bull longhorn turned his way, taking several steps. Rance stood stiff. "Why is it doing that?" The longhorn lowered its horns but stopped its approach.

Jody went off the porch. "That's Brewster. He thinks you're a threat."

"Threat?"

Jody continued to walk to the corral and Les followed. "Yeah. He thinks you're a threat to take his spot. To steal some of his harem of cows."

Rance first looked to Jody with a puzzled face, then back at the bull. "Can he come through this fence?"

"Could if he got all riled up."

"Well, then show him that I want none of his cows. He can have them all."

Jody snickered. "I don't think there's

much to worry about. Now that I think he's got a good look at you, he ain't all that threatened."

Rance finished tethering the reins. "Normally I would resent that remark. But in this instance, I'll let it stand, gladly."

"So, what are you really doing here?"

Rance peeked at Les, then at Jody, pushing his hat back off his brow. "I may have a job for you."

19

"A job?" Jody questioned with surprise.

Les suspected trouble. "What you got yourself into now?"

"Now why say it that way? For all you know, it may be a fine opportunity you'll thank me for later." Neither Jody nor Les were swayed with the positive plea. After Rance flashed his smile for a solid three seconds without reciprocation, he frowned in frustration. About to explain, Jessie Barnes's voice broke his thoughts.

"Jody, are you going to introduce us to your friend?"

This opportunity restored Rance's grin. "Indeed, Jody. Where are your manners?" He looked to Jessie and removed his hat. "My name is Cash, ma'am. Rance Cash. You must be Jody's sister, am I right?"

While Jessie put her hand to her mouth and blushed, Les rolled her eyes, catching sight of Jody shaking his head.

"Don't be fooled, Ma. This one is as slick as a snake."

Jessie looked sternly at her son. "Hush your mouth, boy. If he wants to say nice things, ain't your place to put him down for it." She changed to a more pleasant face while turning to Rance. "Would you like to come in, Mr. Cash? We were just finishing breakfast."

"How neighborly of you. Yes, I believe I would love to enjoy your fine cooking. And, please call me Rance. All my friends do."

"You ain't got no friends," Les muttered. "Tell her what all the others call you."

Rance didn't miss a step despite her insult. He marched up to the porch, squinting slightly in the bright morning light and naturally beaming his broad smile. As he came up the steps, he took Jessie's hand and placed his free palm atop it in a sincere show of respect. "So nice to meet you." He recognized Jody's father in an instant and held out his hand for a firm handshake. "Rance Cash, sir. Pleasure to be in your home."

"Jack Barnes," was the answer and acceptance of the gesture.

"I see where Jody got his gentlemanly manners. A fine son you two have put out for the world to admire."

Les's stomach churned with that sappy sweet remark.

Rance entered the house and continued his compliments. After an invitation to sit, he settled in the chair abandoned by Les. "Oh, I see you were expecting me," he said with a chuckle.

"Here, Rance," said Jessie, scooping more eggs on the plate. "Those must be cold. Let me give you some warm ones." The mother gave Les an instant glare, then dished out the eggs. Les stayed in the doorway.

"All right," Jody said with an honesty-demanding tone. "You got your food. Now, what you got in mind?"

Rance dipped the fork into the eggs, but looked about to all the faces watching him. "Have you good people heard of a man named of Hank Baines?" He shoved the eggs in his mouth.

"Why, yes," Jessie answered. "I've heard that name."

Jack Barnes nodded. "Young man, I think. Has a small place to the east."

"So what about him?" Jody said to remind Rance of the point.

Rance swallowed. "Well, I'm sorry to be the bearer of bad news, but he's now dead." Jessie sucked in air and huffed a hoot of shock. "Yes, I'm sorry to say. He lost at a game of cards that I'm sad to admit I was in, and I guess the loss hit him harder than he could stand. He came back in the Alamo Saloon and tried to kill a man. Red McClain. And, as it turned out, Red's aim was steadier."

"How terrible," Jessie said, almost moved to tears.

"That's a damn shame. Always said there was no good to be found in no saloon."

Jody pointed at Rance. "You got that right."

Les felt a twinge of anger at Jody's finger being pointed when he himself spoke the praises of the fun to be found in a drinking palace. She held her tongue still, not wanting to encourage any more glares her way.

Rance placed his fork at the edge of the plate. "I apologize. I've brought pain to you people and that was not my intent. I'll leave you to the peace that you had before I came." He rose and put on his hat. "Beholden for the taste of fine food, Mrs. Barnes." As he went to the door, chins were left sagging, allowing for reflection on the news of a man's death. Les still held her tongue, recognizing the play for sympathy.

"Wait." Jody's order stopped Rance at the door. "You never got around to talking about this job you came here to tell me about."

A crease of a smile crept over Rance's face. He looked to Les and winked. "Oh, I don't wish to bother you with my plans of restoring Hank Baines's memory to good stature" — he paused only a second — "and helping out his children."

"Children?" Jessie asked with worry.

"Yes, ma'am. Three of them. Two girls and a boy. The oldest is five. All of them living on their own at a shack."

"Good heavens. Those kids can't stay there by themselves."

"Yes, ma'am. I feel the same. But, I am not a family man and have no home of my own. Like you good folks." With just a ploy to increase the stakes, Rance had gotten what he wanted. Les rolled her eyes again and stared at the ceiling as Jessie Barnes took off her apron.

"Jack, hitch the team to the wagon. We need to get to those kids and get them off that place and bring them home."

Morning dissolved into afternoon. Les kept pace near her two friends while Jody's parents weren't far behind in their wagon. As they rode at a steady pace over the rolling green hills, Les's tongue loosened. "Is there really such a place or is this another trick?"

"My." Rance sighed while keeping his eyes

forward. "How did I survive all these weeks without that sweet sound?"

"You ought to try listening to it for morning, noon, and night."

She sneered at Jody's remark, kicked the paint for it to catch up and ride between them, not wanting to miss any faces they were making with their backs turned. "Well, is it?"

"No, dear Leslie, this is no trick. There is really a farm with poor helpless children."

The reminder of the children dulled her sharp tongue, but she couldn't let herself be silenced so easily. "Don't call me that."

"So, how did you come by these kids? Doesn't sound like your usual company."

Rance only glanced at Jody. "I wish I could tell you." He took a long breath and his face cringed a bit like trying to spit up a rock. "Can't rightly say how it came to be. But, once I saw these kids, I knew I couldn't let them live, or worse, stop living out there alone."

The thought struck Les as funny. "Rance Cash, caretaker of the weak and defenseless."

Rance just shrugged off her remark.

They took a path up a long curve that ascended up a grassy ridge. Once they paused only slightly to allow the elder Barneses to catch them. Once they all regrouped, the three riders again took the lead.

"How far you reckon?" Jody asked.

"I recognize some of these trees from this morning," Rance said, pointing. "Maybe three or four miles."

The mid-autumn day was cool but sunny. Enough to have Les break a sweat just riding. She pondered the reason that would drive Rance this far out into the wilderness. "Your conscience put you out this far?"

"Why? You don't think I have one?" When neither she nor Jody could find a fault with the suggestion, Rance waggled his head. "All right, so it wasn't that at first."

Les looked to Jody. "Thought so," they agreed together.

"So, what was it brought you all the way out here? Wasn't no crying for them kids, was it."

"Well, not at first," Rance admitted, kicking the dun up a small hill. "It was actually a horse."

"A horse?" Jody's question had Rance rein in the dun atop the hill. He pointed into the distance. Les strained to see anything in the tall grass.

"There it is," Rance said. "Come on. Let me show you."

With apologies rapidly expressed to the

pokey parents, Jody followed Rance's lead. Les was quick to keep pace, the cool wind soothing her overheated brow as she rode through the prairie grass. As Rance approached, he slowed the dun and held his hand for Jody to do the same. It took several moments for Les to come alongside.

"It's all right. You can come out," Rance said. A few seconds later, a tall, blond lady dressed in a white blouse and long brown skirt emerged from the front doorway. Soon after, a young girl followed, staying close to the lady like chicks to a hen. Another child joined the group and a little boy poked his head from out the door.

Les gulped. All this time she had bet the other way. Despite not knowing for sure what the game was, she really couldn't believe Rance Cash would align himself with the weak and defenseless. In a silent show of her regret for being wrong, she shook her head while still staring at the small kids.

Rance nudged the dun forward and dismounted and removed his hat. He stood for a few seconds allowing for Jody to do the same. Les got off the paint, but saw no reason to continue the respect shown a woman. In little time Jack Barnes pulled the team to a stop and Jessie was quick to hop off the buckboard.

"Mr. and Mrs. Barnes, let me introduce you to Miss Greta Schneider." The women exchanged their greetings.

"Oh, you're a German girl," Jessie said with surprise.

Greta glanced at Rance, appearing uncomfortable for a moment, then she nodded. "Yes, ma'am. From Bavaria."

"Ain't that something," Jack said. "But, don't know that's something I didn't expect. Heard of a heap of folks from there settled all around here." With the friendly exchange exhausted, Jessie focused on the young children. Holding out her arms looking for a hug, the eldest girl shied from the offering behind the tall lady's skirt.

"They are not used to new people. It took me several hours to gain their trust." She touched the hair of the girl. "This is Mary. And this is her sister, Theresa, and that is their brother, Little Hank."

Jessie used her maternal charm to encourage the young children into her arms. Her husband and son, and even Les were pulled closer to get a better view, but Rance stopped Jody with a hand on the shoulder.

"I want you to take a look at something." The two men went to the other side of the house where a rotting wood fence vaguely resembled a corral. Les, not wishing to be told how she could help with the children, followed Jody and Rance. They walked around a four-post stand with a wide plank acting as a roof. Les scampered to keep up as they turned at the end and view inside.

"Oh, lordy," Jody uttered.

"This is the job I had in mind."

"Job? More like a miracle you're asking for." Jody slowly approached the starved horse. Les came closer as each of the men went to opposite sides. Jody only shook his head in despair as he ran his fingers over the bony bumps along the animal's side. "Don't look like he's been away from this tether for some time."

"That's what I figured." Rance gently patted the flank. "I would like to see if you can get him back into some condition."

Jody bobbed his head to one side. "I'm sure it wouldn't be much to get him some hay and oats."

"How long do you think it would take to get it back into a condition to run?" Rance held that crease on his lips like he was holding back a smirk. Les recognized it as the one he showed before just when he was about to show a winning hand.

"To run where?" asked Jody.

"Oh," Rance shrugged. "Maybe a mile." Jody appeared confused at the mention of the short distance, then just like a gust of wind, he cringed.

"Are you telling me this is a racehorse?" The answer was confirmed with a slow nod. However, Jody shook his head. "Ain't no way. I don't know if this one will even survive the walk back to my place."

"It must race again," Rance boldly replied. "It is from a famous line. Sired by the famous Pride of Texas, this one was. And there are many people anxious to get their hands on it. But, in this condition, it won't bring much of a price. What I need is for you to be able to get it to run, to put on a show."

"So these people wanting to buy it will pay top dollar," Les chimed in.

Rance nodded her way. "Now you're learning."

20

Les watched while perched on the strongest beam of the rickety fence. Jody led the horse tenderly around the corral. The slow gait seemed all the horse could manage. Noise twisted her about to see Rance walk from the house. "All that mothering chase you out here?"

"Not my strong point," he said as he leaned into the fence.

"So, you won this horse in a card game?"

"Yeah," he answered with a nod. "Didn't know it at the time, but it seems to be the center point of a local feud."

"How you mean?"

It took time before he replied. "When it happened, I didn't really grasp what it meant. This fellow Baines, he just seemed like a poor farmer. But, then I learned the story."

His hesitation perked her curiosity. "What story?"

"This horse's daddy was a local celebrity of some renown." The fancy words didn't impress Les, but Rancc continued despite. "He was called The Pride of Texas. But the owner wasn't a good businessman and had to sell the horse to a man by the name of Don Pedro Cuellar. Cuellar is of Creole decent, a stubborn man of very rich means waiting for the return of Spanish rule. He also fancies himself a racehorse owner. But, this horse came into the hands of the original family that owned The Pride of Texas. I believe, rather than sell the horse to Cuellar, Hank Baines was wanting to raise enough to money to save this farm."

Les didn't understand all the events in his story, but she recognized his part in it. "So, you're trying to get this horse in a way to sell it to this Cuellar fellow." Rance bobbed his head once in agreement with her statement. Jody walked the horse over to them. "So, what's this one's name?" asked Les.

"Lone Star."

Jody shook his head as he approached. "I don't know if he's going to make it. Might take months to get him back into any condition to run in a pasture. I can't see anything that will put him to racing."

"Haven't got months," Rance replied. "Winter will be here before we know it. I won't be able to keep the interest that long." Jody looked puzzled at the remark. He looked at Les.

"It's a long story," she answered. That thought put another qustion in her mind. "So, how did you get that woman out here. She owe you money?"

With a chuckle, Rance responded. "Actually, she's the one that wanted to come."

"Lucky for you," said Jody. "Where did you find her?"

"She's the cook, er — I mean chef at the Menger Hotel. I met her when I first went in there. And, well, we began a conversation." His coy manner wasn't normal.

"You took a shine to her?" asked Les.

Rance almost appeared embarrassed. However, it only took a few seconds before he resumed his usual cocky behavior. "I wouldn't insult such a lady by speaking about her private moments in public."

Jody hooted. "You devil. She's sweet on you?"

With a shake of the head, Rance dismissed the giddy talk. "Let's concentrate on the horse. What is it going to take to restore its health?"

"Plenty to eat, being worked with every day," was Jody's simple answer.

"Sold." Rance pointed at Jody. "You get

this animal to the point where he can run a race and it will be worth a thousand dollars to you."

Jody's eyes went wide, but Les was the one able to speak. "A thousand dollars! Where would you get that kind of money?"

With a simple smile, Rance looked her way. "You'd be amazed at the amount that pride can cost."

Les didn't comprehend what was meant, but the staggering sum of money was all she cared to know about. She looked at Jody, who still seemed entranced at the figure of Rance's proposal. Finally, he seemed to snap from it, and with several shakes of his head, he gave Rance a stern jaw.

"You better not be just saying that."

"Jody," Rance said with his smile still in place. "My friend, if we can pull this off, you'll be known as the best horse trainer in Texas."

"Pull what off?" asked Les.

"I can't go into it at the moment, but just trust what I say."

"Trust you?" Jody and Les questioned in unison.

Before he could answer, Rance faced about forcing Les to do the same. Out from the house stepped Jessie and Greta, like two lifelong friends, together with the children following them.

"We're going to take the children home," said the mother.

"What a grand idea," Rance said with such surprise. Les again rolled her eyes, knowing that was the ploy all along.

"Who is that?"

Jody's question pulled all attention first to him then to the far hill. Les concentrated but really did not see anything. Not wanting to seem ignorant, she waited for others to tell her what the worry was. Jody wandered to the southern side of the corral, and Rance also got to a position where he could see clearly. The hush only added to the confusion. Jessie looked to her husband to provide the answer, but Jack Barnes only moved closer to where Les sat on the fence. The tall lady appeared more concerned with the children. She made sure all three were close by her side.

Finally with all the staring and no talking, Les had all she could stand of not knowing. "So?"

"Looks to be four riders heading this way," Jody said still staring.

"I count five," Rance spoke in a soft tone. "And I don't like whatever it is they're planning." He took only a moment to meet Jody's eyes. After an instant of thought, they both stood like they were talking but not a word was said. Then both moved just like they were bit by horseflies and began pointing at the others. Rance was the first to give orders. "We need to get away from here fast. Greta, get those kids in the buggy."

"But, they're going with us," Jessie protested.

"Then get them in the wagon, Ma." Jody's loud command made his mother and father move like he was the parent. Les hopped off the fence, figuring she was next to be ordered around. It was Jody who looked her in the eye, but said nothing. She did.

"What do you want me to do?" He passed her without a reply. Her heart sank as he ignored her question, but Rance pulled her shirt.

"Help Greta with the children, will you?"

It took her a moment before she cleared her mind of Jody's snub. When she faced around, she saw the tall lady already in the back of the buckboard, gathering the children in her arms. There wasn't much for Les to do. When she looked to Rance, he went to secure the end board of the small wagon, then put his hand on Greta's shoulder.

"Go with these good people. And hang on." He looked to Jack Barnes in the driver's seat next to Jessie. "Head back to your place as fast as you can." Jack gave an assuring nod and then shook the reins sending the team bolting. As soon as the buckboard was gone, Jody rode out of the corral on his horse leading Lone Star with a rope.

"I guess we'll see how far he can run," said Jody, then he glanced back at the approaching riders and the sun in the western sky. "I don't know how far he'll go."

"Take him as far as you can. When you have to, rest him in the trees."

"I can't rest him," Jody complained with a shake of his head. "They'll be on me too quick."

"No, they won't. I'm going to lead them back toward San Antonio."

"But they'll follow us. They're looking for this horse, you said."

The problem seemed to stop Rance, but for only a moment. "No, they won't. Not if they think that horse is going with me."

"What are you talking about?"

Rance ignored Jody's question. "Just go." He slapped the mount's rump and it charged with Lone Star following the lead. Rance looked to Les. She gulped. She'd seen that look in his eye before. "Come on." He glanced back at the sun once more.

"What are you doing?" He continued by her without an answer. She huffed a breath and followed. "I said, what are you doing?"

He went to the dun and led it to the far side of the house. Behind the house sat a small buggy. "Hurry," he said. "We've got to get this hitched."

"Why? We can just ride out of here."

"Then Jody will be right. They'll catch him. But if we show them a slower target pulling a horse behind, then maybe they'll follow us."

As Rance went to the other side of the harness, Les shook her head and muttered, "Why would we want to do that?"

"We can't have them catch those kids." He cinched one of the straps then gave her a wink. "Besides, you wouldn't want Jody to turn out to be right, would you?"

She knew what was being tried. The attempt to get her goat by appealing to her need to get back at Jody was easy to see. At first, she was reluctant to be so predictable, but the more she thought about it, especially since she was still at the ranch with unknown riders approaching, she was forced to make a decision. She went to the paint and mounted. When she rode over to the buggy, Rance was surprised to see her in the saddle.

It wasn't smart to go along with what he was planning. They could easily keep ahead of the riders on horseback. However, as she stared into his questioning eyes, her blood turned to acid, burning down her throat, throughout her chest, and into the pit of her stomach. If she left him alone, he may get caught, or the riders may follow the Barneses. By the time he could get the dun unhitched from the buggy, he wouldn't have time to get away.

She sighed, wondering why she was always put to these miserable choices, but she had made it. Les slid off the saddle and led the paint to the rear of the buggy. Quickly tying the reins to it, she climbed into the buggy next to him. Rance took a moment to peer into her eyes.

"Well, what are you waiting on?"

Her angered voice made Rance shake the reins. The dun charged, but the weight of the buggy stalled its stride. Rance kept shaking and after only a few trudging steps, the dun gained momentum and Rance steered it toward the road.

Les peeked behind but the rapidly dimming light didn't allow her to spot the pursuing riders. The unknown made her nervous. "Go faster."

"I only have one horse." With that Rance shook the reins even harder. "Where are they?"

"I can't see them. Maybe they're not following us." Les faced forward. She saw Rance draw the revolver. Putting the reins in one hand, he cocked the hammer, pointed the barrel in the air, and pulled the trigger. The blast rung in her ears, and fire spit into the darkening sky.

"What'd you do that for?"

"They're following us now," he yelled above the hum of the wheels.

21

A shot turned Jody's head. He pulled up his mount and twisted it about. An instant's thought was to follow the sound and see if he could help. As he looked to the weak horse a choice had to be made. It wasn't possible to hold on to the rope and make any real distance. The more he thought about it, the less chance he figured he had of making it to his friends to make a difference.

It was only a single shot. If there was any real shooting he'd have heard a dozen more by now. Yet, the idea that others were covering for him didn't put him to ease. Especially when it was Les out there. That girl was too headstrong for her own good. She should have joined him. He should have told her to. He bit his lip at the mistake, concluding she wouldn't likely have listened much less heeded his orders. She never listened.

Every time he tried to tell her something,

all he ever got in return were reasons why she shouldn't have to do it. He had brought that girl to his family's place. Gave her a roof over her head and food to eat. More times than not, he was sorry for bringing her.

He looked in the direction of the shot again. He shook his head, trying to clear his mind. Les was his friend. Like it or not, he was fond of the girl he had first thought to be a boy. Now, she was out there with that damn fool gambler. He glanced ahead. The roll of the buckboard could barely be heard. If he didn't turn to follow he would have to race at a gallop, too much for this weak horse at this time. The sun was setting fast and to try to find them in the dark might put himself in a bad spot. There was also his ma and pa to think about. And then there was the foreign woman. And them kids.

He steered the mount back to the west. He tugged at the rope to get the racehorse's attention. The respite was over. Unsure what course he might take if he heard more shots, he nudged the mount to catch the buckboard.

Les clutched the thin iron rail of the buggy seat. Rance had the dun at a gallop, swerving to the left and right, crashing over the bumpy ground. She glanced back at the paint, which also was running as fast as possible just to keep slack in the reins. She hoped it didn't miss a step and have the bit ripped from its head. She didn't want anything to happen to that paint. While she thought about it, she hoped not to fall out herself.

"Can you see anything?" Rance's question faced her forward.

"Not yet. Do you think they were just riding by? You know, meant no harm?"

"Not likely." He gritted his teeth, straining to keep the buggy from toppling over. "I kind of made someone mad this morning."

"What!? Oh, that's just fine. I see you haven't changed your habits none."

He smiled. "Just my nature, I guess." He pulled hard on left rein, but the right front wheel smashed into a stone, sending that side up and at an angle. Les was flung from the seat, her fingers firmly wrapped around the thin rail the only reason she wasn't cast into the weeds. She hung dangling from the side of the buggy as it rolled on. Rance's hand grabbed her wrist and he pulled back on the brake. The spring mechanism shattered as it hit the wheels. There was nothing to stop the buggy with the dun at a full gallop.

With only a single hand on the reins,

Rance couldn't pull hard enough to slow the horse. The jagged ground scraped against her trousers, keeping her off balance and interfering with progress to get back in the seat.

"Hang on!"

She reached for his hand, but just slackening her grip on the rail forced her farther away. She grasped it with all her strength. Her muscles cramped from the constant pressure. Unable to keep them bent anymore, she realized that she was about to be strewn into pieces when she fell under the wheels.

Les glanced to the right. She couldn't see in the darkness, but felt the ground rise farther up her legs. Soon, her hip drug against the dirt. It was a hill and the buggy tipped up on the right, lifting her into the air. Another jarring jolt flung her back across the seat, falling onto Rance's lap.

"Are you all right?"

"I don't know for sure." Still lying across his lap, she straightened up to peek behind. The mixed white coat of the paint could barely be seen. "I don't think anybody is behind us."

"Good. Tell the dun that!"

She helped Rance pull back on the reins, and in a few seconds, the exhausted horse slowed to a stop. Still trying to capture her breath, Les panted while rubbing her sore thighs. Rance noticed and checked her legs. She grabbed his hands.

"I'm trying to feel if something is broken."

"I don't care what you're feeling for. You keep your hands off me."

"Have it your way," he said, angered. He stood and peered into the darkness. Despite some throbbing, Les couldn't hold back her curiosity.

"See anything?"

"No," was the answer. "But it's fairly plain we ain't going far. Not with these horses. We'll have to rest them." He sat back in the seat. She couldn't see his face as she continued rubbing. "I can't see a thing," he said.

"Maybe those riders weren't even coming our way. Maybe they were just passing by." Her snide tone was answered by his.

"Maybe they were coming to give us a party."

"Well, I'm just saying that we didn't know for sure."

"And if we stayed there, what would we do surrounded by a half dozen guns?"

"You said there were only five."

"I only counted five. They might have been six. There might have been a full dozen that hadn't come over the hill yet. Either

258

way, I didn't feel like putting ourselves in danger."

"Oh, and scampering off into the dark wilderness is safer?"

"Safer than being in that situation."

"You weren't the one hanging off the buggy," she shouted. He clasped his hand over her mouth.

"Hush up or they find us just the same." He slackened his hand.

"If they're even there."

"Just be quiet."

She heard him breathe, but couldn't focus on anything about him. He was just a voice in the dark. As they sat, the night air began to sink into her skin. The chill made her more nervous than the ordeal hanging off the buggy. "So what are we going to do now?"

"I don't know."

She chuckled. "The great Rance Cash not knowing what his next play is?"

"If you're just going to be a nuisance, why don't you just start walking somewhere. Damn, now I regret talking you into staying with me. I should have let you go with Jody."

His sharp remark stole her wind. Her mind turned to the suggestion and it stung. "He wouldn't want me there, neither." Her words hung in the brisk air. She sensed

Rance was a bit surprised.

"You two still fighting over you dressing as a boy?"

She nodded, even though she realized the answer couldn't be seen. "He don't see me as anything else. One time he'll tell me I'm a girl and can't do something because of that. The next time, he's looking at them gals that like to scoot up close to him and fill his head with their giggly talk. Makes my insides flip up and down when I have to be around that. And him."

"Well, you know what that is." He dangled the question as squeaks abounded while he climbed from the buggy. She felt the weight swing his way then bounce from the relief.

"What are you talking about?"

"Sounds like the two of you have something to say to each other that neither of you has the courage to tell each other."

His voice wasn't as strong as before so in order to hear better and confront his remark, she eased out of the buggy. "What are you trying to say? And don't make it into a heap of fancy words that I ain't going to know." Her eyes adjusted to the dim light and she recognized the flash of a white shirt near the dun. The longer he said nothing, the higher her blood boiled into her head.

"It's clear to see."

"See what?"

"That the two of you have feelings for each other." He paused again and she heard the jangle of the hitch. Still, she didn't have the wind to speak. All she could do was listen. "I see it in him, too. Jody doesn't know what to make of you, mostly because of you. You act like you're a cowhand, so he treats you like one. By what I saw of you at the house, you don't appear much for washing shirts." He unfastened the last of the straps and the dun walked from the hitch. "So, while you act like a boy, he's going to treat you like one. Plus, you're a kid. Not the same as he."

"So?"

"So, when he tries to help you, you snap at him like a dog." Rance walked the dun about. Les needed some time to think of an answer why he was wrong, so she went to the rear and untied the tether. Soon, Rance brought the dun to the rear and lifted the saddle from the back of the buggy.

"If you're trying to say that I have feelings for Jody Barnes as a beau, then you're plumb crazy."

"Say that if you want," he replied as he threw the saddle on top of the dun. "But, that just shows my point."

"What point? What's a point?"

"That you're hooked."

"Hooked?"

"Like a fish."

She shook her head. "What do you mean hooked?" Despite the dimness, she recognized that gleaming smile.

"You can't get him out of your head. I'd bet each time you're with him you're unsure of what to say or what to do and find yourself feeling worse when you can't pick which. And then there's times when you figure what Jody is going to do, and when he doesn't, you find yourself even more lost in your decisions. Am I right?" While he tended to the cinch, she huffed about, finally deciding to take out her frustration on the stirrup by kicking it about several times as she tried to mount the paint. Despite trying to find a reason why Rance was talking nonsense, she couldn't find an excuse to make that what was said wasn't right. He had her pegged. And she felt even worse. As she reminded herself of the times when she was with Jody, it was the flutter in her heart that sent blood pounding through her veins. Even in a silent agreement, she couldn't admit it.

Rance finished the cinch and climbed into the saddle of the dun. "Are you okay to ride?"

"Oh," she answered, her sharp tone spitting off her tongue. "I never felt better. Especially after talking with you." She heard his laugh and noticed him turn the dun and nudge it forward. When she did the same to follow, she took notice of the buggy. "Hey, you just going to leave this here?"

His answer came just when he moved beyond her sight. "It's a rental."

22

The opening of a door drew attention to the front entrance. Expected news brought anticipation; however, when the drawn faces of Alfredo and Stefan appeared from around the corner, he knew there was no good news. All three stood in the den for a silent moment of eyes meeting eyes. The question had to be asked.

"El caballo?"

A shake of the head from Stefan confirmed the expected answer. *"It was not there when we arrived. The children are gone, also."*

A long exhale and single nod allowed reflection. *"This is not what I wanted, but I should have expected this to happen. However, I am surprised to learn he took the children. Señor Cash didn't appear to be a man concerned with the health of those that did not belong to him."* He looked to his two employees. Confidence needed to be restored. *"Fol-*

low their tracks. Discover where they have taken the horse. Then, we will have more to say about the dealings of Señor Rance Cash."

Another tight squint renewed his eyes for another few moments. Despite traveling with the most lovely woman he knew of in the whole entire state, Rance just wanted a little rest in a comfortable bed, and that was all. The loan of the Barneses' buckboard provided him the means to get her back to her home and her employer, but the night had been long and the early dawn only reminded him of an eventful night he'd soon wish to forget.

The Menger's white facade lit up like a lantern in the dim light. Rance pulled up on the team's reins. "Well," he said with an exhausted tone. "Here you are. Safe at last." His mind strained for an attempt at levity, but no comment came to mind. Instead, he decided to make amends, and without the courage to meet her eyes, he kept them on the rumps in front. "My apology for what occurred. I feel in a poor state for having put your safety in such jeopardy. It was hardly what I planned."

"You are right," she replied, sticking another needle into his already sore gut. "And I wouldn't have changed a thing." It took a moment before he repeated what she said so not to misunderstand. In so doing, he faced her and saw a heavenly grin. "You are a good man, Rance. I was not certain of that until I saw you defend the children as you did. Now, they are safe in a good home of your friend." Rance grunted his throat clear, about to explain exactly what kind of friend Jody really was, but Greta continued before he had a chance. "It was very exciting. I normally do not get to feel my blood rush so fast."

"You enjoy that?"

"Very much," she said with a nod. "And I would like also to give you a good meal tonight."

The invitation sent his heart pounding. Suddenly, fatigue vanished and a renewed spirit filled his lungs. "How delightful. I cannot think of a better way to spend an evening." He let his pompous tone sag to one of sincerity. "I would really enjoy that, Greta." He looked deep into her eyes, only taking a peek at those delicious lips. Encouraged by her mood, he thought to lean her way and steal a kiss, but again, she trumped his play with a quick smooch to his cheek.

Stunned by the show of affection by the proper woman, he was seized in reaction when she left the buckboard. Shamed by not escorting her from the small wagon, he watched as she went into the front door, once again glancing his way and brushing the back of her skirt.

As she went inside, he gave thought of chasing after her and continuing the brief interlude, which might bloom into a more private meeting. A second thought convinced him not to press his luck. After all, he had a date with her when she and he would be rested and refreshed.

A glance to his soiled suit reminded him that she wasn't an admirer of his choice of clothes. When he thought about it, neither was he. Determined to make the best impression, he sought the best haberdashery. A shake of the reins put the buckboard in motion. Crossing the river bridge, he went into the heart of town. Through the dirt streets he searched as the sun slowly grew into the eastern sky. No shops appeared open.

During his journey, a familiar figure appeared on the shaded boardwalk. In very little time, Rance's good mood waned upon recognition of Rodney Sartain. The annoying agent waved with a wide smile. Southern manners didn't allow Rance to continue on and pass him.

"Rance Cash, good to see you, sir. How did your meeting go with Don Pedro Cuellar?"

The truth was easy to recall, but it wasn't a matter of public knowledge. "Oh, it was quite an experience enjoying that man's company." About to shake the reins, another inquiry held his hands firm.

"Did you have an opportunity to discuss the matter of the horse?"

Rance nodded. "We did." Desiring to conclude any conversation on the subject, Rance decided to change it. "You'll have to excuse me, Rodney. I am in search of new clothes."

"Clothes?" A chuckle broke a smile on Sartain's face. "I don't believe you'll discover any of the latest fashion in San Antonio." Ignoring the comment despite sharing in the opinion, Rance simply nodded and again prepared to shake the reins. Sartain's voice stopped him once more. "Why don't you allow me to provide you with some of my wardrobe. I confess I have a love for fine apparel and wouldn't mind sharing some of those I no longer find useful since I have worn them once."

The swagger in the voice was ample enough for Rance to refuse the offer. A quick glance confirmed the unlikelihood of any of the man's suits being the proper size. However, since he had few if any options, he gave the idea enough consideration to think of a solution and accept. "Why, Rodney, I find that a capital proposal."

"Good," Sartain said with some amazement. He climbed off the boardwalk and into the buckboard. "I am staying at a small establishment just down the street here. I am sure I can find something in my trunk befitting a man of your stature."

Being so close to the slimy agent could have been worse, but no parallels came immediately to mind. Rance moved as far away as the small seat would allow and finally sent the team forward.

Les went outside and found Jody already at work with that horse. Normally once late to bed she didn't wake until near noon, but her mind wouldn't let her sleep. Slowly, she crept down to the side of the house to the small corral. Jody led the horse around in a circle. Les folded her arms on the top rail and watched. During the short night, her conversation with Rance hounded her head. As she looked to Jody now, she decided maybe it was time to be less nuisance and more help.

"What are you doing?"

"Get him used to walking." He shook his head in disgust. "It's been so long since he's done any, it's going to take time for him to get the feeling back."

His words applied to more than just the horse. She tried to ease into the conversation. "Do you think you can get him to run like Rance wants?"

That head kept shaking. "No. Not running no races. Might make a decent saddle pony with time. But not run no races."

She looked off into the sky. "Then that will be a shame. I guess Rance will be proved wrong."

"That won't be the first time for him." Jody kept walking the horse. "What is it this time?"

"That you can train this horse to run."

The announcement stopped Jody in his tracks. "When did he say that?"

"He told me at that farm. He said, 'If anybody can make this horse run like the wind, then it will be Jody Barnes.'" She knew the boast had caught more than Jody's attention, but more was needed to stick it firmly in his craw. Mere encouragement likely would leave room for doubt. It was always easier to disclaim the praises of others as fool notions, allowing for the ease of failure. If it was just a matter of Jody trying but not achieving success, then it wouldn't be him that was wrong, rather Rance. As she watched him resume leading the horse, she knew what would get his goat and make it worse than a dare. "I told him he was wrong. That if there was somebody going to get that nag to run again, it wasn't you."

The bold remark stopped him in his tracks. He looked at her and appeared hurt by the words. In an instant, she wanted to take them back, but if they were to do any good, she'd have to let them stand. Les waited for him to fill with spite, but the only expression that came from his lips was a curled frown. More was needed to defend the opinion.

"I'm just spouting the truth. Ain't never seen you nurse an animal to health, and by what I seen around here you never treat none of them the way that one's got to be so to get back to running."

She paused, waiting for a mean comment. Maybe one on how she was just a fool kid and ain't seen nothing to give her opinion any value. Instead, Jody went about his routine of leading the horse around the corral, not even sending so much as a glare her way. The churning in her stomach was now worse than when she had stepped out of the house.

Rance looked into the trunk at the row of folded suits. His anticipation sank when he saw the limited choices of acceptable wardrobe. "Perhaps this was a bad idea."

"On the contrary," said Sartain. "I believe these bring out the success in the man."

Despite the boast, Rance wasn't deterred from the gloomy outlook with each of the suits Sartain removed and proposed. Each of them came at best to the top of his ankle. About to dismiss the entire endeavor as folly, he caught sight of a copper suit that he couldn't get his attention away from. When he reached for it, Sartain was quick to embellish the choice. "Fine selection. I've always liked that one. Wore it at a formal gathering with the baroness of Austria during my stay in Baltimore some years ago."

Not impressed with the boast, Rance sized the garment to his figure and decided this was the one. "I'll take it."

"Grand," Sartain agreed. "But you'll need a hat." Reaching over into another trunk, the agent opened the lid and began a search. "So, what will be your plans for that horse, Cash?"

The unexpected question took Rance from his inspection of the suit. "I'm going to sell it."

"Sell it?" Sartain rose with a matching small-brimmed derby in his hand. "To whom? Don Pedro, no doubt."

First putting on the derby — which to his

amazement fit well, and led to his conclusion that despite Sartain's short stature his head was swelled beyond proportion — Rance shrugged. "Perhaps so, or not. Something tells me there is a greater number of people interested in the purchase other than that gentleman." Satisfied with the match, he looked to Sartain. "What do I owe you?"

"Oh, let's call it a loan. The first of many perhaps which may include reciprocal benefits?"

Rance understood the suggestion, and not one to be obliged to return favors, he admitted he was one to ask for them. "Very kind of you, Rodney. Yes, there may be something I can do for you in the future."

"I am certain you might." As they walked toward the door, Rance was disappointed to notice the agent following. "So, when do you believe you might start asking for a price?"

Rance opened the door and proceeded down the narrow hall to the single flight of stairs. He didn't like sharing his plans; however, he needed the suit and feared a coy answer might recall the gesture. "Well, I still need to see what I've got. At the moment the animal isn't as valuable as I envisioned. I'm planning on bringing him back into racing form."

"Racing form?" Sartain yelped as they

went down the stairs. "That would mean you plan on racing him?"

"Could be." Rance saw the buckboard through the window. Only a few more feet and he would be free of the agent.

"That would mean you would require a rider. A jockey."

Off the stairs, he had the knob in hand and turned. "Indeed. Know of any? If so, have them see me. I'll be at the Menger later this evening." He opened the door and lifted his leg to proceed through the threshold.

"I don't know of any that would dare to become part of an enterprise against Don Pedro."

Slowly, Rance closed the door in front of him and faced about. "What?" he said with a polite tone.

"Well," Sartain said with his hands tucked into his vest. "It is obvious you plan to bring this horse back into condition to compete, am I right?"

"Go on."

"That would mean you will require a rider to train this horse. All the ones I know of here are Mexican and in no way would risk competing against Cuellar. After all, they all want to work for him since he is the single richest horse owner in the state. To cross him would be foolhardy."

"Money tends to change peoples' minds. Good day, Rodney." Turning the knob once more and opening the door, Rance went to the boardwalk.

"Yes, and no one has more than Don Pedro Cuellar."

23

Rance Cash emerged from the Cullums' store. Once again, Mary Cullum had performed her magic with needle and thread and tailored the copper suit to his form. With a wave, he bid a grateful farewell to the skilled seamstress and ignored her concentration on his lower extremities. Her fascination with his physique was a small price to endure for the end result.

He placed the derby on his head and walked down the boardwalk feeling like a new man. No longer was he wearing the garb of the dead. Even the .44 felt a bit more snug and the pepperbox sat better concealed in the longer coat. The sun was bright in the center of the sky and the autumn season had refreshed the air to give him a spry step.

The town was about its business of hauling freight and selling goods along Crockett Street. While strolling, he tried to rid his brain of Sartain's pessimistic prediction. Surely there would be men willing to ride for him. Especially with the promise of being well paid. Confident he had nothing to worry about, he recognized the welcome smell of food. In close range, the aroma of roasted meat and baking corn flour wafted to his nose. He followed it to a quaint cantina. With a few coins in his pocket, he decided to satisfy his appetite.

Upon entering, he soon found himself alone in a room of about thirty. Thirty of the brown-skin natives. Not wishing to appear impolite or intimidated, he continued inside and found a table near the rear corner. The solid mud masonry radiated heat and made for a comfortable haven.

A young Mexican girl came to him, mumbling in her language what he hoped was the fare of the day. Completely ignorant of Spanish, he shrugged then nodded in acceptance of what she said. Certain it had to be some sort of food and it might even be tasty, he resolved to explore new cuisine and not allow his good mood to dissolve.

Reclined in the stiff chair, he let his mind wander to the evening meal yet to come. There would be Greta, *her long blond hair flowing over her shoulders. Candlelight reflecting off her big blue eyes, her collar scan-*

dalously undone, allowing for a better view of the pristine skin of her neck and just a hint of a suggestion of what lay only inches below. Her face, filled with desire and anticipation as she walked his way, scratching her beard —

Rance shook his head. A Mexican man scrubbed the thick black hairs of his beard over the tray he held with his other hand. With a friendly smile, he placed the plate of tortillas and mashed beans in front of Rance.

"Salud."

The man left Rance with the less-than-appetizing food. Nonetheless, for the last few days he hadn't eaten but a few bites of egg at the Barnes home and even less as a guest of Don Pedro Cuellar. He picked up one of the three tortillas and spied the other patrons in the room. Noticing the technique of rolling the flat corn cake into a tube, he did so and ran the open end like a scoop into the beans. A deep breath was needed before taking a bite. Once he did, he chewed off the end and was immediately relieved at the spicy flavor. These beans didn't have the muddy taste of the those he was forced to eat on the trail to Texas. These actually held the familar seasoning he'd enjoyed in the cafes of New Orleans.

Each bite only fueled his hunger. He finished the first tortilla and quickly rolled another. While he was doing so, another beard caught his eye. This one belonged to Red McClain passing by the front of the cantina. As luck would have it, McClain also noticed Rance through the dirty front glass. Suddenly the tortillas and beans lost their flavor.

After serving breakfast and dinner, Greta was too nervous to take a short nap. She'd been up most of the night and had hurried through the meal preparations, however, she was still distracted by her plans for the evening supper. Once in the kitchen, she searched for the essential ingredient for her candied yam soufflé. She had no yams. Once she considered how long it'd been since she made the dish, it was little wonder why she hadn't any. No matter.

She put on her shawl, left the kitchen and went into the main lobby. She only gave Calvin a glance, but he hurried around the counter. "Where are you going?"

"I need something." She paused, not wanting to reveal the purpose of the trip, which without doubt would lead to more questions. "Salt."

"Salt?" he asked. "I thought I saw kegs of it."

"That is not the kind I need," she lied. "I need German salt."

"German salt?" Calvin's shoulders slumped. "I am not stupid. There isn't any such thing as German salt. Is this another excuse for you not to be here? I can't have my cook galloping off with that gambler Rance Cash to see to the needs of a few Mexican runts while we have paying guests who want to be served."

Greta held her tongue civil despite the urge to put the small man in his place. "No. That is not what I am doing. I will be here for the evening supper, Calvin. The guests will be served as they are always. I need the special salt for the ham I am cooking, which will bring out the Bavarian flavor. They do not sell the salt, but I can make it with the kind that is sold in the store. Not the kind that comes in the keg." She finished with a smile, and although most of what she said she didn't even understand, her sincere smile wilted away the clerk's resolve to object. Without more from him, she left the lobby and went out the front door.

She crossed the street, nodding to the men tipping their hats and smiling at the women and children. She turned the corner and went to the only store where she knew the owners and was certain of having the yams. When she found the shop, she entered to the chime of bells. "Hello, Mrs. Cullum."

"Hello, Miss Greta. How you be?"

"Very good, thank you." She went to the counter where Mary Cullum stood. "I am needing some yams. Do you have some?"

Mary gave a wink and came around the counter. "I think we got some in just yesterday from East Texas." She led Greta to the row of hoop barrels filled with bean pods, onions, various fruit, and finally orange yams. "Here they are."

Greta was relieved to find the main ingredient to her supper. "Oh very good. These will do very good."

"Planning on something special?"

"Yes," she said with a giggle, inspecting the yams so as to pick the plumpest.

"Look at you. You're a-blushing. Must be you've got something planned for a gentleman friend maybe?" Greta raised her brow and bobbed her head from side to side, resisting the feminine nature to gossip, although she wanted to very much. "And what is the name of this fellow?"

"Oh, Mrs. Cullum, in my country it is a custom not to talk about such things." Having chosen three yams, she searched for three more in order to make a large pan of the delicacy.

"I understand, honey. I was young once. I know what it was like to have a man say nice things about you, bring you flowers, sit and hold your hand, maybe even get in some necking."

"Mrs. Cullum," Greta said with some shock, but she really didn't mind the idea.

"Oh, don't let these gray hairs fool you. There is still some heat in the oven, if you know what I mean." Greta cringed at the vision in her head, not wanting to say anything that might encourage more, but Mary continued. "There was a man in here just today. I have to admit to thinking about such things." Mary snapped her fingers. "Hey, he said he was staying at the Menger. Maybe you've seen him."

"Oh, I don't know." Greta ran through her memory any recollection of an elder guest at the hotel.

"Oh, this one is quite a looker. Dark hair, slim build. You know what is said about slim men. Oh, and that smile." Mary wandered farther into the store, while Greta found the fourth yam. "Got the manners of a real Southern gentleman, and that charm could really put a young girl in a daze, and before she knew it she might find herself compromising her virtues. Believe me, he's no prim and proper dandy with nothing to back it up when it comes to being a man. He's got the goods. I had an occasion to seam some britches for him and have to admit to peeking. He could put the same smile on a woman's face as the one he's a-wearing."

Greta stopped her search for a moment, having now five yams in hand and faced about at the older lady's enchantment. Still in amazement, she stood amused by the frank admissions. Yet, she didn't recognize the description as anyone she'd seen at any of the meals or even walking the halls.

"Yes," she sighed. "His fiancée is a lucky girl."

"Oh," Greta moaned. "He is a man to be married and you talk about him that way. Shame on you, Mrs. Cullum," she added in a joking tone.

Mary shrugged. It was evident she held no shame for her thoughts. "You know. I am surprised you haven't met this fellow. Has a real distinctive name. Hard to forget."

Yet to find an elusive sixth yam, Greta responded casually with her focus of attention on the numerous tubers. "Well, I might have heard of him. What is his name?"

"Rance Cash."

Red McClain's loud voice stopped Rance in midchew. "Howdy, Red," he mumbled with his mouth full.

"I almost didn't recognize you with them

new duds. I haven't seen you since I saved your life, boy. Where you been?"

Rance took the time to finish chewing and swallowed. "I believe it was actually your life you were saving. All the bullets were headed in your direction."

Slowly a grin grew on the big thug's face. He pulled out a chair and sat, hastening many of the patrons to prematurely conclude their meal and head for the door, tossing coins on their tables. The loud scratch of chair legs against the floor drew noticeable attention, but McClain only chuckled slightly at the fear he cast.

"Word is, Cash, that you turned down the don. Is it true?"

Rance leaned back in the chair, freeing his right hand of the tortilla. "Let's say I still have something to sell. Why do you ask? Are you interested in making an offer?"

"You know, by rights, that should be my horse. I'm the one that forced old Hank to put it into the game. And since it was me that brought about the end to old Hank, I figured you owe it to me."

Rance chuckled at the suggestion. "How did I know that would be your way of thinking." Rance picked up the tortilla with his left hand, rolled it round while keeping an eye on McClain's right hand, then dabbed it into the mashed beans. "No." He bit off the end and chewed.

"No?" McClain raised a eyebrow. "What does that mean?"

Still chewing, Rance shook his head. "No. I don't agree. We were both in that game and I won the horse, fair and square. Now, if you truly want it, then I'll accept bids in a few days."

The refusal wiped the smile from McClain's face, but he blinked several times as if stunned by a punch. "Why a few days?"

Rance took another bite but continued to speak. "Let's say I'm not ready to sell. Not just yet."

"Going to run up the price, are you?"

Taking another bite and his mouth completely full, Rance just nodded. Once swallowing, he had a question of his own. "Tell me, Red. Why do you want the horse? You never struck me as much for the sport. Am I wrong?"

Several moments went by before another sly grin grew across McClain's face. "Let's say I have my reasons." He inhaled deeply, a sign of the big man restraining himself. Rance wasn't about to take a chance and rested his hand on his belly within inches of the .44 pistol. "You ain't dumb, Cash. I ain't neither. You know what that horse means to the don. A man could kind of set himself up for the rest of his life with the right amount of money. I can't say that I would mind doing that."

Rance smiled but made sure to show respect. "Right you are, Red. On all counts. So, I guess it is something we share in common. The desire for wealth. However, it is a fact that I possess the horse and am the one to reap the benefits. Now, forgive me if I am rude, but you don't impress me as the one with enough means with which to supply the sum I will be asking for. No offense."

Despite the pre-apology, the big thug's mean exterior showed itself as he rose from the chair. He spoke in a calm but ominous tone. "We're going to meet again, Cash. At a time when you don't see me coming. And then," he said with a nod, "I'm going to get what's coming to me."

24

Rance watched Red McClain leave the cantina. Only once the big man was through the door did he exhale. He looked to the young Mexican girl and the one with the beard. Although he didn't speak their language, he saw their eyes urge him to leave before further trouble came into their door. He rose from the table, rolled the last tortilla, dabbed it into the beans, and took a bite. A hand in the pocket drew payment for the food with a tip for the disturbance caused.

Out into the sunshine, he headed for the part of San Antonio he knew the best. With some food in his belly he walked at a lazy pace into a masoned archway leading to a shaded walkway beneath a wooden balcony. A glance to the north showed a tall white building under construction on the other side of the river. As he proceeded, there were ever increasing signs of the frontier village filled with architectural relics of its Spanish past giving way to its new American identity.

Soon he arrived at the point in the whole town he knew the best. Believing himself due a celebratory libation, he marched toward the Alamo Saloon. As he was about to cross the street, a familiar figure drew his attention to the square. Under the shade of the broad elm sat that old man and his rooster.

"Where have you been, old man?"

Dudley arched a mean brow his way, then resumed his attention to the checkerboard. "You see, Chuck. I told you this peace and quiet wouldn't last long."

Amused, Rance approached and sat by the nervous chicken. A quick scan of the board revealed that once again the old man was on the run from his feathered opponent. "I think you might want to surrender now before he makes a bigger fool of you."

"No suggestions from the spectators. Besides, from what I've heard you're not one to talk."

The amusement slowly faded away to curiosity to outright concern. "What are you talking about?"

Dudley put his finger on a piece and nudged it to the next square. "I'm not the one that put himself between Don Pedro Cuellar and what he wants."

An attempt to pet Chuck only produced a protesting squawk. Rance held up his hand in apology. "Well, that man can't have everything on his terms."

Dudley peered up from the board. "Oh no?" He chuckled in the same manner as Red McClain. It was unsettling. Wanting to learn more, his question was delayed when Chuck once again flapped his wings to the disgust of Dudley. The old-timer took one of the bird's pieces and jumped two of his own. With a break in the game, Dudley leaned back and cast a wary eye at Rance. "Where did you get them?"

Rance threw back his shoulders and put his hands on his lapels. "Do you like it?"

With a single shake of the head Dudley leaned forward to the bird. "He looks like an old penny."

Accustomed to insults, Rance wasn't alarmed. "Have it your way, old man. I'm in a good mood and I even was thinking of buying you a drink of your choice. But not if you're going to poke fun at me."

"Keep your liquor." Dudley pushed another piece forward. "I give it up years back."

It wasn't the first time he heard of abstaining from spirits. Especially if it held a firm grip on the soul. The answer spawned another curiosity. "Just how old are you?"

"Old enough to know better than to make myself a target."

"What does that mean?"

Another wave of disgust at the board signaled the end to the game. He looked at Rance with a reflective expression. "This may be part of the States now, but it's a very old town. Folks around here have been dealing with outsiders for near three hundred years. First it was the Spanish nosing around to see what was here. There was rumor of stacks of gold somewhere around here, but the Indians that was here then knew how to point the greedy interlopers in another direction. Missionaries thought about staying and working their religion to settle the land. Comanches put an end to that and run them off. Mexicans took over and let the whites come on in so to kill the Comanches and pay taxes. But the whites weren't any more for taking orders from Mexicans than the Comanches. That's what the Alamo was all about. Two different kind of folks mixing together, one not taking to the ways of the other. That's what you're trying to do."

As before when talking to the old man, Rance sat in a daze. "So, what are you telling me?"

"What I'm saying is you best beware of

those that don't care for you being here and getting in the middle of their mess."

Rance had heard this before. He shook his head. "It's all a part of the game."

"This ain't no game." Dudley's words hung in the air for a moment. They didn't hold the tone of a crotchety old man but rather the stern warning of a growling dog. Yet, Rance wasn't going to let it affect his good mood.

"Well, old man, I'll take what you have to say to heart. In fact, I may just spread a little of my influence in the form of free drinks for my friends in there." He rose and went to the saloon, confident he had accounted for all obstacles in his way.

Jody rode around the open pasture, leading the horse about in easy circles. He didn't want to admit it, but the animal seemed to be responding to the running. Ears perked showed attention, which was a good sign. Maybe, with all the fresh oats and ample supply of food it might be possible for him to run again. However, it was too soon to be making plans for that. If he was to say so, then it would play into that girl's hands.

A glance at the distant house didn't reveal her figure. Likely she had been given chores to tend and that was fine with him. Her nagging eyes only served to rub him raw worse than a thorn caught in his britches. It wasn't just her complaining, but what stung worse was her picking at him as bad as mosquitoes in the dead of August. The wide circle complete, it was time to turn for the house. As he glanced behind, the horse kept the same loping gait, but it wouldn't be long before it might lag behind. Jody reined in to slow him down gradually and keep the breathing at a steady rate. When Jody saw the house and his gut felt queasy, he turned once more for a slow walk. Les could come out at any minute and he wasn't ready.

Why did she bother him so much? He shook his head in confusion. If she didn't want to be there, then why not leave? He didn't like telling her so, and he'd never admit he even liked talking to her, at times, mostly when she was a boy. Ever since she turned girl, he never could keep his wind with her around. He shook his head again. It didn't make sense.

As darkness crept over the door of the Alamo Saloon, Rance threw in the last of his minimal stack. His luck hadn't been the best for the last few hours and he decided it needed a spark. With only a pair of sixes, his hand showed little promise as had the previous thirty he'd been dealt.

When it was time to show the cards, it was only a pair of eights that took the pot. However, all faces appeared friendly. The warnings cast upon him concerning restless natives didn't appear to hold any water. When he rose from the table, there were a few complaints at the loss of his presence and more likely the loss of his money. Despite having forfeited more than a hundred dollars, he understood the yearning for more. A bit ashamed for letting these locals take his spending money, he resolved that it was all an investment. There would be another game on another day. A baited hole attracts more fish.

He left the saloon, holding the doors to steady his legs, then proceeded across the darkening street. He noticed the absence of the checker game under the elm. The hour must have turned too late for the old man. Another sign not to pay too much heed to those ramblings.

When he got to the front portico, he stopped and straightened his coat. A deep breath was needed to settle his quivering. He felt like a child awaiting a birthday gift. Through the doors, his enthusiasm sank a bit when he saw Calvin.

"Rance," was the shrill call. Even with a

quicker gait toward the restaurant, there was no escape from the determined clerk. "Rance, I need to have a word with you."

Resigned to the fact that he couldn't outrun the clerk, Rance faced about with a proud posture. "Calvin! How are you this fine evening?"

"Cut the sweet talk. I'll not fall victim to your banter. I have a stack of bills sent to the hotel claiming they are owed for services tended to you. I've got one for a hundred and thirty-two dollars for a rented buggy that was never returned. Now, listen, the owners have been delayed another month due to winter weather in the north. It's a saving grace for you and for me. If I don't get all these matters settled before they get back it will mean my job. I ain't going back to emptying spittoons in McClusky's barbershop."

"Calvin, Calvin," he said, placing a comforting palm on the clerk's shoulder. "Calm yourself. I'll make good my debts all in good time. As a matter of fact, I am currently in the midst of a rather large enterprise that will make those petty bills a mere annoyance." He wrapped his arm around Calvin's shoulders and walked toward the restaurant. "Now, here is what I propose you do. Go ahead and make payment on those and put them on my bill."

"Your bill!?"

He nodded with a sly smile. "Yes, I plan to stay here for the next few days. That way, the hotel doesn't compromise its good standing. We wouldn't want that. And in short order, I'll satisfy the bill with a substantial gratuity for you and your help." He patted the back of the clerk. Calvin wasn't smiling.

"I've heard that from you before."

"And you're likely to hear it again." Rance drew the remaining bills from his wallet and spread the large denominations like a hand of cards. "As you see I have amassed a small amount of capital." Calvin's eyes lit up and reached for the currency, but Rance rapidly collapsed the bills back in the wallet. "And with that, I will compound the success and be able to pay those bills thrice over."

Achieving exactly the effect he sought, Rance smiled at Calvin, who stood confused as to whether Rance was able to pay now or not. He again slapped the back of the slick-haired innkeeper and went into the restaurant. Most of the guests had enjoyed their meal and left. Rance took his customary seat at the table in the rear of the room. He didn't see Greta and that was fine since he wanted to clearly see the surprise on her face when she emerged from the kitchen. He drew a match and lit the candle on the table, ready to see her eyes glisten. Again straightening his lapels, he leaned back in the chair in a comfortable and confident posture.

In short time, Greta entered the room, dressed as he expected in her long skirt and white blouse with the tightly buttoned collar. He waited for her to notice him as she inspected the empty tables, brushing the tops with a rag. Finally, during her duty, she peeked up and stopped upon sighting him. He couldn't help but smile.

She only showed her proud demeanor, pretending not to be overly excited at his presence. He sat confident she would soon join him at the table. She cleared another table and went into the kitchen. Surely, she must have prepared that special meal she promised and went to retrieve it. Rance rubbed his hands together in delighted anticipation.

His breath was taken when the kitchen door swung open again. He watched Greta slowly approach with a single plate. The dim light didn't reveal the contents but he was sure it was delicious. Perhaps as delicious as she would be later, but he didn't let his mind get that far ahead.

He took a deep breath when she came near, expecting her to lean close enough for him to smell the food and her skin. Slowly, she lowered the plate and placed it in front of him. He gazed down upon it and his smile gradually eroded away at the recognition of a heap of scraps. Confused, he looked up at her.

She slapped his face in anger. It stung just a bit, but it wasn't the first time. He'd been hit harder, but the loss of an expected evening alone with her hurt worse.

"Arschloch!" she sternly spoke in her choppy accent. "If you act like a dog, then you can eat like one."

Rance's vision cleared enough to raise his eyebrows. "What did I do?"

"You are to be married to another woman. And you come here to share a meal with me. Do you have no respect for her? Or for me? You think of me as a hussy?"

"Hussy," he said, shaking his head. "I don't know what you are . . ." He paused as his mind quickly recalled one of his little white lies spread in attempt to gain the help of others. "Oh." He smiled, hoping to explain. "That! You don't understand. I'm really not engaged, if that's what you think. I was just saying —"

She slapped him again. "Now, you deny it. Americans, you have no honor." She faced about and marched toward the kitchen. She faced about for only an instant. "Never come here again. I do not want to see you ever."

Watching her leave the room, Rance felt his heart sink, regretful his careless charm might have cost him one of the most beautiful women he'd ever laid eyes on. A moment's consideration of going after her to explain was quickly overruled. His cheek was starting to really sting and unless she became left-handed, he couldn't sustain another slap. He sniffed at the heap of scraps and despite the lack of any real meal in days decided not to attempt to pick. A peek at the remaining patrons showed their shock. Some left the room immediately due to embarrassment. There was no chance of being elected governor now.

25

Les pulled the rope, trying to ignore the pain in her back. Drawing water from a well had become a daily toil that didn't live up to her expectation of life on a quiet farm. It wasn't the only thing less than dreamy. With the bucket at the top, she struggled to balance it on the ledge of the wooden top and prepared to tote it to the house. Unenthused about lugging the weight, she scanned about for help. Jody was nowhere to be found. She knew why and it was her fault.

Had she not planted a spur under his skin to train that horse, then he'd be about more often and might even take enough pity on her to help with this water bucket. Resigned to the fact she'd get no help, she grabbed the handle and lifted.

"Need a hand with that?"

The voice startled her so that she lost her grip on the bucket and before she could salvage the grasp, the bucket tumbled back down the hole. She turned about in exasperation. The clothes were different, but that face still held that boyish charm.

"Rance? What are you doing here?"

He came to stand next to her and tugged on the rope. "Oh, I just thought I would come and visit and see how my investment was doing."

"Dressed like that? Seems kind of fancy to come all the way out here." When he kept pulling and didn't snap back with a sharp retort, she suspected there was more. "What's the truth?"

"Oh," he stretched longer than needed. "I believe it's better to lay a little low for a while."

"That German woman found out what a low-down scoundrel you really are?" He looked to her with a false face of spirit, but she knew a nerve had been pricked. Finally, his shoulders slumped when the bucket came to the top.

"She hates me," he sighed. "But," he said, taking hold of the handle, "what she heard wasn't true. They were all lies and rumors." He paused, peeking at the sky. "Of course, they were started by me."

"You? What did you tell her?"

He wagged his head. "I told a few folks

that I was engaged to be married so to gain a little help with a few items."

"And it came around to bite you, didn't it." A few steps toward the house were taken before there was an answer.

"Right in the posterior."

The big word wasn't one Les recognized, but she didn't let it get in the way. "So what are you going to do now?"

"I really did think I should come and see what the condition of the horse was. Speaking of which, I didn't see it on my way in."

"Jody's been working with it. Every waking moment. Since he brought it here, he's been leading it around getting it used to running."

"Running?"

"Not at a full gallop. He ain't got that far."

"Still," he said with a bit of a grin, "that's the best news I've heard in some time."

"Is that you, Rance?" Jessie Barnes stood on the front porch, wiping her hands on her apron. Rance's grin instantly widened.

"Why, Mrs. Barnes, you look lovelier each time I have the privilege to see you."

Jessie blushed at the compliment while Les felt her stomach turn over. As the slick gambler approached the porch with water bucket in hand, Les lagged behind, knowing somehow she wasn't as welcome.

301

■ ■ ■ ■

Red McClain peeked at the sun. If there was anything he disliked it was leaving a successful card game to be left waiting under a tree five miles out of town. The rumble of wheels turned him around in all directions. The rolling hills didn't allow him to see far. He gripped the revolver tucked in his belt, unsure if this meeting was for only one benefit. As the noise came near, he faced about and saw the bronze carriage and that young gunman who never strayed far. Soon he saw the man who'd summoned him to the meeting. In the clean duds of a fancy dude, the old man forced a respectful smile.

"Señor McClain, it pleases me that you have come."

"Yeah." He dismissed the politeness with a shrug. "Let's get down to business. Why you want me?"

With a long pause, the don tilted his head to the side. "As you wish. I have called you because I want you to help the both of us. As you know, there is a man who has come to our home and he has his eyes on stealing what is not his."

"Rance Cash? That's who you're talking about?"

The don simply nodded. "I do not wish to

mention names, but you have an idea of the one."

"Yeah, but what's he stole? I don't like admitting that I saw him win that horse in a game of cards."

"Yes," was the answer with a quick nod. "Of that I am aware. It is not only that. If he is allowed to hold what he has, then he will seek to take more."

McClain chuckled. "And you think he might start taking a little more of what you've got. Like maybe buying some land around here. Turning folks against you."

"Let us say that would not benefit both of us." He paused again, and peeked at the sky. "Such good weather for so late in the autumn, don't you think?"

"Get to what you want."

The don faced him with a determined scowl. "I wish for you to make for events not in this man's favor. I do not wish to know how you plan. Only that you are successful."

"And why would I do that?"

"What is not good for me" — he paused, staring straight into McClain's eyes — "is not good for you."

The warning had sand. Enough to put to mind what could be done. "I have to say that I don't cotton to him. But what can I do?"

The don glanced at his mounted rider. "I

have discovered that the horse is at a ranch to the west. Jack Barnes's ranch. Perhaps there is something to happen there?"

McClain nodded. An idea of what was the worst to happen to a ranch came to mind. "And what if I do what you're saying?"

"Oh," the don said, his face changing to a pleasant repose. "I believe certain rewards should accompany such work. Perhaps a grateful commission upon recovery of what should belong to me."

"Like what?" McClain demanded.

"Two thousand American dollars when I have the horse at my hacienda."

The offer was reasonable, but he needed more for the moment. "Nothing right now?"

The don chuckled, glancing about to his driver and rider. "Señor McClain, my word is my bond."

Not one who cared to be laughed at, Red McClain sat on his horse, his mood turning foul by the second. The urge to pull the revolver and send lead at the smile was tempting, but it wouldn't get him any richer. There was more time left to take that smile right off that face.

Rance looked about at the happy faces at the table. The three children eagerly ate Jessie Barnes's supper. Even Mary's penetrating stare seemed to ease. He looked to his own plate of fried chicken. Although it took a full day, he finally enjoyed the decent meal he had longed for.

"Mrs. Barnes, may I say this is absolutely divine." He gazed about to the agreeing faces until he saw Les's sneer. Undeterred, he continued his cheery tone. "It is a shame your son isn't here to enjoy it. Where is Jody?"

"Still working that horse," said Jack Barnes. "Don't know what's got into that boy. It seems like the devil himself is whipping him to bring that horse around."

"Oh, Jack," said Jessie. "Don't speak against it. Haven't seen him so determined since he left here to go with the drive to Kansas. It's good he has something to work for."

Rance peeked at Les and she at him. He had an idea what might be spurring the young Texan.

Jack reached for a chicken leg. "There's still a fence needing mending. Can't ignore his chores."

"Well, I thank you both for letting him help me restore the horse's health."

"Happy to oblige, Rance," answered Jessie. "Besides, it brought us these little darlings to our home." She smiled at all, but

changed when she got to Les. It didn't go un-
noticed.

"I'd like to go outside and get some air,"
said Les, putting down her food. Before she
was given permission, she rose from her
chair and went outside. The uneasy mood
hung over the table.

Rance didn't believe more of his compliments would settle feelings. "Excuse me,
Mrs. Barnes. I believe I might step out myself. Perhaps I can see if Les might be feeling poorly." He went outside to scan about
in the dark. Sniffles were enough for him
to follow and find her on the side of the
house. "You're going to get chills out
here."

"I don't care. Maybe catch cold and die
right here. Outside of the house with the rest
of the varmints."

This wasn't going to be easy. So, Rance
went next to her and leaned against the
house. "I'm sure you're exaggerating."

"No, I'm not. You saw the way she looks at
me. She hates me. I'm just a bother to her."

"No. I meant catching cold. It's not that
chilly." When he found he was alone in
chuckling, he changed his tone. "You're
not a bother. I see this all different than
you."

The sniffling ceased. "How you see that?"

"I see a jealous mother. She sees a young girl in her house and fears she might be losing her son."

"Me? Jody? Ain't going that way. He ain't looking at me as nothing more than a kid."

"Maybe. If that's what you think he wants to see."

"What does that mean?"

Not usually comfortable counseling the emotions of females, he approached the subject with simplicity. "Imagine you're a young filly."

"Now I'm a horse. Is that what you're saying?"

He tried to think of a different approach. While pondering, the pounding of hooves came near. His thoughts broken, he listened for the direction. He concentrated, leaning to the side. As the noise became louder, Les spoke.

"It's just Jody, hurrying for supper cause he knows he's late and don't want his ma mad."

A gunshot ripped into the night.

Rance drew the .44 and rose off the ground. "She must take it personal." Another blast drew their attention to the front of the house. Rance squinted into the darkness, but his attention was drawn to the side with Jack Barnes's emergence, lantern in one hand and shotgun in the other.

"Put out that light," Rance yelled. A bullet splintered the wood garnish around the door. Jack knelt and let loose with his own blast. Sparks flew into the dark. Rance only faced about a moment to yell at Les. "You keep down back here. If you see something, let out a shout."

"What are you going to do?"

"I'm going out here to find out who's shooting." He crept around to the front, pistol in front. From the north, four torches came near in a hurry. Rance cocked the pistol and prepared to fire. When the first rider came around the corral he pointed the barrel and pulled the trigger. The recoil from the heavy gun jerked his arm high. The rider kept coming. The torch was flung to the roof of the house.

The second rider arrived in an instant and whirled the torch above the head like a whip. Another blast came from behind. The torch fell to the ground, but the rider still stayed mounted. Rance twisted about to see Jack holding the smoking shotgun.

With the other two attackers rounding the far side of the corral, Rance pulled back the hammer and fired toward the distant riders. The shot again jolted his aim so bad, he gripped the .44 with both hands and fired. The riders kept riding. A yellow glow lit up the night.

Rance turned to see the fire licking at the wooden roof. Fearing for Jessie and the kids inside, he ran for the well. While on the run, he saw Les behind him. "I told you to stay put."

"I've got the bucket!"

They both arrived at the well. She hooked the handle to the rope and threw it down the hole. Rance holstered the .44 and grabbed the rope. The splash meant to haul it up. More gunshots turned his attention. With both hands on the rope, he couldn't pull and try to fire. He yanked as fast as he could move his hands.

"That you, Cash?"

The voice turned his head, but in the flickering light he couldn't see the face, but he knew who it was. A rider charged ahead at him. The glow shone off the metal of a pistol pointed at both of them. Rance pushed Les behind the well, expecting a bullet to pierce his body. A shot rang out.

Still quivering from the expectation, he didn't feel any pain. In the dim light he saw the rider cringe. The mount shied and turned around to gallop away. Rance twisted back and saw Jody holding the rifle.

Grateful, he attempted a grin, but the rising flames reminded him to haul up the bucket. Jody ran to his side. Rance had the bucket on the ledge and handed it to him. "Thanks," he said.

"Just keep getting water." Jody ran the bucket up to the house. Les ran after him. Rance watched as the children were scurried out of the house along with Jessie. Jody gave the bucket to Jack and Les ran back with another. She gave it to Rance and Jody returned quickly with the emptied bucket. No words were needed. One bucketful after another were tossed on the fire.

The morning light showed the smoldering wood. The house still stood, but the fire had eaten a hole in the roof. Jack Barnes carefully crawled atop the house and examined the damage. "Ain't as bad as I thought. Looks like we stopped it in time."

"Thank the lord," said Jessie, still hugging the three children.

Rance looked to Jody approaching. "I'm beholden to you for helping my family."

"Actually, it's me that has to thank you. If you'd not shot, I'd be the one in worse shape than the house."

"Who were they?" asked Les.

"I have a good idea. The one Jody shot was Red McClain. He's a local strongboy of the saloon."

"I heard that name. More like an outlaw is what I know it for. Been a lot a folks talking about missing cattle that mention his name."

Rance nodded at Jody. "Well, it seems he wasn't satisfied with just cattle. What happened to the other two?"

"I think I winged another one, and when that one ran, the other followed. Must have turned yellow when they had lead flying their way."

"Hey," Jack Barnes called. "All three of you need to stop your talking and grab some boards and a hammer and some nails." With the command, Rance shed his coat and went to the barn to comply.

The day passed with the sawing of lumber and hammering of nails. The next day continued with more of the same. During the short breaks, Jody went to the barn and led out that horse. As he walked it around, it was evident the health of the animal had improved dramatically and its trainer truly enjoyed the progress.

Days went by with repairs to the house. Shingles were cut from the scraps and the charred edges on the interior were replaced. Rance watched, feeling a bit more satisfied with himself. It wasn't a game he had to scheme to win. Here, he was part of a sort of family that began out of the same type of remnants used to construct the roof. He eyed the children playing in the front under the watchful eye of Jessie. Jack continued the trimming of structure. And then there was Jody and Les. As each day passed, he saw them working, feeding, and watering the horse just as if it were a child. The animal responded with youthful energy to their care.

Inside of a week, the horse showed more signs of recovery. Jody rode to the side, galloping in short spurts. As he watched, Rance saw what might have been a plan in shambles rise from ashes.

Jody led the horse to the rails of the corral. Les joined them and climbed atop the top board. "So, what do you think about him now?" asked Jody with some pride. Rance inspected the muscular flanks and shoulders.

"I have to admit, I wouldn't recognize him from when I first saw him three weeks ago. You've done good work."

"Well," Jody said, casting an eye at Les. "There were some people didn't think it could be done."

Rance noticed the intent of the remark. "More reason not to listen to doubters." He looked to Les, watching for any sign of her taking offense, but she held a smug grin, almost as if she held a certain pride at Jody's success. While he looked to her, Rance saw another image creep from the back of his mind. One that as it formed appeared more certain, more correct, and more perfect in its fit. "Speaking of not listening to doubters, I have another issue to overcome." He looked to the two of them, each looking at the other in equal confusion. "While I was spending time in town, I was told of a detail that might cause trouble."

"Such as what?" asked Jody.

"Well, you see," he said, propping a boot on the low rail. "The only way to make any money from your hard work is to get top dollar for Lone Star here."

"Lone Star," Jody giggled. "All this time this horse had a name."

"Well, yes. But as I was saying."

"Why didn't you tell us that? We were trying to think up names for the thing. Harold, Henry, Horace."

"I knew it. I told you I didn't like that one," Les barked.

"Listen to me." Rance's call for order took time before it was obeyed. "Now, as I was saying. The way to profit from all of this and make good on what I promised is to show what the horse is capable of. To do that, he'll have to run."

"Yah, you told us that weeks ago," sniped Jody.

"Well," Rance answered in kind. "To do that, he'll have to have a rider. A horse jockey."

"So?" Jody asked. "Bring one out here and we'll put him to work."

The idea wasn't one Rance hadn't thought about. "There's one small problem with that. It appears the man we're looking to sell the horse to apparently has scared away all the known jockeys for fear they may not ever ride again. Or walk for that matter." He let his eyes stray to Les. While it appeared she was thinking of a solution, Rance knew the answer all the time. Slowly, she noticed his stare. Seconds passed by before she gradually began shaking her head.

"Oh no. No, no, no. I ain't no *jockey*."

"What are you saying?" Jody asked in wonder. "Les?" He chuckled. "You can't have no girl ride the horse."

Rance shook his head once. "No. You're right. Not a girl. It wouldn't be allowed." Again it took a moment before the suggestion was clear.

"No," she answered sternly. "I ain't doing that again. Not me. Not again."

"But, Les," Rance pleaded. "Think about what could come from it."

"You're wanting her to pretend to be a man?" They both looked to Jody for an instant, then back at each other.

"There's a bag of money to be made."

While Les kept shaking her head, Jody began his laugh. "You're thinking she can pass for a man again? And ride a horse. This horse? A racehorse?" He shook his head. "Ain't no way she can do that."

Les glanced at him with disdain, then back at Rance, but still shaking her head. "I can't do it."

"And why?" asked Rance. "If you truly want to get back to Kansas, then this can get you there. With the profit made on the sale, I'll personally pay you enough for the trip."

"'Cause I ain't going to be a boy again. Not for you." She looked to Jody. "Not for him." Tears built in her eyes. "Damn the day I put on those clothes. It's all what you think of me." She heaved breath, obviously straining not to break down.

Rance sighed and looked to Jody. The cowboy just shook his head in a manner agreeing with Les. Twisting about, Rance glanced at the house where Jessie scrubbed the children in a metal wash tub. "I understand what you're saying, Les. But, if you won't do it for me, then do it for them. They have a stake in this, too. It was their father that risked their future on this horse. Lone Star was the one chance they had for a better life." He turned to her. "And don't forget. They're orphans, too." He knew it was a low-down trick. The link to her own past as a waif sent on a train west was meant to tug at her heart. As he let the words hang about, he saw the decision gnaw away at her gut. She stared at him, then at the children, then at Lone Star.

26

Despite the sun brightly shining in the cloudless sky, the air held a hint of winter. Rance walked about like a nervous father-to-be. He continually scanned about, looking for a sign the plan was taking shape. When he first sighted Jody coming over the rise, he felt a smile crease his face, but soon it faded when he saw no figure following. What had happened? Another change? Could it have been stolen? His pulse resumed when he saw the loping stride of Lone Star come over a second later, but he had no rider. A moment later he saw who he'd feared about the most bob her head from behind Jody's shoulder. Finally, Rance took another breath.

"What took so long?" he asked with spite. Jody arched his thumb behind. Les poked her head out again. When Jody reined the mount to a stop, he pulled up on the long leader rope to slow down Lone Star. Les slid off the far side of the saddle and hid.

"What's wrong?" Rance asked.

"I look like one of them clowns in the circus."

Rance examined her dressed in billowed hip riding pants to the knee with thin boots covering her long socks. A red striped shirt was too large, but allowed for more freedom of motion. A small billed cap concealed her lengthening hair. "I don't see a problem. You look like a jockey."

"I feel like a fool."

"If you knew how much money that outfit cost me, you'd change your mind. I look like a fool. Those cost me a hundred and fifty dollars."

"Still looks mighty strange," said Jody, cinching the riding saddle.

"Don't add to the problem," Rance said. Les walked past him to Lone Star.

"How do you expect me to stay on that?"

"That's an English riding saddle. Very expensive."

"Where did you get this?" Jody asked as he tightened the cinch.

Before he answered, Rance looked to the far side of the hill. There he recognized a bronze carriage. The man he most wanted to attend was seated next to his daughter. A late rendezvous during the week provided the opportunity to procure the necessary items for a racehorse. Especially a saddle so light it allowed for a full stride. The meager cost was a few flowery words and an hour at one of her accomplice's homes in San Antonio. "Let's say it's just one of two in the area." He turned and spotted another familiar face. "Rodney Sartain," he said with some disguised disappointment.

"Yes, I only learned of this from rumor in town."

"Well, it's not really for public display. I was just going to test the horse's stamina."

Sartain tilted his head to the side. "Yes, of course. I see Don Pedro is here. Tricky of you, Rance. How did you get word to him that you would be here?"

Remembering the very rendezvous, he answered truthfully while glancing back at the bronze carriage. "Oh, I whispered it in someone's ear." He faced around and looked to Jody, who nodded. The horse was ready. It was just a matter of the rider. "Find a spot to watch, Sartain." He slapped the agent's shoulder, then went to Les. "Are you ready?"

"I feel sick. Like I'm going to toss up breakfast."

"Good," he said, hugging her shoulder. "That means you're ready. Now let's get you on your horse."

Jody cupped his hand like a stirrup. Les peered at him, appearing unsure whether to trust him. They looked each other in the eye. "I'm doing this for them kids. And the money." She stepped into his hands and he lifted her up into the saddle. She settled into it and put her boots into the iron stirrups.

Rance came close to her. "Now, you only need ride him down by the river and back up around that grove of trees. It's near a mile, and it's important he make it in two minutes."

"Two minutes? How fast is that?"

"Fast enough to get the price we want. Just let him do the running. All you have to do is hang on."

Jody led Lone Star in line with a large bare cottonwood. Rance wanted to follow, but didn't want to spook the horse or the rider any worse. When they got to the point, Jody looked up to Les.

"Remember to stay off his back. Stand in the stirrups and stay low. Tuck your knees above his shoulders. Keep your back arched and eyes on what's ahead. The more free he can run, the better. He's got a lot of spirit, but sometimes he loses his way. Just keep him looking ahead and not off to the side. I ain't sure how far he can run, so if he starts slowing up smack him with this," he said, handing her a short flexible stick wrapped in leather. "And stay on." He patted the horse but still held the bit firmly.

Rance took in a deep breath, looking from side to side. The way was clear. It was time. He drew his watch and waited for the second hand to strike twelve. Within five seconds, he raised his arm. Three, two, one. He dropped his arm. Jody smacked its rump and released the bridle.

Lone Star bolted. Les gripped the reins as the brisk wind blew in her face. At first it was like when she first rode the paint at a gallop, but soon the speed proved that she'd never traveled so far so fast. The graceful stride kept her in the center over the saddle. Les stood balanced in the stirrups, rolling her shoulders in time with the horse so when he strode she stretched. As they passed by the folks amassed on the hill, Lone Star leaped through the air, only letting hooves touch ground for a blink of an eye, then leaped again.

Rance watched as the horse and rider galloped down the stretch as if shot from a cannon. He looked to Jody, who didn't show his usual gleeful smile. Rance couldn't even force his own. He peeked at the watch and saw ten seconds had elapsed. Although he saw nothing but dirt kicked up in the air, the pace wasn't what it seemed it should be.

With his own heart beating ten times inside of each tick of the watch, he tried to steady his breath so as not to faint. He'd be much more confident at a table with cards. That way, he could always stall the outcome. By a glance at the watch, he saw there was no stalling the time. He glimpsed the bronze carriage on the far hill. No doubt the gentleman was also timing the horse and would be ever more interested should the course be run in time. "Go," he muttered under his breath.

"They're at the river," Jody said nervously.

Les shifted her weight as she angled Lone Star to the left. The mushy ground slowed the horse's gait. "Keep going, boy," she yelled over the noise of the mush being sprayed. Just as she spoke, Lone Star stumbled and lost its stride. Her arms ran out of rhythm with his lunge forward. "Come on, boy. Get through it." Quickly, Lone Star resumed its stride but had lost near all its speed. Through the spotted shade of trees not yet shedding all their leaves she guided him to the narrow path where the ground was the most level.

She gripped the reins and pushed against

Lone Star's head, trying to get him back to the speed they were at just moments before.

"Seems to be slowing up a bit."

Sartain's observation only spiked Rance's blood, but he couldn't ignore the truth of it. He needed to act in control with confidence. If he didn't believe the horse could do it, it might lower the price. "Just a mere pause. You wait. He'll tear up the ground when they come back this way." He glanced at Jody, hoping for a reflection of his confidence. He didn't read any on the cowboy's face. Rance peeked at the watch. Fifty seconds were gone and they weren't halfway through the course.

Above the pounding hooves Les heard the lumbering breath. She bobbed her head to the side between strides, remembering what Jody had said. "Come on, boy."

She moved the crop into her hand, not wanting to use it, but she saw that the ground wasn't passing as fast as before. She didn't know how long they had been running but it was a long way back to Rance and Jody.

"Come on, boy." Lone Star seemed to slow with her encouragement. Maybe if she got mad he'd go faster. "Go, you buzzard bait of a horse."

They angled around the far hill. From the corner of her eye she saw people above but couldn't recognize who they were. Instead, she pushed its head, but the heavy breath got louder. It must have been too soon to run him. This was a mistake. Soon, he'd slow down so she could hop off and hit the ground without taking an extra step.

As they angled beyond the hill, they were turning for Rance and Jody. They stood a far piece from her. She regripped the crop and inhaled courage to do what she didn't want.

One minute thirty seconds. Rance couldn't bear to look at the watch or his horse. Surely Don Pedro had noticed and would be satisfied now to lower the one-thousand-dollar offer to a mere hundred, maybe less.

"He's going to come running. Just smack him once and he'll come a-running." Jody's prediction heightened Rance's mood.

"Too bad, Cash," Sartain chimed. "It appears your horse is all promise but no delivery as it were."

The remark boiled Rance's blood. Although it didn't appear wise, he couldn't let this whiny agent get the better of him. If Jody believed, he'd believe. He faced about. "Fifty dollars he makes it here in two minutes."

Sartain nodded back. "Wager accepted." He drew a glass flask from his long coat. "The easiest fifty I've ever made." He pulled out the cork. "Excuse me for celebrating early."

Rance glanced down. One minute forty seconds.

About to swing the crop, Les yelled the same as Rance had taunted her. "Think of them kids." Lone Star didn't react, but didn't lose any more speed. Now from under the bank of trees and in the bright light, she yelled again. "Do it for them." On flat ground, Lone Star picked up speed. She felt him go faster and just a touch to the flanks might get him there in time. She brushed his side with the crop. Like pulling a trigger, Lone Star galloped faster. The increase in speed nearly tore Les from the saddle. The wind again buzzed in her ears. Lone Star ran like when they first started out. "That's the way, boy. Make your daddy proud!"

Dispirited, Rance hung his head, now certain that on top of the paltry hundred-dollar sale of the horse, his impulse had cut that in half.

"Here he comes!"

Jody's voice brought Rance's head back

up. Lone Star charged in the middle of the field, each stride quicker than the one before. He felt his heart beat again and then pound through his chest. "Go," he muttered once more, risking a peek at the watch. Seven seconds left. "Go!"

Les concentrated on staying on her feet, staying in time with the horse's stride, and most important, staying on top of the horse. She arched her back, tucked her knees over the shoulders and pushed her chin as low as she could and still see the bare cottonwood tree. She'd done all she could. The rest was all up to the horse.

Rance watched as Lone Star passed by them. From the corner of his eye he saw Jody's head turn as his did, and also Sartain's. When the horse ran past the bare cottonwood at a full sprint, Rance felt that smile crease his face. He peeked once more at the timepiece. "One minute fifty-eight seconds."

Jody hooted and threw his hat.

Sartain dropped his flask to shatter on a protruding stone.

As Jody ran after Les and the horse, Rance tucked his hand inside his coat in a profound gesture of gloating. "Mr. Sartain, it is customary to settle all wagers on demand." He held out his hand. "I'll accept payment now." The disgruntled agent slowly drew his wallet from his coat and thumbed out the bills to satisfy the bet. "Pleasure doing business with you, sir." He suppressed a chuckle and faced away from the small-statured man. He went to where Les had stopped the horse and Jody held the bit.

"Did we make it?" she asked with excited worry.

Rance nodded with joy. "With two seconds to spare."

The news etched Les's face as the happiest he'd ever seen. She hugged Lone Star's neck. "He got tired around that far bend, but I kept talking to him, not letting him forget who he was running for."

"Yes, well, now it's time for us to collect." Rance again patted Jody's shoulder and while Les continued her story of the ride, he went to the dun. He needed to get to the far hill in time before his mark had time to leave. Quickly he got onto his mount and steered in the direction of the bronze carriage. He got to the far hill nearly as fast as Lone Star had run the course. Up the incline he caught the carriage on its way.

"Oh," he said with false surprise. "What a coincidence meeting you out here in the middle of the wilderness."

The gentleman grinned politely. Rance respected the restraint of temper, even though he silently reveled in the achievement. "I congratulate you with what you've done to the horse."

"Yes," he said, glancing back in the direction and averting his eyes from Catarina batting hers. "I had a great trainer and rider."

"Yes, I noticed. Who was that?"

"Les." He paused. "Is *his* name."

The announcement raised eyebrows. "I must meet him. I may want him to help train some of my horses."

The conversation wasn't going the way he planned. "He is . . . very shy. Not one to try to prosper by success. I doubt he would want to do that," he finished, with pursed lips and a shake of the head. "Actually, sir. I was more interested in the matter concerning the sale of the horse."

"Oh? You are selling? I would think a man like you would want to test your animal against another. Of course, if you have the courage to do so."

"Courage?" The word cut into his gut. "What do you mean courage?"

Don Pedro smiled. Rance couldn't help but feel he was a fly in a spider's web. His plans of selling Lone Star for ten thousand dollars were vanishing before him.

"I propose that there be a race. My horse and the one you currently own. A match race. In one week. Winner take all."

"A race? Winner take all?" Rance mumbled the words over and over in his head. The proposal hung like a dare. Don Pedro raised his brow like a challenge. As Rance stared him in the eye, he relied on his instincts and raised the stakes. "No," he said shaking his head. "I think we can do better."

Now Don Pedro appeared confused. "Better?"

"I'll accept your proposal of winner take all. And when I win, and I will," he said, leaning forward in the saddle, "it'll take ten thousand dollars to gain back your horse and another ten to get back what you've wanted all this time."

With the effect of a punch, Don Pedro's cheeks puffed out. "What do you say?"

"You heard what I said." Rance looked to Catarina and remembered his manners to tip his hat. She smirked at his bold dare to her father. He took the sign as more evidence that he'd struck a nerve of the father. "Well, sir? Are you game? Or should I seek another player?" His held his jaw firm and locked eyes with the old man. If he flinched, it would soften the impact and might give time to consider or stall. When at a table, it was best to call when you had a better hand. Finally, to salt the bet, he again tipped his hat to Catarina, then pulled the reins on the dun in a gesture of leaving and thus calling into question Don Pedro's courage.

"We have a wager."

The acceptance made him pull back the reins. Rance looked back at the gentleman and flashed his smile. "Very well, then. In one week, sir." He again tipped his hat and steered the dun back to Jody and Les. He let out a long-held breath. All he had to do was come up with a better hand.

27

"You did what?" Les shrieked.

"Keep your voice down. He'll be able to hear you all the way at his home." Rance glanced back as they rode back toward the Barneses' place.

"Oh no," she said, shaking her head. "You said if I was to ride, then I get paid enough to get back to Kansas."

"And you will," he said. "Matter of fact, I'm thinking of upping the fee to where you can take a stage from here all the way up there."

"How else would I get there?"

Rance scrambled for reasons to keep her interested. "Well, how about you're the only one in there? Look, we knew this was going to happen."

"What do you mean, we?" Jody added.

"We're all in together?" He looked at the two frowns. "Aren't we?" Even pleading didn't sway them to his side. "Lone Star did it once, he can do it again."

"Ain't sure about that," said Jody. "He's got a wheeze. Might be his lungs haven't got used to sucking that much wind."

"Well, you got him ready for this time. I have confidence you two can get him ready for one more time."

His two friends now looked away from him. "Sounds like we ain't getting paid, Les."

Deciding it best to keep his mouth shut, he focused on the path and also on what it would take to ensure winning the race. Nothing came to mind.

A night's sleep on straw didn't provide for much rest but did give him time to think. He woke early and spread his optimism around the breakfast table, even if he was the only one who believed it. He got on the dun and spent the rest of the morning traveling to San Antonio.

He first arrived on the town and rode past the Spanish governor's palace. The long white building with its barred windows resembled a jail and ate away into his confidence. He nudged the dun a little faster. Through the narrow paths that led to the city, he crossed the river and soon found Crockett Street.

As he prepared to dismount, he ran through his plan. In order to insulate himself from total catastrophe, he needed to lay off some of the amount by placing side bets with those around town who enjoyed taking a chance.

At first, he boasted about *El Magnifico Hijo*. With that name and the legacy of the sire, Rance soon took in enough to start spreading the news on the other end of the street about Lone Star. The hardest issue to overcome was that he held all the money. A short trip to the San Antonio Bank gave faith that the money wouldn't be headed to Mexico. The afternoon was getting long, and a libation was in order. He had half the cash to cover the bet and exceeded his expectations. However, there were still more details and but just a few days to see them done.

While approaching the Menger, he gave thought to going inside to see Greta. A quick second thought convinced him that too much damage had been done. He stood on the portico and shook his head. Instead, he headed down the boardwalk to the Alamo Saloon where he knew the crowd would be friendly. While on his way, he saw an old friend and his bird.

"Still testing your game?"

Dudley only gave him a glance. "What you been up to?"

"Well, I have a horse in a race. Haven't you heard?"

The old-timer pushed a piece to the next square. "Oh, I heard. Even got wind that your horse might win. Some yahoos around here have been throwing in their money at some fellow at the other end of town bragging about your horse. Wouldn't be you, would it?"

Rance shrugged. "One must be confident."

"Figures," he said, resuming concentration on the board. As he looked about and Chuck bobbed his head about, Rance's thirst drew him to the saloon. "Don't think there's going to be no race no way," was muttered.

Rance faced about. "What was that?"

With an innocent face, Dudley poked his head from his concentration. "Oh, I was just repeating what Chuck had said."

"Chuck? Chuck said this?" He closed his eyes knowing he'd later ask himself why he pursued this silly conversation. "And, why would he say that?"

Dudley, with the surety of a scholar, began nodding his head. "Well, he did make a good point. He says that Spanish fellow is not used to losing. He may have more in mind than just a fair race. Might have something up his sleeve, ain't that right, Chuck?" The bird clucked in a manner like an old fool laughing. Dudley moved one of Chuck's pieces.

At first dismissing the absurd notion of a rooster with thoughts, Rance stood in wait for another comment. The longer he stood, the more he recalled the raid on the Barnes place. "You mean like trying to steal my horse?"

"Could be?"

"Hah," Rance said with spite. "Well, I'm here to tell you that's already been tried and we put lead in those that tried."

"Who was it that tried?"

"Red McClain. Saw him myself take a bullet and ride off into the night. Likely dead by now, or have you seen him?"

Dudley shook his head. "No. No, I can't say I have."

Rance's confidence swelled in his chest. "Proves me right. Now, I'll not listen to any more of your nonsense." He faced about.

"Yeah, I agree with you, Chuck."

Rance spun around on his heels. "What now?"

"Oh, I was just agreeing with Chuck," said Dudley, pushing another piece forward.

"And, just what did he say?"

335

"That just when you're sure the henhouse is safe, along comes a fox that sneaks in the back."

The analogy piqued his curiosity. "And what does he mean by that?"

"That you haven't thought of everything." With that, Chuck flapped his wings to Dudley's chagrin. The old-timer moved a piece toward him and removed one of his own.

"If you have some advice, please make it plain so I can get on with my drinking."

Dudley jumped a piece and chortled. "Maybe you ought to consider what your opponent has to lose more than what you have to win."

"What does that mean?"

Chuck squawked. Dudley jumped three more of his own pieces. "Damn you, I'm losing again."

"I'm leaving."

"Suit yourself. Don't listen to him."

"I'm not. Especially since he talks in the same riddles as you." About to continue his trek to the bawdy tavern, he hesitated only long enough to hear Chuck crow and hop off the crate to scamper across the street. Rance glanced at the sunset.

"See there. You made him mad. And he was just trying to help you."

"Help me?"

"Yes. He's just trying to tell you that he knows of a plan to steal your money and that it's best not to put all your eggs in one coop."

"Plot to steal my money? How? When?"

Dudley shrugged and folded the checkerboard. "Don't know. He never said exactly."

"Well, can't you ask him? He's just over there somewhere."

"Oh no." He tucked the folded checkerboard under his arm and limped toward the street. "There's no talking to him when he's mad. You'd be best served to heed his warning, young fellow."

In panic, Rance tried to view into the dim light of dusk. "Well, when will he be back? Can you ask him then?"

Dudley shrugged once more. "How should I know? He's a damn chicken, man."

Throughout the week, Rance couldn't sleep, eat, or even drink. He was shook. The foreboding of Chuck the soothsayer had him examining every detail of the race, much to the irritation of Les and Jody.

The pair had reluctantly joined him in the venture to win the race and from his own novice opinion had Lone Star in fine condition for today. As they proceeded toward the grounds, the assembling crowd along the way shouted encouragement or sought advice on which horse to bet. Rance projected his normal confident facade, all the while trying to keep an eye on any suspected trouble. When they reached the grounds, a white ribbon had been stretched between two trees.

"What's that for?" asked Les.

"My guess is that's the distance. A quarter mile. Four times around."

Les and Jody began to saddle Lone Star. While doing so, Don Pedro arrived in his bronze carriage, but without Catarina. Rance took that as a bad sign. If there was shooting, the gentleman obviously didn't want his daughter about. Feeling the need to be a sporting man, he availed himself to walk over and bid goodwill and perhaps find out more.

"Ah, Señor Cash, I am pleased to see you here."

"I am a man of my word, sir." The two shook hands just as the competition came into view. Aboard *El Magnifico Hijo* was a slight man of minute height in his racing uniform and looking all the part of a professional.

"I would like you to meet Jaime Lopez. He is the best rider of racehorses in the Southwest. He has come all the way from Monterey just for this race."

With all the force he could muster, Rance

338

put on a confident face. "Pleased to meet you," he said with the tip of his hat. The stern-jawed jockey made no move in kind.

"He does not speak your language."

"Oh, sorry. No English?"

"No. He doesn't understand courtesy to the opposition. He has never lost."

Rance gulped. "Always a first time."

"I do not think so," Don Pedro answered. He patted a bag on the floorboard of the carriage. "I have made good my part of the wager. I assume you have as well?"

Rance patted his thin wallet inside the copper coat. "Of course. Every penny." He grinned until his own mouth tired. "Well, I need to return to my horse. I'll see you at the end of the race."

Don Pedro nodded. "Of course. I'll have a man ready to take him when we are done here."

Rance continued the smile until he turned about, then rubbed his aching cheeks. He neared Jody and Les with a casual walk. "Well, they've brought in some amateur to race against you. They're terribly overconfident. Never raced before in his life."

"Really?" Les questioned. "He sure looks like he knows what he's doing."

"Appearances can be fooling. He thinks you're a man."

Les glared at him, but for only a moment. "What's his name?"

Rance shrugged. "Something Lopez, I didn't really listen."

"Well, I hope you were listening when they explained the rules," Jody said, finishing with the cinch.

"Huh?" Rance said. "Oh, yes, they went over them earlier. I'm sure it's your standard policy. First horse wins." His simple explanation only served to roll the eyes of both of them. "Well, it's time to get you aboard."

Jody bent down and cupped his hands. Les paused before stepping into them. "I'm doing this for the money." The cowboy straightened up and put his hands on his hips. "What do you think I'm doing it for? You?"

"Well, I sure ain't doing this for anything you done."

"Fine with me." He walked past them both. "You two can do it without me. I'm going back to the ranch."

"Jody, wait," Rance pleaded but there was nothing to stop the mad Texan on his way to his horse. Fearing time was being lost and with the crowd surrounding them, Rance cupped his hands. "Come on. Let's go."

Les peered back at Jody once, then quickly stepped into Rance's hold. On Lone Star, she led him out to the course to the cheer of the crowd.

"What's that other horse's name?"

"What?"

"I need to tell Lone Star." Now Rance rolled his eyes and with his knowledge of the Spanish language, he translated. "He's called 'The Son.'"

"But, Lone Star is a son of The Pride of Texas, too."

"Not in their eyes." He walked the horse to the start where a portly gentleman of good standing stood holding a pistol. Soon, Lopez guided his mount to the same line. As the shouts from the masses grew louder, Rance leaned closer to Les. "Remember what Jody told you?"

"Yeah," she answered only glancing in the direction where Jody left. "I remember."

"Good. Do everything you can to win." He pointed at Lopez. "He will." Rance went to the hill, his heart beating through his sweaty shirt despite the mild early winter temperature. Once at the top to get a good view, he took a deep breath, then looked to Les and Lone Star.

The starter raised his pistol. Rance inhaled.

BANG.

28

The blast startled Les and Lone Star. When they flinched, squinting her eyes, Les finally saw that Lopez had three strides on them. She kicked Lone Star after them. The first stride was strong and long. The second was equal. By the third, she felt the air whip her face, just as when she rode him before, just the same as when she was on the back of the paint the first time it bolted. All in her mind was the determination to go faster and her mount had the same idea.

She peeked ahead. Lopez was a full two lengths in front. Running the lessons through her mind, she lifted her weight onto her legs, bending her knees over the shoulders, arching her back, pointing her nose just above the mane and propping her rear in the air. Hooves pounding dirt filled her ears. Lone Star's graceful stride propelled them through the air like a bullet.

With one eye cast at the waving tail of The Son, she kept tight grip on the reins to keep Lone Star on pace. The distance behind didn't concern her; she'd seen how fast he could run when he wanted. All she needed to do was stay close.

Despite the cheers from the crowd for his horse, Rance didn't have the spit to say a word. Never had he been so worried. Not at cards, with the spin of a wheel, the roll of the dice, alone with beautiful women, or facing down the muzzle of a gun. With those circumstances, at least he was the one making the decisions, except for some of the women. Now his fortune was hinged on a spiteful sixteen-year-old girl and a bastard-born horse.

Bonnets and hats obstructed his view. He bobbed his head from one side to the other. Once he had a clear line of sight, he saw that Lone Star was at least two lengths behind. His heart pounded acid through his veins. He strained to get breath while watching the horses gallop away to the first turn. Wanting to watch as much as he could, he squeezed through the maze of chests and elbows. However, each time he moved, the new perch provided less of a view. Finally, he marched to the front of the crowd in time to see that at least his horse hadn't lost any more ground.

Accepting relief from the minor victory, the new position in the crowd gave him fresher air to breathe, and also an unwanted voice of advice.

"Well, at least you're giving him a spirited race," said Rodney Sartain.

Rance didn't want to be distracted, so he kept his eyes on the horses while replying. "We're giving him more than that. We intend on winning."

"Winning?" Sartain answered. His tone had one of surprise, but not one of sincerity. "Of course you do, Cash. That's what you have to tell all the rest. Good show."

Les kept Lone Star on course. She saw the tree of the first turn and wanted to stay as close to it as she could. Lopez had the same idea. He moved his mount closer to the inside and finally in front of hers. With ideas of swinging wide and letting Lone Star run past on the right, she decided better so as not to lose ground and speed, much less tire him too quickly.

With the first tree so near, she prepared to slightly pull the reins left. As she approached, Lopez pulled hard on his reins, stopping The Son abruptly. Lone Star reared, head flying up in front of her and popping her in the mouth. When Les shook her head, Lone Star had lost all his speed while Lopez had made the turn and sent his mount down the far side. With just a nudge she prodded Lone Star to resume the pace, but now he was at least four lengths behind with three more turns yet to come.

Back in the riding position, she again felt the whip of the wind passing over her face and mouth, but a tacky taste seeped on her tongue. Her own blood smacked on her lips. Despite the little pain, it was the sting of having been tricked that burned in her now. She regripped the reins and wrapped the end of her fingers into the long hairs of the mane, pushing with each stride. She was going to catch the no-good rascal.

His heart squeezed a little tighter when Les had to pull up. Yet, she seemed to have survived and was back on the pace with The Son. "What do you mean, 'show'?" Rance's question irritated him more than the one asked by Sartain. "This race isn't a show. It is sport. A contest."

Sartain spoke over his shoulder, not allowing his own eyes to leave the spyglass for very long. "I am sure that is what you think it is."

"Think?" Now he took his eyes off the

horses. "What are you talking about, man?"

"Money wagered on any outcome is at the very least a business investment."

Worry over the race put Rance's sight back on the two horses. "What does that mean? And, please get to your point. If it's one thing that I cannot abide it is one charlatan trying to impress wisdom upon another. Trust me, I know when I'm hearing it." With eyes firmly glued to the competition, Rance's concentration wasn't so focused as to not allow for Sartain's voice.

"To most of these people, this is a fair event. The outcome unknown. They're betting on their knowledge and opinion as to which is the better horse."

"Yes, I know. I'm familiar with the game. It's paying for these clothes."

"Then you must also know that to the few, this is an opportunity."

"Opportunity? To wager money? You think I don't see that? Damn you, Sartain. You're as confusing as an old man and a bird I know." Despite the frustration building inside him, Rance was still listening.

"An opportunity to seize the outcome before it is known."

It was no revelation. He just hoped he'd hadn't been outsmarted. "Do you think he's gotten to my horse?" whispered Rance as he watched. His heart beat a bit faster when he saw Les gaining ground. From his side, he saw Sartain put the spyglass to the eye.

"No. Something more basic than that."

The Son's tail was so close she could have grabbed it. Lone Star had run as fast as she knew he could. When she was at the leader's flank, Lopez glanced behind, then switched the crop from his left hand to the right. When even with the side, Lopez swiped at Lone Star's nose, but her horse didn't miss a step.

"Hey!" she yelled.

Lopez swiped again, and again missed by only a hair. If that leather struck Lone Star's nose, certainly he'd slow, maybe even cower enough to a sudden stop and throw her. Les pulled him out of range of the crop, but the tactic cost her distance. As she moved Lone Star farther to the outside, the second turn was upon her. Lopez swung The Son around the tree. Les steered her horse to take the turn at the full gait. When she cleared the tree, The Son had taken too wide a turn. With a few strides they were running by each other's side. She was even.

He couldn't help shaking his fist by his side. He could hardly breathe. Saliva tasted like gravel when he swallowed. Yet, he couldn't keep his mind firmly on the race. "Basic? What's more basic than messing with my horse?" The more he saw Lone Star running alongside The Son, the less he was able to hear Sartain over the exuberance of the mass. The response came as a jumble of noise. "What was that?"

"I said, there are rules."

"Rules? Yes, I'm sure there are rules. And it looks like they are breaking most of them. Their jockey is swatting at my horse. Don't tell me about rules."

The two horses stampeded as if hitched together as a team. Rance couldn't help but cheer silently, still too nervous to shout his encouragement aloud as most around him. What he was watching was too good to be true. His luck usually wasn't this good. Normally his advantages were gained through sleight of hand, but what he was seeing was actually happening.

The horse he'd won in a poker game, one that was fit to be food for scavengers, nursed back to health in such a short time, despite the considerable cost, ridden by a girl who once again was able to fool grown men into believing she was a man, much less a horse jockey, and was holding her own against a skilled opponent in a match race of the best versus the best. Rance couldn't help but glance at Don Pedro in his carriage. The distinguished man had a worried face. Rance had to shake his head at his own disbelief. When he shook his head, he barely heard the mumble for Sartain over the noise from the cheers. "What was that?"

"There are basic rules in this sport."

"Such as winning?" He chuckled at his own response.

Sartain turned to him with solemn face. "Such as the winning horse must have a rider." Rance's heart stopped. This wasn't humor. Only then did he realize it wasn't meant so when there was no relief in Sartain's firm jaw. "Think about what he wants. After all, he wouldn't hurt the horse."

Every muscle jittered for an instant. It couldn't be true. There were too many people. What had he done? This wasn't meant to be. He glanced out at the horses as they approached the third turn. If Les was losing, there wasn't a need for any action. But, if she was leading?

He sucked in wind. There was only one possible solution. "JODY!"

Les ducked from another of Lopez's swipes and let go with one of her own, landing the strike in the ribs. The blow cringed Lopez enough to make him lose his balance and sag in the saddle for an instant. Les swatted Lone Star on the left flank and picked up speed. Barely a nose ahead, she watched as Lopez swung once more. She flinched and held up her crop in defense. The crops clashed like swords, jarring each from their respective holds.

With a hand free, she gripped them both on the reins and tucked her heels into Lone Star. The horse responded, striding, huffing, flying down the long stretch toward the finish. Not wanting to lose any concentration, she only allowed for a peek to the side. The Son was at her side, but Lone Star was ahead by a neck.

Focusing ahead she could see the finish. Fearful that anything she did wrong might ruin the race, she made sure her boots were firm in the stirrups, her grip tight on the reins, her arms in rhythm with Lone Star's stride. The finish was getting closer. She didn't dare look behind or anywhere else. She was going to win.

Rance pushed and clawed his way through the mass. He had to get to a spot where he could see the entire field. If there was a threat it would come from where no one expected. Past the last of the rows, he again glanced at Don Pedro. The old man still looked to the race, but Rance couldn't afford to pause and watch. He concentrated for any sign, any motion for an assassin to act. However, he only sat still in the carriage. If Les was to win, then the order must be to see that she didn't.

He scanned left then right. All were on their feet. Les was within a hundred feet of the win. His breath was trapped in his chest or he'd yell for her to pull up. The money was one thing, but it wasn't worth her life. What had he done?

29

Jody couldn't keep from watching. There was the bag of bones he'd made run again. And that girl he couldn't get out of his mind. Nobody would notice him. Astride the saddle at the top of the far north hill, he felt safe in the distance from the action. His blood pumped a bit faster in anticipation of the horse taking the race. His mind pondered when he was in the rodeo and how he had enjoyed the comfort of controlling his own fate; he noticed the current twitch in his nerves was different. However, a rustle from the right took away those thoughts.

He turned to see a large live oak. The broad limbs were thick with leaves that waved just as from a gust of wind. The one next to it didn't move. He glanced at the race and Les was just ahead of the other horse. The shake of the tree, although for only an instant, intrigued him enough to steer toward it.

As he neared, a figure formed between the limbs, the color of which didn't match the green and brown of the leaves. It wasn't a form he recognized. Even a bobcat wouldn't be making such a ruckus. If it was a puma claiming a kill in the trees, it might not take so kindly to a rider's approach. Jody pulled the Henry from the scabbard. About to dismount, he caught sight of a black-and-red pattern. Nothing in nature sported such colors at that size. "Hey! What you doing up there?"

A shot rippled through the air.

Jody flinched from the percussion. He looked to the tree, then to the race. Both horses still ran.

Rance heard a shot ripple through the air. His heart stopped. Almost fearful to look, he forced a glance at Les. She was still aboard Lone Star. An instant's thought brought his view to The Son. It, too, still was in stride.

A quick glance to Don Pedro showed no reaction. Rance blinked twice to be sure it wasn't a blur. Had some rowdy just celebrated the race too soon with a shot in the air. A quick glance didn't spot any puff of smoke. Should he search further for a possible attack? Go to Les and get her off that horse? Charge at Don Pedro? The safest place from a shooter would be to be near him.

All the choices left him with no decisions but to stand stiff.

Jody raised the yellow boy and steadied it at the tree. "Come out of there!"

More rustle of the leaves only eased his trigger finger, but when another shot ripped through the foliage and popped dirt next to him, Jody fired into the live oak. Before taking the chance of missing the shot, he levered again and put the barrel in line again. Another shake of leaves was all the signal he needed to put another bullet into the leaves. A shot came from the top of the canopy.

Thinking there could be two of whoever was up there, Jody dove from the saddle, propped himself on one knee and let loose levering and firing. One, two, three, four. He couldn't see anything to aim at except the huge green-and-yellow target. By the time he'd squeezed off six rounds, he levered once more but held his finger steady. There was no return fire. There was no more shake of the leaves.

Cautiously, he rose and walked toward the live oak, rifle in continuous aim at the bulk of the leaves. He no longer saw the black-and-red pattern, but couldn't trust the idea the shooter wasn't about in the branches. One side step after another, he kept an eye above while only allowing an occasional glimpse at the tall grass in case another of this one's friends were targeting him. The closer he came, the more the leaves revealed the shape behind them. He crept, slowing his approach, ready to blast away if anything were to move. However, when he stood next to the trunk, he bobbed his head side to side to see blood dripping on the thick limbs.

He pointed the rifle up into the branches, fearing that even a wounded animal normally became most dangerous when panicked. About to send another piece of lead up into the leaves just to be certain and safe, he eased his finger from the trigger guard. Above him he recognized the agonized face of death staring back at him in the form of a man with a black-and-red-checkered coat that dangled as a drape surrounding the body. A mild but steady drip of blood pelted wood and dirt.

He scanned about looking for any who might take a shot at him, but saw none. All he heard was the roar of a crowd.

■ ■ ■ ■

She could hear the heavy breath of the horse to her left. Every step lasted hours in her mind. Only a few more feet were needed. Through the bouncing tangle of the mane she stared at the end. Les kept Lone Star on the same course, not wanting to veer left or right to block The Son from the same path, but rather get there first on their own. "Come on, boy."

With one gaping stride after another, Lone Star huffed at the strain. Come on, come on, she repeated in her head, knowing the next stride may be his last. The groan echoed in her ears.

With a final kick to the side, she pushed Lone Star to the end. Allowing just a peek to the side, there was still the nose of The Son, but in front of that showed the white painted line. A quick glance showed Lone Star's hoof stomping on it. The horse had crossed. She had crossed. They had won.

Relief cascaded through every nerve. At last she could breathe. She eased her grip on the reins and stood in the irons. Her first glance was to the masses on the right. The first figure she saw was Rance Cash standing on the top of the hill.

Rance smiled at Les. It was the first motion his nerves allowed in over a minute and was no act. He genuinely was delighted not only that she won but that she was alive.

With normal breathing restored, he turned his attention to the man in the carriage. With a proud strut, he marched his way down the slope toward Don Pedro, who continued to wear a firm jaw, not reflecting either disappointment or raging anger. Undeterred, Rance felt it only right to address the matter of the initial wager.

"Exciting race, wouldn't you say?"

The answer took time coming. "Yes, it was quite an entertaining spectacle." He grunted his throat. "Of course, I was expecting a different outcome."

"Of course. But, that is why they race, isn't that the saying?" The remark didn't gain a response, nor did it advance the subject at hand. Rance wiped the sheepish grin from his lips and attempted to gather as much respect as possible. After all, this man owed him a sizable sum. "Sir, I believe payment is due. Ten thousand dollars to be exact."

Again, it took time before any answer or any respectable eye contact came about. When Don Pedro finally looked his way, Rance's attention was drawn to the left. Les rode Lone Star toward him. Business could wait.

He went to her. She wore a big smile. He

reacted in kind. "You did great," he said, letting her lean to him, then hugging her. A peek at Don Pedro's confused face brought the reminder of how odd this must seem. Things might be said about men embracing and he didn't need people to talk about Les, or him for that matter. He released his hug and peered into her eyes. "Well, kid, you did it. You beat him."

"He beat him," she replied, patting Lone Star. "He's the one did all the running."

Rance was amused at her modesty. He patted the winning horse also, then was reminded about the winnings. "Find Jody. I'll meet you back at the Alamo Saloon."

Her sprightly mood quickly changed. "Jody? He ain't here."

Rance nodded. "Yes, he is. I have a feeling. He's here. Somewhere. You need to find him and have him take you."

"I ain't no kid. I don't need —"

"Les," he said, staring her in the eye. "Just do it." Realizing he didn't need to explain for fear of frightening her, he took an instant to think, then pointed at Lone Star. "Do it for the horse." He read in her face an understanding. Now since the concern was for the animal, she straightened in the saddle.

Rance faced about to resume his collection.

The image in front of him made him reach for the Walker Colt, but the muzzle pointed at him seized his hand. "Make a move for it and I'll blow you in half," said Big Red Mc-Clain, holding a Remington revolver in line with Rance's gut.

"But," he mumbled, confused, first looking at Don Pedro, who appeared perturbed at the intrusion, then at McClain. "You're dead? Aren't you?"

"Never felt better." The thug turned the pistol at Don Pedro, "Now, I'm going to get what's coming to me." He reached into the carriage and lifted a cloth bag.

"Wait," Rance said with a bit of due exasperation. "That wouldn't be what's coming to me, is it?"

"Ain't got your name on it." McClain waved the pistol at the bystanders, who quickly receded. Rance stood firm.

"It wasn't you at the ranch?"

McClain held his mug grin. "Yeah, I was there. But it was Fred Spillman who took that lead." He shook his head. "Poor Fred. I'll be thinking about him on my way across the border." He turned his attention to Don Pedro. "And for you." He waved the pistol at him. "This is my part of our little deal."

"What?" Rance shouted. "What deal? You and McClain had a deal to steal my money."

"I have no agreement with this man," said the gentleman. "He is a liar."

"Liar, huh?"

"Who is the one holding a weapon to my head? I think the good people of San Antonio will help me track you down and have you hanged."

McClain laughed. "Tell that to Fred's brother Ferris. He's the one out there shooting from the trees. He's got me covered and will shoot any one of you if any of you try to stop us."

"Not no more," Jody shouted from up the hill, levering the Henry and aiming it at McClain. "He's dead in that tree, and you'll be the same if you don't drop that pistol."

McClain stood stiff. Don Pedro quickly grabbed the pistol, but Rance rapidly grabbed the bag.

30

While leaning back in his chair, Rance Cash allowed himself a sigh of relief. He closed his eyes and absorbed the giddy laughter of celebration that surrounded him in the Alamo Saloon. When the day started he hadn't expected to hear his name mentioned with such praise, or for that matter even hear anything again, nor send Big Red McClain to jail.

Slaps to his shoulder woke him from the trance. He shook the congratulatory hands and nodded with a contented smile. When he faced the front his ears went deaf to the continued rejoicing. When Greta stepped through the swing doors, he shot out of his chair, cloth money bag in hand, to rescue her from the drunken pandemonium.

"You came," he said with surprise. She seemed surprised herself, but when she didn't reply with words but only a simple nod, he escorted her back to the table. His gentlemanly manners instantly flowed, pulling out the rickety wooden chair, taking out a cloth from his pocket and swatting away the dust. Greta sat and he scooted her in, then quickly settled into his own. "I didn't believe I would see you in here."

By her reaction, she thought the same. After a moment to clear her throat, she gazed about the room, then looked at him. "Maybe it is time for me to go to the places I have not been." She kept her eyes firmly aimed into his. Initially, Rance took the comment to reflect an inner need for self-discovery. Once she didn't blink, his mind wandered to consider that perhaps it wasn't just a comment, but maybe an offer. He wanted to take her hand at that instant to see if his guess was right, but an eruption of cheers drew both their attention to the doors.

Les entered, still dressed in her rider garb and hat, squinting to adjust her eyes to the darkness. The crowd smacked her back and shouted their admiration into her ears. Rance wanted to continue his conversation with Greta, but he couldn't concentrate with Les appearing so lost in the bawdy forest. He held up a single finger for Greta to keep her thoughts where they were, then rose to signal Les to the table. She stood still for a moment in a pose of uncertainty. Rance pointed at the open chair, but when Greta arched a brow at him, he stood in effort to make up for his lapse of manners. Les was too quick and pulled out her own chair and sat. A quick glimpse at Greta wasn't reassuring. He cringed. Certainly her mood must have changed.

"Why are all these people in here?" asked Les, leaning over the table to be heard.

"To celebrate their winnings," answered Rance. "They bet a heap of money on you."

"Me?" Les scanned about at the crowd, some who stared back. "It was Lone Star that did the running."

"Yes, but they can't buy the horse a drink, now can they?" Rance signaled for the bartender, who gladly came around the wooden bar. About to order a bottle of the best mash whiskey in the place, he cast an eye at Greta, then at Les. "Do you have any champagne?"

The bartender nodded. "We have some down in the cellar."

Rance winked and held up two fingers. The order was confirmed with a wink back and the man left the table. When he turned his attention back to Greta, another cheer went up when Jody came into the place. As he came closer to the table, Les seemed to cower from the Texan's approach. A stumbling drunk tried to whisper in Jody's ear, but lack of balance fell him like a tree. Jody snatched the mug of beer without spilling a drop before a thud rumbled through the wooden floor.

"Am I the only one drinking?" Jody asked with a smile.

"We're waiting on" — Rance paused, casting an eye at Greta — "something else." He looked at Jody. The two locked eyes, but the cowboy's brow seemed to ease.

"So, now that you're a famous horse owner, are you thinking of staying in Texas?"

It took a moment before Rance replied with a shake of the head. The bartender arrived with two dark and dusty bottles. Rance took one and gently unwrapped the cork. "No. I'm not the kind that can appreciate a fine animal. Nurturing its development." When he pressed his thumbs against the cork, it shot to the ceiling. About to pour the fine wine into the glass in front of Greta, he sensed disappointment at his announcement. When he filled the glass, he decided to improve her mood. "I think the children might be better suited as owners." A surprised smile grew across the German woman's face. He filled another glass and put it in front of Les. "Of course they will need guidance, so I'm sure the two of you could serve as managers of their assets." He glanced an eye at Greta. "As long as you consult their guardian." Now certain he'd restored her mood, his minor victory was interrupted by Les.

"I don't have need to take care of no horse."

Jody stole Rance's reply. "But you're the rider. You and the horse belong together."

"I agree. I can't believe Lone Star finishes first without you." Despite the compliments, Les showed no change of heart.

"I don't have plans on staying." She picked up the glass and sniffed at the bubbling wine. "You said you'd pay me enough to get to Kansas in a stagecoach by myself." She took a sip and her face soured.

Puzzled by her answer, Rance looked quickly at Greta, then at Jody. He lifted his glass to Les. "That was the agreement. You earned the reward. You can do with it as you wish." As Rance tasted the tart champagne, he couldn't help notice Jody standing stiff. After a moment, the cowboy glanced at the mug of beer.

"If that's what you want, I'll help you get there."

Sensing the continual bitterness between the two, Rance thought to change the mood.

"But, you're not leaving today. So, drink up."
He lifted up his own glass. "A toast. To defying the odds." About to take a sip, he observed confusion. A second realization was that he might be the only one to appreciate the financial significance. Their victory represented something a bit more important. A glance showed the accuracy of the assumption etched on Greta's face, then on Les's and Jody's also. "And let us not forget the overcoming of obstacles in order to accomplish a greater good." He paused and raised his glass again. "To Mary, Theresa, and Little Hank. And to Lone Star. All children who proved the lineage and heritage. All sharing and showing their pride." About to drink, one more thought came to mind. "Their Texas pride."

Chuckles and smiles mildly came over the four of them. However, soon Les showed her restlessness. As she gazed about, it was apparent she wasn't comfortable with the surroundings. "I think I'm going to go back to the house. I'm tired. I just want to go to sleep." When she got up, Jody was busy accepting handshakes. Rance noticed and rose from his chair. Les, standing at the table, looked to Greta. "I'm happy to meet you." She cast an eye as Rance rounded the table. "He ain't that bad. For a man." She leaned closer to the German woman. "Just don't let him know it."

Rance nodded at the remark he wasn't expected to hear. He took her shoulder and turned her for the door, turning his head for an instant to Greta. "I'll be right back." While Les was pointed outside through the maze of shoulders, Rance tapped Jody's shoulder to show him Les was leaving. Jody just shrugged.

Following close, Rance and Les emerged through the swinging doors. Several men stood on the boardwalk so he steered her farther from their leers. "I would gladly pay for an escort, but I don't spot any prospective candidates."

"That's all right. Ain't like I don't know the way."

"Yes, but you shouldn't be alone. It wouldn't be right for a young girl to travel by yourself. There's still some people with hard feelings over the race." He wasn't sure, but Les didn't show her usual spite at the reminder of her gender. She took more a somber stance. Her face lost any resolve to argue.

"Maybe nobody will notice me."

Rance forced a grin and put his arm around her shoulder. "Now, don't talk like that. Many a man will take considerable notice when I make good your part of the bargain. I should have the funds just as soon as I make my rounds of collecting debts." Despite his encouragement, she didn't seem swayed by the prospect of future wealth.

"No," she answered. "I think I can make it home by myself."

Rance peered down at her. "Jody's home."

After a short hesitation, she looked up at him, then shook her head. "No. Home in Kansas."

"It sure is a long way from here." He put his hands on her shoulders. "Take time to think about it." He bent forward and gave her a smooch on her forehead. Les repelled from the gesture.

"What are you doing?"

A voice came from behind. "Would you stop your bellyaching." Rance faced about to see Jody standing behind, sensing his cue to retreat back to Greta and stepped aside.

Les looked to Jody and took a deep breath. "What are you doing here?"

"I'm taking you home," he said, walking past her toward his horse.

"I don't need nobody taking me home."

Jody stopped and faced her. In a stern tone he ordered, "Yes, you do. I been listening to you for nearly six months now complain and nag." He took her hand but not

368

with the grasp of a cowboy handling a calf, but with the touch of an unsure gentleman.

Before she took a step, she held his arm stiff, but she didn't release his hand. "I ain't sure I'll be staying long."

He glanced at the sun, then pushed his hat back. "Well, that will be up to you. Winter is coming. Up north it's snowing up a storm. Wouldn't make sense to leave before spring. If you still want to leave, you can leave."

Les took that step that frightened her before. "We'll see."

With a firm grip on the bag, Rance Cash stepped through the swing doors. More happy faces offered him a drink, but through the bobbing heads, he saw Greta had left. His heart sank. Determined not to let the one opportunity pass, he turned back through the doors and walked outside. His eyes first caught sight of Dudley. Seeking information, he ran to him.

"Hey, old-timer, did you see a tall, blond woman pass by?

He pointed at the Menger. "Went in there."

Rance smiled. "Much obliged to you," he said, only pausing to notice the absence of that rooster. "Where's Chuck?" When he looked closer, something didn't seem right about the scruffy beard. It wasn't even.

"He's headed west. Heard a tale of lost Confederate gold. Never could tame his adventurous heart."

Rance laughed. "Here's some advice. The same tale brought me here. Let me tell you. There is no Texas gold. It's just a hoax."

Dudley nodded. "Captain Broussard tell you that?" About to nod, Rance was caught in half thought about why this old man would ask that question. "You better hurry, young fellow. That woman could be waiting on you." Dudley rose and walked with a little firmer stance than Rance remembered. However, the warning was enough to bring his mind to Greta.

Through the front doors of the Menger, he quickly stepped by the counter. Calvin noticed and Rance took another deep breath. "Rance, my friend. I heard of your good fortune. Let me express my congratulations." Rance kept walking toward the restaurant. "If you're looking for Greta, she's not there."

"Where is she?" he asked in more form of an order.

"Well, I could tell you, but first, I would like to talk to you about settling those bills we talked about."

"Calvin," he eased his tone. "Tell me

370

where she is or I'll stick around long enough to tell the owners how you endangered the hotel's image by trusting a reputed gambler."

The clerk pointed to the stairwell. "She's in her room."

Before the man had a chance to utter another sound, Rance ran to the stairs and took them two at a time. At the second floor, he walked down the hall uncertain of which to enter. As he went, he noticed a door not fully closed. Trusting his instincts, he went to it and rapped on the wooden door. When two seconds elapsed without an answer, he felt his heart stop.

Gradually, the door opened and the most beautiful woman in Texas stood in the doorway, her collar unbuttoned, gazing into his eyes with a desire he hadn't seen before. "I thought you were leaving town?"

He leaned closer to her mouth. "Well, not today." He kissed her lips and she didn't resist. She tasted like a fine wine, warm, full of body, with a sweet taste that begged for more. He wrapped his mouth around hers and sensed her slowly retreat inside into the room, dropping the bag and kicking the door closed.

Together, he spent the first time in two months in a soft bed. And after one of the most surprising interludes, he discovered Greta held no inhibitions toward finding her inner womanhood, and that he still couldn't get any sleep.

As he watched her curled in only the sheets, he rose and reflected on the day. In a relatively short time, he had entered San Antonio with only three dollars and now he stood in a beautiful woman's room holding more money than he'd ever had in his life.

He thought to enjoy one of Don Pedro's cigars as the perfect end to a perfect day. As his mind wandered about where he placed those cigars, he wondered where he had placed other important items. He saw his coat, pants, both pistols in the custom-made holsters, shoes, and nothing else. His heart stopped.

Fate froze him in the window peering outside on the street. There he saw a man boarding a stagecoach, appearing like Rodney Sartain holding Don Pedro's bag. The bag with ten thousand dollars in it. Sartain faced around and locked eyes with him, but the beard and face were those of Dudley. He jumped into the coach and the driver shook the reins to send the team galloping down the street toward the Texas west.

ABOUT THE AUTHOR

Tim McGuire's vivid imagination and fascination with history formed an early ambition to be a writer. He lives in Grand Prairie, Texas. Learn more about the author at www.timmcguire.com.